"I CAN TAKE CARE OF MYSELF. WITHOUT YOU."

Jarrod's mouth tugged into a smile. "Where does that leave me?" He smoothed back her hair, dislodging her hood as he did so. Unable to resist, he brushed his lips across her forehead. The delicate scent of water lilies filled his senses.

"With no political or business ties between us." Dia's response sounded a trifle breathless.

"What about personal ones?" His mouth worked its way over her eyes, down her cheek, along her throat to the enticing hollow at the base.

"We're both free agents. Ties of any kind can prove tricky, though." She moved her head, finding his mouth with hers.

"You're telling me," he muttered. His hand slid beneath her cloak as he dragged her against himself.

"It's cold out here." Her cheek brushed his as she nuzzled her face in his hair.

"You'd better go in." He pushed her through the doorway, but she kept hold of his hand, drawing him after her into her room.

"I'll still be cold—without you."

The longing in her voice proved too much for what little control he retained. He swept her tightly into one arm, the other groping at her throat for the tie to her cape. It slid with a feathery rustle to the tiled floor, and her soft sigh sounded in his ears . . .

AMETHYST MOON

JANICE BENNETT

PINNACLE BOOKS
KENSINGTON PUBLISHING CORP.

PINNACLE BOOKS are published by

Kensington Publishing Corp.
850 Third Avenue
New York, NY 10022

Pinnacle and the P logo Reg. U.S. Pat. & TM Off.

First Printing: August, 1995

Printed in the United States of America

For Rob and Matt

Chapter One

Gasping for breath, Dialora caught hold of the rough plasti-planking of an empty berth. For a long moment she rested her aching muscles, too exhausted to do more than cling to the floating dock, grateful just to be alive.

Flashes of explosions and the searing streaks of laser fire illumined the midnight sky, obliterating the glow of the three moons and the canopy of stars called the Great Net. The purple waters of the Kerrinian sea roiled with the movement of the terrified sea creatures about her. Nowhere could they find sufficient shelter beneath the maze of wharves, walkways, bridges and houseboats that formed the floating city about the obsidian-based winter palace at Kerrian-Isla.

Silken tendrils twined about Dia's legs, and a large, gelatinous body pressed against her thigh. A panic-stricken Columbine jell fish, seeking comfort. Its empathic images jumbled into her mind, pure emotion, pure terror. She couldn't soothe the giant, intelligent creature; instead, she mentally urged it deeper under cover. With a last, clinging caress, it slid away.

If only she could do the same. If only Linore and Edrick— She fought back thoughts of them, of her laughing cousin Linore, and Linore's energetic, enthusiastic fiancé. There'd been nothing she could do. The explosion that shattered their outrigger— their lives—had done too thorough a job.

Another explosion flared through the night. Off to the left, perhaps a kilometer away. The merchants' quarter. Now, with the ocean no longer roaring in her ears, she could hear the shouts, the booted feet as they ran along the plasti-floats, the muffled hiss of the laser rifles and the tingling, ringing pitch of the vicious alien cell imploders that melted the flesh.

With a tremendous effort, Dia dragged herself up, out of the water and onto the narrow walkway surrounding the berth. She'd managed to find the one spot of near calm in the midst of this nightmarish chaos. The tourist quarter. No true Kerrinian, no matter how mad he might have run, would risk the planet's major industry.

Just how mad had people run this night? It couldn't be invasion, there'd been no warnings. Was it—could it be—revolution? She had to reach the palace, find out what happened, somehow stop it. Her father—

The scuff of a sandal on the weathered plasti-planks was her only warning. She tensed, but before she could react, before her aching muscles could roll her back into the safety of the dark purple waters, her assailant swooped down on her. The sharp point of a dagger pressed against the back of her neck.

"Don't move." A deep voice breathed the words near her ear.

She couldn't, she realized in disgust, no matter how hard she tried. She had nothing left in her after that swim. She lay still, frustrated, as a hand ran over the wet silk of her torn sarong.

"If you're looking for a weapon," she said through gritted teeth, "I haven't got one." She twisted her head, trying to see her captor.

She could also see her rys-bracelet, the thick tracery of silver that looped over her fingers, criss-crossing along her hand and arm all the way to her elbow, connected by chains at her wrist to allow her movement. Its tiny bead of amethyst coral—Dahmla coral—that sat on the back of her hand remained quiescent, though she could arm the tiny laser pistol that pointed along her index finger with only a flick of her wrist. That simple movement would drop the coral into the jellactic acid contained in the hidden compartment beneath, where it would dissolve. Not quite weaponless, and few knew the true power of this seemingly innocent jewelry.

The man's hand finished its cursory search and he sat back on his heels. "Get up." The dagger eased its pressure, but remained touching her.

She pulled herself into a sitting position and tugged her mass of dripping, knee-length black hair from beneath her. She'd cut it in an instant if it weren't part of the image she projected for the tourists. If there'd be any more, after tonight.

The man studied her, peering through a darkness broken all too often by illuminating flashes from the explosions. Smoke hovered about them, an acrid fug too heavy to be dispelled by the soft tropical breeze. She couldn't make out his features in the uncertain light, but he wore a loose tunic, a style favored by off-worlders vacationing here. A tourist.

She had to get away from him, reach the palace—but not by any of the regular entrances. If someone had blown up her boat, then they'd probably targeted her father, too. She'd do no one any good, making a present of herself to her enemies. Linore and Edrick— She hugged herself, sick with dread that her father, too, had fallen victim. But she couldn't let this man see her fears.

The way he looked at her, she doubted he'd miss anything. Her chin thrust out. "Well? Satisfied?" she demanded.

A slow smile tugged at the grim corners of his mouth. "Yes. Very much so." His words held a slow, tantalizing drawl. "What, by the Sacred Fire, were you doing in the water?"

"Swimming," came her flippant response. She straightened, tugging the remnants of her tattered lavender flowered sarong about her; it exposed far too much of her honey-colored skin for her liking.

She'd already let this damned tourist detain her too long. She rose shakily to her feet, and a muttered oath escaped her lips as her legs buckled beneath her. She'd swum more than five kilometers from the smoldering ruins of her outrigger.

The man caught her by the arm, steadying her. "*Why* were you swimming?" he pursued.

She threw him an irritated glance. "Have you ever tried walking out there?" She pulled free and took an unsteady step away from him. From the crackle of weapon fire and the mingling shouts of fear and battle, the fighting must be all over the city now, on the floating walkways, the bridges, even the back alleys. Yet she had to get through it, reach the palace. She took another faltering step.

"Not so fast." The man caught her again, and this time his grip bit into her arm.

"Look, if you don't mind, now's not the time for me to give you a guided tour of the local water sports." She pulled, but he wasn't letting go.

A glimmer of amusement lit his shadowed eyes. "It's not the time for taking walks around here, either."

An explosion punctuated his words and set the dock on which they stood swinging. She fell against him, and his arm wrapped about her shoulders, holding her close. Her face pressed firmly against the soft, smooth cloth of his over tunic, and she drew in a lungful of a pungent, yet strongly masculine, herb. It overpowered even the brine that permeated everything on this water planet. It tantalized her senses, oddly familiar yet elusive. Beneath it, she encountered the man's own scent, the solidity of a powerfully muscled chest, the coarse tickling of the tightly curled hairs not quite covered by his tunic.

She pulled away. "I've got to—" She broke off.

"Got to what?" The crease in his brow deepened.

She couldn't make out his features clearly, for mist mingled with the smoke, hanging low over the water, obliterating the brilliance of the stars and moons. He was a shape, an occasional fleeting expression—a hindrance. She wasn't about to trust him with the truth.

"I'll see you safe." He caught her by the elbow and pulled her along the dock, toward the sheltering shadows of a floating building.

She stumbled after him, refusing to acknowledge the ache in her legs—or in her heart. Not now. Not yet. When this was over, she could grieve. Now she had to prevent further catastrophes.

The man drew her against the rough wall of one of the numerous inns that made up this quarter of town. Just meters from them, people huddled in groups, only a few Kerrinians in their picturesque, tourist-pleasing sarongs. Most were garbed in a variety of gaudy holiday costumes: off-worlders, come for the water sports offered by this planet where only one tenth of one percent of the surface was *not* covered by ocean. Their voices rumbled, low and nervous.

Dia crept nearer, trying to hear if any had news. Her companion remained at her side, and she sensed his listening silence.

". . . taken the palace." One man, from Ceres Alpha by his accent and dress, shifted uneasily.

A woman—a Rualdan—mouthed a response, but the words faded beneath an onslaught of explosions. The groups scattered, running for shelter.

Taken the palace? Dia drew back, shielding herself with the wall. *What had become of her father?* She forced her tired legs to carry her forward, to run toward the shouts and screams and searing of the weapons. She had to reach the palace. She stumbled, pitched forward onto her knee, and tears of exhaustion stung her eyes.

Hands caught her about the waist, and her forgotten companion's voice sounded in her ear. "Only fools run toward danger." His strong arms lifted her to her feet, then turned her back the way she'd come.

"No." She pulled away, only to have his hand close about her wrist like a steel band.

"There's a revolution going on, if you haven't realized." Grim humor touched his voice. "By the Sacred Fire, girl, you're a native. If you have any sense, you'll go into hiding until we know what this is about."

"You don't understand—" Dia shook her head,

for the moment unable to protest more strongly. This was no time to give way to weakness, not when her world—her planet—shattered about her.

The man swung her up into his arms. "No time for protests, my girl." He carried her away from the sounds of battle, across an oiled skin bridge, then up the gangplank of a tavern. The door remained firmly closed, though he kicked it with his sandaled foot. "Great Artis," he shouted, "open up!"

A Gavonian oath. That fact finally clicked into place. She hadn't been able to see his features, but now she placed his accent. And the scent that clung to his tunic. Pine. An image flashed in her mind of the elderly Gavonian ambassador, handing her a branch from a pine tree as a present. She'd been only seven, had no idea what the strange, prickly, divinely scented thing could be.

An explosion blew them forward against the door. Dia rolled away from the man, her head throbbing. Complete silence—deafness. Then sound filtered back and lights danced before her eyes.

The man. She bent over his unconscious body, running trembling hands along his temple and forehead. A bruise, swelling rapidly, but nothing shattered. A low moan broke from him and he turned to his side, dragging himself up to his elbows only to collapse again.

Dia looked about, desperate. That must have been a launched grenade; the fighters would be close behind. She couldn't leave him here to be killed. She had to get him—both of them—to shelter. She caught his arm and tugged. "Can you hear me? Can you stand? We can't stay here."

"You finally realized that." The words sounded faint and slurred, as if he forced them out. He pulled himself into a sitting position, shook his head slowly as if making sure nothing rattled, then clutched it. "Fires," he muttered.

"Come on." She helped him to rise. The effort sent her reeling backward into the tavern's door, which remained firmly bolted against them. "Where—" She broke off, gasping for breath.

"Not far." He wrapped an arm about her waist, half supporting her, half leaning on her. His other hand massaged his forehead. She fell against him, draping her own arm about him, and together they stumbled down the ramp and along the rolling dock, back toward the heart of the tourist quarter.

At the third inn they reached, he paused to check the wooden sign that swung overhead. A painted pelican stared down at them from above a beak full of fish. The man stumbled on to the next, which displayed a porpoise leaping high above the waves. With a grunt of satisfaction, he turned in and hammered on the bolted door.

Behind them, the sounds of battle raged louder. Dia glanced over her shoulder, every nerve on edge. A shadowy figure darted along the floating walkway, only to disappear into an inn across from them. No one else. Then fighters burst across the head of the alley, lasers searing the midnight darkness.

The door inched open on its heavy chain, then closed again. Dia's companion began an impressive string of curses, then broke off as the door swung wide to allow them admittance. The proprietor, still garbed in his elaborate apron, stood aside while they pushed within. He slammed and bolted the door behind them.

"You shouldn't have gone out, sir." The proprietor

peered through the paned window as more lights flashed.

"Food." Dia's companion tightened his arm about her. "We've had a bad night. Anything hot will do."

The proprietor turned toward them, and Dia buried her face against her companion's shoulder. The last thing she needed now was for someone to recognize her, before she knew exactly what happened, where she stood.

Her companion dragged her forward toward the stairs leading to the rooms above. "Bring it up, as quick as you can," he called as he supported Dia up the steps.

At their head, he turned to the right and palmed open the door of the first room. Dia crossed the threshold, her bare feet sinking into the thick carpet. She dropped into the first chair she reached and closed her eyes, allowing herself a moment to recover. She drew three slow, deep breaths, and found her world settling.

Looking up, she saw the man had sprawled in a huge upholstered chair opposite her, his feet supported on a stool. He watched her through half-lidded eyes as his fingers massaged his forehead. A tall man, she noted. Solidly built and very much an offworlder. A Gavonian, as she'd guessed, fair-complected with sandy-brown hair, gray eyes and rough-hewn features, so very different from the delicate ones that characterized most native Kerrinians. Strong features. Something about the set of his jaw fascinated her, as did the tiny lines—smile lines—that etched the corners of his eyes. A very attractive face.

She might find it easy to relax here with him, if

she didn't have so much on her mind, if she weren't so desperate to learn what had happened to her father. Surely she'd know if he'd been killed, know with that dull, aching certainty she'd experienced when her mother drowned. She'd been on the other side of the planet at the time with a party of diplomats, but distance made no difference.

Severe injury, though, could be another matter. That, she wouldn't know. Her father could be wounded, in need of aid. She shivered.

The man surged to his feet, steadied himself for a moment, then disappeared through a doorway to the left. He re-emerged a moment later carrying a plush robe of deep purple, which he draped over her. "That help?"

"Thanks." Dia shuddered, and snuggled into the soft folds of the fabric, glad of its warmth. Standard issue for the luxury inns, part of her mind registered. She glanced about, for the first time noting the size and appointments of the room. Definitely, the upper rent district.

The Gavonian settled on the edge of his footstool and studied her face. Warmth flooded her cheeks, and she found herself looking back, her gaze resting on each feature, assessing—liking what she saw. Especially his eyes, compelling, drawing her in as if they sought an answer to some unasked question.

She gave her head a quick shake. Now wasn't the time to let herself be beguiled. Not with her world collapsing about her, with her cousin dead, and her father—*where was he?* She struggled against the weight of this personal side of the catastrophe, of the chaos that raged outside. It threatened not just the life she'd known, but the government, the safety of her people, even the future of her entire planet.

The man rose once more, wincing, and went to a cabinet beneath the window through which flashes, almost like the lightning that accented the summer storms, lit up the sky. From the bottom shelf he produced a bottle and poured some of the deep amber liquid into two glasses. He handed one to Dia, then resumed his seat on the stool. "Why were you out swimming? And you've already used your joke about walking on water."

Dia took a sip—not a synthetic, but real Gavonian brandy—and allowed the warmth to flow through her veins. "We—" She broke off and clutched the glass. "We were celebrating the Amethyst Moon. My cousin, her fiancé and I. They were to be married in two days' time. It's—it's an omen of good fortune, to be married under it, you know." A shaky, derisive laugh escaped her. "We were in my outrigger, heading for Cyrene Atoll to make the midnight offering. It—the boat—blew up." She gulped down a mouthful of the burning liquor, fighting back the barrage of nightmarish images.

"They were killed." Her companion made it a statement. "Great Artis." He rose and strode once more to the window where he stood for a long moment, staring out. "Have you other family?"

"I—I don't know any more." *Had* her father survived? Just because she'd known with her mother was no guarantee her awareness worked with her father, as well. If this were indeed a revolution, he would have been one of the first targets. The death of the king would be a priority. "I'd better go, I've got to find out—"

He turned from the window, frowning. "It's not safe out there yet."

She straightened her shoulders. "I have to. I can't just sit here, doing nothing. There's so much—"

He held up his hand. "Stay here until it's safe. By morning, at the latest, things should have settled. I'm surprised the fighting's lasted this long."

She opened her mouth, then closed it again. The warmth of the room, the aura of safety and companionship, tempted her to remain. In here, she could almost convince herself the fighting was an illusion, the explosions merely fireworks. Almost.

A knock sounded on the door, and the man crossed to it and palmed it open. The proprietor bustled in, bearing a covered tray. Dia averted her face while he set his burden on a table. With a slight ching of metal he lifted the lid, and enticing aromas wafted forth. Not until she heard the door close did she dare turn around once more.

The man set chairs before the table. "Come eat something." He broke off. "We haven't even introduced ourselves. I'm—" He hesitated. "Jarrod," he finished simply.

"Di—" She broke off. She didn't dare say more, admit to being Dialora rys Pauaia, daughter of King Harryl and princess of this water planet.

"Dee," he repeated, misinterpreting her name. "Will you join me?"

Acting the host seemed to come easily to him. She hesitated, nerves raging at her not to stay but to do something, anything, to end the violence outside. Yet, exhaustion left her too weak to think clearly. With only a brief struggle, common sense won out. She needed to eat, to renew her strength after that draining swim. She still had a long night ahead of her.

She sat at the table and accepted the steaming platter of fish and hydroponically grown root tubers Jarrod handed her. She had no appetite, though. She looked across the filled, aromatic plates, as he took a large mouthful. "What have you heard? Did you go out to collect news?"

He nodded, then swallowed. "A revolution."

She clenched her hands. "Great Net," she whispered. "And—and the king?"

"Dead, I hear. The princess, too. Which leaves no one in charge of the royal guard. They'll surrender in short order." His voice rang with certainty.

She closed her eyes. Her father, dead. No, she couldn't comprehend it, couldn't—wouldn't!—believe it. She hadn't seen his body torn apart by an explosion, hadn't seen what was left floating, bloodied and face down, like Linore. . . .

His hand clasped her shoulder, and she blinked back tears, refusing to give in to them. Not yet. After all, rumors weren't necessarily true. Maybe her father *wasn't* dead. *She* wasn't, after all.

And that meant there *was* someone to take charge—provided she could reach the communications room in the palace. She knew the secret passages that honeycombed the volcanic rock upon which the winter palace had been built. She just had to reach the hidden entrance—and soon. She had to take command of the guards.

"Dee? I'm sorry." A gentle note warmed his voice.

She looked up, meeting his concerned gaze, and drew in a slow, steadying breath. She could lose herself in those eyes. They made her feel safe, welcomed, protected.

A spark lit their charcoal depths, igniting unexpected embers. His expression underwent a subtle alteration, becoming more intense, more encompassing. The pressure on her shoulder increased, and she found herself leaning forward across the table. Toward him. The thought drifted through her mind, that under other circumstances. . . .

Abruptly Jarrod released her and rose, staring at the window. He crossed to it, then threw it wide, leaning out. Dia blinked, bewildered and shaken by his withdrawal. Then she had it. What had caught his attention. What was so different from just a minute before. Silence. No sounds of fighting, no explosions of light and terror. Nothing.

"It's over." Jarrod closed the window and turned back into the room. "The guard must have surrendered. That's it, then." He crossed to the table and resumed his seat, his rugged features now set in a considering frown. "I suppose there'll be a new government established quickly."

"I—" Dia rose, and found her legs trembled. "I have to go."

His brow snapped down. "That's not a good idea, not yet, at least. There'll still be revolutionary soldiers patrolling."

She shook her head. "You don't understand. I *need* to go."

"Worried about staying alone with me?" His lips twitched into a wry smile. He returned to where she stood beside the table. "I promise, you're quite safe. I doubt my head will stop ringing before morning."

A teasing note crept into his voice, enticing her back toward the intimacy they'd shared only minutes before. It would be so easy to let herself forget everything in his arms.

But that wouldn't make the revolution go away. Only her actions, right now, could do that.

Firmly, she shook her head. "I've got to find out what's happened. My family." She crossed to the door.

"Wait." He followed, and put a restraining hand on her shoulder. "I'll go with you."

"There's no need. And think of your poor head." She palmed the door open.

"I am." He didn't release her. "And my conscience. I'm not letting you out on the streets alone. You—" He broke off, his mouth setting in a stubborn line. "You're a damned sight too tempting, even for a man who isn't caught up in battle lust. If you go out that door, so do I."

She caught her lower lip between her teeth. He was rather tempting, himself. But she didn't dare betray herself by letting him see where she went. She lowered her head, then nodded, pretending acquiescence. "Take something for your head," she advised. "It's a bit of a walk."

"Good girl." With one finger under her chin, he raised her face to look up into his. "Two minutes," he promised. The finger trailed along the line of her jaw, then he turned and headed toward the bathroom.

For a long moment, she stood mesmerized, then gave herself a shake. Two minutes. Not much time. She darted out the door. At least, she'd recovered from her exhaustion; her legs functioned once more. Now, if only her mind would recover from the shock. Or, maybe it was just as well if it didn't. To face up to the death and destruction of this night— No, not yet. Far better remember the lingering sensations caused by Jarrod's touch.

She reached the ground floor, and to her relief saw no one. Jarrod would look for her out the front door first; therefore, she'd find a back way. She darted around the tables and chairs of the taproom, ducked behind the bar, and found the kitchen. Still, no one.

From the room behind her, she heard Jarrod's call. With a touch of regret, she let herself out into the night, onto a narrow floating walkway. Keeping deep in the shadows, she made her way to the alley-street, then studied the night sky. Clouds of smoke lingered, making it hard to identify the constellations. Rhysta rode high and full in the sky, though, shadowed by Mehrtis and tiny Vergan, all three moons only gray hazes rather than showing their tinges of rich color. Still, they were sufficient to point her way east, toward the palace.

Chapter Two

Dialora hurried along the swaying pathways, hugging the shadows of the floating inns and taverns. Over the first oil-skin bridge and still no sign of revolutionaries. She darted across the walkway to the other side and stumbled over something.

No, not something. Someone. She drew back, stifling a scream. The uniform— She swallowed, her throat dry. One of her father's guard. She stooped to check his pulse, and her fingers encountered the cool, sticky dampness that had once been his forearm. She was too late to help.

Too late. She forced the despair from her heart. As long as she still lived, it wasn't too late.

A shaky, hysterical laugh set her shoulders quaking, but she stifled it before it could break out, loud against the quiet of the night. Jarrod thought she only had to get home to be safe. If he knew the truth! Home—the palace—had to be the one place that *wasn't* safe for Dia.

For that matter, the whole floating resort city of
Kerrian-Isla would be dangerous. She rose, moving
on, her thoughts racing. Here, in the winter capital,
the revolutionaries had slaughtered the guard. Here,
she might well find no supporters who would dare
to step forward and help her reclaim the planet. Here,
she realized with a sick lurch of her heart, no sane
gambler would bet so much as a single credit on her
chances of survival.

She eased into the sheltering alcove of a doorway,
balanced herself, and took three calming breaths.
Her hands flowed through the ritual cleansing
motions, freeing her mind to think clearly again. No,
remaining in Kerrian-Isla would be foolhardy. She
had to return to the government center far to the
frozen north, to Waianoa, to gather more guards.
Perhaps the revolution hadn't penetrated there. The
capital city would be heavy with snow, its innumerable
waterways frozen solid. It would be her best chance.

Her decision made, she altered her course to the
south, toward the Recreation Quarter with its count-
less water craft. She wouldn't have far to go. After
all, the city had been laid out for the convenience of
the tourists. She crept through the network of floating
docks and bridges, at last reaching the wider spaces
with the swinging signs advertising the various sports
available.

She wanted something with speed boats. Preferably
an operator who had converted one of his crafts to
coral fuel.

Dahmla coral fuel. By the Great Net, she wished
its power had never been discovered. Although, it
would be to her advantage now, of course. If she
found a hydro-plane converted to its use, she could

accomplish the three thousand kilometer journey in less than one of Kerrian's twenty-hour days.

She cast a cursory glance over the selection of glass-bottomed boats tied at the first dock, then made her way to the next. Canoes, outriggers, kayaks—nothing of use here. She returned to the main wharf and headed to the next section. She needed to find an affluent business, one that sacrificed the picturesque for prestige. One like—

One like this. No swaying wooden sign, here. Crisp, clean letters proclaimed "Coral-Power." The snob. With a curled lip, Dia ducked under the gate and hurried along the arm of the dock, examining the available craft. The fifth, the one nearest the end, was a hydro-plane, sleek and serviceable. With a nod of satisfaction, she stooped to ease the line from its anchoring cleat.

"Here!" A deep, guttural cry sounded from the wharf, and booted footsteps thudded along the creaking plasti-planks.

Dia spun into a crouch, raising her arm. With a deft flick of her wrist, the chamber guard on her rys-bracelet slid open. The coral hissed as it dropped into the jellactic acid. No wonder the royal family reserved the sole right to wear that little attachment to the otherwise traditional Kerrinian bracelet. The tiny laser throbbed with growing power . . . she needed it to hurry. . . . When fully charged, it could be fired for several hours, non-stop. But it took valuable seconds to begin dissolving, to build sufficient power to arm itself. . . .

The man wore a Kerrinian sarong, and strands of shell necklaces hung about his thick neck, bouncing as he ran. His features—no! This was no native Kerrinian. An alien. A mercenary? Hired for the revolution? She pointed her index finger, sighting along it, waiting. Her tiny laser bracelet had an effective range of no more than four meters.

He swung his weapon to his shoulder, leveling it at her head. A cell imploder. Great. She'd rather it had been anything else. The thought of every cell touched collapsing inward on itself, melting away, left her ill.

The implosion chamber on the rys-bracelet throbbed softly on the back of her hand, ready at last. She touched the firing pin with her thumb, and power crackled from the tiny pistol.

With a strangled exclamation, half surprise and half pain, the mercenary dropped his imploder. He stumbled forward, one hand gripping the other, as his weapon slid across the wet planks. Only the softest splash announced its dropping into the ocean.

Dia didn't wait to shoot again. She scrambled into the hydro-plane, tugging the line free as her feet touched the fiberboard bottom. She shoved against the pier, easing the boat away from its dockage, then lunged for the controls. A single tap on the starter brought the engine to life with a roar that faded at once to the soft purr of coral power. Behind her, the mercenary shouted, but she concentrated on steering a path through the crowded dock.

Beyond, the artificial bay sparkled deep purple, reflecting the light from the multitude of stars and from the three moons. They stood in alignment this night, with ruby Rhysta and sapphire Mehrtis casting their colored glows over ivory Vergan, creating the Amethyst Moon. New Year's. Somehow, that sounded too prophetic for comfort.

She slowed the engine, peering ahead to spot the

numerous buoys that marked the path to the open seas. At the height of the tourist season, these channels—even the bay—were necessary to manage the heavy traffic of water craft, to guide the planet's visitors to the correct wharf without endangering the lives of the local workers. Now, the floats were only in her way. Once she was sure of a clear run, she could open the throttle, allow the boat to rise on its skis.

The course narrowed, leading toward the mouth of a harbor that existed only because of the joined buoys. Almost free. Past that last marker.

Spot lights flooded the night, hitting directly in her eyes, one on either side of the bobbing float that identified this as Kerrian-Isla. Cut off. Dia quieted the engine to lowest power and ducked down, peering over the side.

"Stop your engine and prepare to be boarded." The disembodied words, deep and reverberating, boomed over a loudspeaker like a death knell.

They didn't even ask for identification. Their sole job was to cut off escape. She couldn't get around them.

The loudspeaker crackled, then boomed forth once more. "If you do not comply at once, we will fire upon you."

By the Great Net, she'd already been in one exploding boat tonight. She couldn't get past, evasion would do no good, going back was pointless—She wedged the boat hook through the wheel to hold the craft on course, opened the throttle full out, and dove overboard.

She stroked for the unreachable bottom, but the explosion still sent her head-over-heels. At least the hydro-plane hadn't been right on top of her. Her lungs aching for lack of oxygen, she pulled toward the air. She needed her artificial gill, but that had been lost with the outrigger, and Linore and Edrick.

Her head broke the surface, but she barely gasped in a lungful of air before diving once more, heading as far from the wreckage as she could get before her oxygen-deprived body forced her once more to the top. This time she risked a look behind her. One of the patrol boats now circled the flaming remains of her craft, its spotlight scanning the debris. They'd realize all too soon she hadn't been aboard.

Quiet surrounded her, a stillness broken only by the gentle lapping of the wavelets and the hum of the patrol boat's engine. She rolled to her side and pulled herself silently through the dark waters, buffeted by too many shocks to think clearly.

She was alone. The thought kept hammering into her mind. Alone. No one to turn to for aid, cut off from the guards, from the government officials who remained in the capital of Waianoa. Alone, and her planet was being taken over by a mercenary-manned revolution.

Her hands clenched, and the water slipped through her tensed fingers. Alone, but not giving up. Not while she still had breath. She would not permit this alien invasion of her home. After all, she only had to reclaim her palace, quell the rebellion, and appear strong for the coral treaty negotiations. Not much. Her shoulders trembled with her hollow laugh.

The patroller's engine revved, and she struck out again, heading not toward the shore but outward, toward the harbor's mouth. They'd be less likely to suspect her of going that way. It wouldn't be wise for her to return to the Recreation Quarter. That mercenary must have raised an alarm by now. She'd go— Well, that would take some thought.

The searchlight swept in a slow circle, seeking her out. If they'd only concentrate toward shore. . . . The patroller turned, heading away from her, and began a spiraling course that would take it to the docks.

She reached the marker-buoys, dove under the floats that delineated the ''harbors,'' and breathed a sigh of relief. Commercial Quarter, now. She'd be cut off from reaching Waianoa on this side; she wouldn't find any vessels capable of reaching there in the hurry she needed. Which left her no choice. The palace it would have to be.

Mehrtis, the nearest of the three moons, arced low in the western sky, nearing its descent below the horizon. Its two mates followed in close pursuit. There would shortly be a brief period of darkness, then the sun would begin its ascent and dawn would illumine the battle-ravaged city. Time slipped through her fingers as rapidly as did the water through which she swam.

As she neared the commercial wharves, allowing the waves to sweep her along, the muffled sound of voices reached her. Fishermen, preparing to start their day's work? Or mercenaries, patrolling to make certain no one escaped? She allowed herself to drift next to a hull.

She couldn't see any sign of the huge gulls who slumbered here during the night, waiting to raid the bait nets. No jells, either, or seals or gyriks, or any of the other warm-water mammals who made an easy living by raiding the commercial catches. She strained her ears, but only the sound of heavy footfalls reached her, accompanied by the creaking of the docks.

The faint crackling of a portable comm unit interrupted the murmuring, and a heavily accented, non-Kerrinian voice announced: "Watch Five reporting in, sir. All quiet."

"Keep to your rounds, soldier," a male voice snapped back. A different accent.

"Waste of time, if you ask me." A female this time, Gavonian by her accent.

"I didn't." Her companion's tone held a touch of anger. "Been too easy, so far."

"What did you expect?" The woman moved into Dia's line of vision. Tall, graceful, very non-Kerrinian in spite of her sarong, a cell imploder clasped lightly in her hand. "This is a tourist-industry planet, for crying out loud. Bad for business to have a military."

"But it's their home. There's going to be more of a fight yet, you mark my words." The man strode off, apparently to continue his own rounds.

The woman lifted her arm toward his departing back, but Dia couldn't make out the gesture she made in the dim light. Probably just as well. But no matter what the woman seemed to think, the man had been right. Dia was going to give them a fight.

She eased around the back of the boat, then along the line of trawlers until she reached an area where the dock was narrow enough for her to swim under. She came up in front of two packing sheds. An acrid odor lingered here. Burning. There must have been fires.

She pulled herself from the dark waters and shivered as the pre-dawn breezes caressed the tatters of her dripping sarong. No one around, at least. She doubted if the fishing fleets would go out this day. She ran along the bobbing walkways, headed toward the central hub, the volcanic mountain on which her

ancestor had constructed his picturesque palace—
more a fairy-tale castle, for her long-gone relative
had possessed a discerning eye for tourist attraction
potential. He hadn't received the nickname of Symon
the Mercenary for his fighting abilities.

As she passed through the shops on the outer
perimeter of the Commercial Quarter, she slowed.
There'd be guards surrounding the palace; she didn't
need to scout ahead to be certain of that. Even though
her rys-bracelet vibrated with the power that continued to build as the coral slowly dissolved, she wasn't
prepared to take on an entire mercenary army.

She eased herself over the edge of the dock, back
into the lapping waters beside an elite boutique boat.
She needed light to guide her and air to breath. The
former was a lost hope; the latter she'd have to obtain
as best she could. At least she didn't have far to go.

The entrance to the underwater cavern lay just over
five hundred meters to the east, beyond the palace
perimeter in the Government Services Quarter.
Beneath a school. She worked her way amid the rafts
and houseboats, well into the sector. Then she dove,
striking out hard, and surfaced between two floating
classrooms. The sky, she noted, softened as morning
light crept across the horizon. She'd made it, without
any time to spare. She drew a deep lungful of air and
dove again, this time pulling herself downward.

The high mineral content of the water stung her
eyes as she opened them, searching for the cavern.
There. She caught a glimpse of the softly glowing
lamp that burned just within the entrance. Closing
her eyes to ease their pain, she struck out toward the
opening.

Her hand brushed against the sharp volcanic
pumice and she grabbed the rock, ignoring the tear-

ing in her palm as she used it to hurl herself forward, out of the water, to where oxygen awaited her aching lungs. At least the mercenaries hadn't shut down any of the emergency power stations, or her haven here would have flooded back to its normal high water level.

Stepping carefully, all too aware of her bare feet, she crept over the slick obsidian floor of the tunnel, upward to the small cavern. The chill damp bit at her lungs, and the air smelled of brine and disuse. By the dim glow of the entryway lamp, she could just make out the row of lanterns that hung in an orderly line against the back wall. She tested the first, found it heavy with fuel, and flicked the switch. Light blazed in a three meter arc about her. A check of the supply cabinet revealed sandals, cloaks, towels, and an array of artificial gills. She would have welcomed the latter any time this night.

The former, though, she welcomed now. She removed the remains of her sarong, dried herself on a thick towel, then donned a lightweight cloak that she belted about her waist with its cord. In the past, she'd always considered checking the supplies down here in the emergency cavern as a waste of time. Now she was grateful that she herself had replaced the ration packs only two months before. Not enough to supply an entire resistance movement, but it provided a safe hideout for a handful of people. No beds, though; this was meant for escaping the palace in case of just such an event as this revolution.

Escaping the palace. . . . She spun back into the low-ceilinged chamber. Had her father had time? But nothing appeared disturbed except by her. No gills missing, no carrysacks torn from their place on the shelf. He hadn't made it to this shelter.

Now wasn't the time to give in to worry or grief, she reminded herself fiercely. She had work to do.

She adjusted her lantern to a low glow and started forward through the maze of interconnecting tunnels and chambers. Some had been narrow once, and so low in spots a person had to crawl, but her wily ancestor had assured the ease of his emergency escape route. She slowed, casting her light around the obsidian cavern in which she currently stood. Provided food could be smuggled in and provided the entrance within the palace remained undiscovered, she *could* shelter a small fighting force here.

The darkness seemed to stretch on forever as her light sent the shadows dancing backwards. She shivered in the cold dampness and hugged the cloak about herself. Not much further, she assured herself. Any moment now.

A plasti-rail gleamed in the darkness. The stairs. Relieved, she hurried forward and set a cautious foot on the first dura-plast step. Good old Symon. He hadn't spared the expenses, even where it wouldn't return a profit. Of course, he'd placed a high value on his own skin. Unless—Yes, she'd be willing to bet he'd intended to someday open the caverns—for a hefty admission price—for the tourists to come and gawk at the royal labyrinth.

The stairs spiraled upward to a landing at the level of the palace basement. The door before her would lead her into the wine cellar. She continued upward, no longer in the volcanic chambers but inside the castle wall itself. She climbed higher, beyond the reception floor, past the next with the government chambers and then on until the stairs ended at another door. On the opposite side stood her father's massive closet/dressing room, the entrance well hidden in the oak paneling imported from Darius V, her ancestral planet and Symon the Mercenary's original home.

She extinguished her lamp, then stilled her rapid breath with the ritual movements of her hands. For a long moment, she stood, gathering her courage and then she eased the panel free. Only the softest of clicks announced her presence. She stepped through and then froze as the sound of voices reached her from the room beyond. Her father's spacious bed-chamber.

Her father! Hope flooded through her, and she had to bite back a cry of excitement. She couldn't take chances.

She eased aside the garment preservation bags protecting her father's ceremonial sarong and cape with their rich decoration of furs, feathers, pearls and corals. There were even a few pieces of amethyst Dahmla coral among the variously colored pieces. She'd remember that if her bracelet needed more fuel.

His other garments crowded along the wall, and she ducked under a selection of silk fabric—probably sarongs—and emerged into the center clearing. Too dark to see anything in this windowless chamber. She crept toward the door as a man's voice rose in anger.

"*I* am now ruler of Kerrian!" The voice trembled. "You will do as I order and spare me the arguments."

Whether trepidation or frustration shook the voice, Dia couldn't tell. She recognized it, though. Bailan bor Alleia, her mother's nephew, and third in line for the succession to the throne after Dia herself and her cousin Linore. Her cousin Linore, who died in that fiery explosion only hours before, an explosion that should have claimed Dia as well. . . .

Bailan! The shock left her weak.

"You'll never rule this planet." Agathas, the elderly housekeeper, sounded amazingly calm.

"Who is there to challenge me?" A note of barely restrained triumph colored Bailan's words.

"Your mercenaries. And your new friends," came the prompt response.

"Be careful, woman. My cousins put up with a great deal of insolence from you, but I warn you, I won't. You can be replaced easily."

Agathas gave a short, angry laugh. "With so many ambassadors and their staffs arriving for the treaty negotiations? But, of course, you know best. Go ahead. Fire me. Or kill me, the way your masters killed the *true* king and princess. It makes no difference."

Masters? Dia leaned closer, straining to hear. What had been going on?

"*I* am master!" Bailan cried.

Agathas sniffed. "Go ahead and think so if you want. It won't do you any good. You're nothing but a puppet of Gavin-Secundus, and in your heart, you know it. Why do you think they arranged this revolt for you? Because Harryl and Dialora were too shrewd to have been taken in by—"

Dia's stomach clenched. Gavin-Secundus, their oldest ally—their oldest friend—behind this.?

"Enough!" Fabric rustled and a chair creaked, as if Bailan surged to his feet. "Get back to your work, and don't bother me with nonsense. I've got to meet with the Gavonian ambassador in an hour. Then you'll see a proper show of respect." Footsteps sounded, crossing the heavy carpet, and the outer door creaked in opening, then slammed.

"Wampa bait!" Agathas threw the insult after him.

Dia inched the dressing room door open and cast a rapid glance about the spacious, comfortable chamber. Empty, except for Agathas. Safe for the moment.

She must have made a sound, for the woman spun to face her. For a long moment Agathas stared at her, mouth open, then with a muffled cry the wiry little housekeeper ran across the room and enveloped Dia in an unexpected embrace.

"You're alive." The woman held Dia at arm's length, gave a short nod and released her. "He said you'd been killed."

"I nearly was. Linore and Edrick—"

Agathas's expression darkened. "Damn him. Well, since it's too late to save them, we'll have to avenge them. Them and your father."

"It's true, then? I—" Dia shook her head, wanting the woman to deny the rumors.

Agathas led her to the bed and pushed her down to sit on the edge. "Bailan wouldn't dare come in here otherwise. But at least we've got *you* safe." She broke off, frowning. "Well, we'll just have to keep you that way, won't we?"

"I tried to get a hydro–plane to get to Waianoa—"

Agathas shook her head. "No good. Not yet. You'd never get clear of the harbor. No, the safest place for you will be right here, under everyone's noses where they'd never think to find you, while we try to get a message to the ministers."

Dia nodded. "Are the staff all right? Was anyone—"

"No, why should soldiers kill servants?" A gleam lit the wiry little woman's lavender eyes. "They need people to wait on them, too, you know. Only the guards were slaughtered."

Slaughtered. Like the one she'd stumbled over in that alleyway. Like Linore and Edrick . . . and her father. . . . "We'll give them all a proper send-off, a whole platoon of flaming canoes, once we've dealt with this mess," she said through gritted teeth.

Agathas nodded. "That we will."

"Are they loyal? The servants, I mean? Will they support me, or whoever is currently running things? I don't think I could blame them if they just wanted to avoid any more bloodshed around here."

Agathas snorted. "They can't stand Bailan. Call him the Whiner. They aren't fighters—don't think we can make an army out of them to drive these mercenaries off—but they won't betray you. You'll be safe enough, hiding among them."

Dia met the housekeeper's solemn gaze. "Is Gavin really behind this?"

Agathas gave a short nod. "Your cousin let it slip. Someone on Gavin arranged everything for him, even the hiring of the mercenaries. Now," she put her hands on her hips, frowning. "It's too late to look back. We'd better concentrate on keeping you safe. If we make you an upstairs maid, you'd probably be more comfortable. But there's more chance you'll run into that cousin of yours."

Dia closed her eyes. Gavin. She still couldn't believe it. Close ties bound their planets. Her father's oldest friend, her "Uncle" Dysart, ruled Gavin as its tharl. Dysart's tempestuous son, Lomax, made Kerrian his second home, entertaining prospective clients on the pleasure yachts or venting the frustrations from some soured enterprise through the more vigorous water sports. Gavin. . . .

No, best not think of it now. She concentrated on the dangers—and needs—of the moment. "I want to be able to move around. Get to the comm room. How about making me kitchen help? I can deliver food anywhere in the palace without arousing comment.''

"Especially with so many people coming in today. They haven't called off the talks, and those ambassadors are still willing to come.''

Dia's mouth tightened. "Of course, the talks will go on. They're what this whole revolution's about, after all. Coral." She spat out the word. "We should have expected something like this.''

"Greed." Agathas gave a knowing nod. "These outsiders I can understand, but not our own people going along with it. The whole planet was going to benefit from the treaties, not just you and your father. Everyone knew that.''

Dia fingered the warm fabric of her cloak. "We weren't going to ask for much in the treaty negotiations." She looked up, seeking answers she knew Agathas didn't possess. "We weren't going to *give* the coral away, of course, it's so rare and the jells only produce such a little amount of acid, though they're generous with it. But our planet doesn't *need* much. We've been happy catering to the tourist trade. That's what we all know.''

Agathas folded her arms. "There's always those who want more, who can never get enough. Like that cousin of yours.''

"I wish we'd never realized what the coral was capable of." Dia hugged herself.

"That Doctor Aldric, she meant it for the best," Agathas reminded Dia, though her tone was grudging. "You have to admit, it's a boon to every system in the galaxy.''

"And a plague to us!" Dia surged to her feet and paced across the spacious chamber. "What I wouldn't

give to go back just four months, before she made
that first test on a hydro-plane. If only—''

She broke off, frustrated. Four short months since
the galaxy-wide announcement of the incredible
energy released by the Dahmla coral's chemical reaction in the acidic fluid produced by the giant, intelligent Columbine jell fish. Four short months which
had catapulted Kerrian from its sleepy status as an
obscure planet valued only as a water-recreation
resort by inhabitants of the neighboring systems, to
the center of galactic attention.

Only fifteen grams of this rare coral, that was all
that was necessary. Fifteen tiny grams, combined in
an implosion chamber with no more than two scant
liters of jellactic acid, could power a battle cruiser to
one side of the galaxy and back again—with fuel to
spare.

But the coral was rare, very rare. And the jellactic
acid could not be exploited. While the jells didn't
express themselves with words, they communicated
through emotions, making their curiosity and intelli-
gence abundantly clear. Jells possessed full rights on
this planet, a fact that more than one tourist had
to have forcibly explained. The humans on Kerrian
respected and held in deep affection their planet's
indigenous species.

Dia stopped before the housekeeper. ''We have to
protect the jells.'' A plea crept into her voice.

Agathas nodded. ''You just follow your father's
plan, and you'll come off all right.''

''Plan! He—'' She bit back the words. She couldn't
admit to the housekeeper that her father had no plan
beyond making treaties with everyone as quickly as
possible. The mere thought of his new position of

galactic importance had given him sleepless nights. All he'd ever negotiated before had been tourist industry licenses. If Agathas's faith in Dia's leadership abilities were shattered, she might withdraw her support—and that of the entire staff. Better to serve a puppet of strong Gavonian masters than the faltering, if rightful, heir of the house of rys Pauaia.

Dia straightened her shoulders. "I'll need my father's schedule of meetings. The ambassador from Gavin-Secundus—" She broke off, the betrayal of their long-time ally making itself felt again. The ambassador supposedly had been coming to serve as advisor in the negotiations with the representatives of the first four planets to apply for treaties. "It's not Lomax, is it? He's shrewd enough. No," she corrected herself before Agathas could speak. "He doesn't know the meaning of the word 'altruism.' Uncle Dysart would never send us someone who'd demand a percentage in exchange for his help."

Agathas's mouth thinned. "Their ambassador may be an impostor, here to make sure his revolution goes as planned."

"Or he may be the real one, here for that same reason." Dia drew in a shaky breath. "I don't dare trust anyone."

Agathas nodded. "Your father was right. You'll need to arrange treaties with every neighboring planet, and as soon as possible, or we'll have every fuel-hungry system in the galaxy trying to take us over."

"We won't let them. We'll have to act fast, that's all. Has that ambassador arrived yet?"

"About fifteen minutes ago." The woman's eyes narrowed as her gaze rested on Dia's face. "The revolution kept his delegation away from the palace last night. But as soon as they arrived, I came to tell—Bailan.''

No derogatory epithet added to his name. Did that mean Agathas had begun to doubt Dia's abilities? Dia's chin thrust forward in defiance. ''If he possesses any honor, he won't deal with Bailan once he knows I'm still alive. I wish I knew if this revolt had the backing of the Gavonian government, or only some rich opportunists who want to control our coral.''

Agathas pursed her mouth. ''Will it matter? Don't you forget that tharlship of theirs is a warrior-chieftain job, not a ceremonial royalty like what's handed down in your family. Their government may recognize a kingship won in battle.''

''Not if I have anything to say to it! Let's go.'' She started for the door, driven by the certain knowledge she had very little time. ''I've got to get to the comm room before Bailan makes any disastrous agreements.''

Agathas's snort of disapproval stopped her. ''You can't be seen in that cloak, not if you don't want anyone paying attention to you. Wait here while I get you a maid's uniform.''

What she'd like to do, Dia reflected as the little woman slipped out into the corridor, would be to go to her own room at the opposite end of the hall. So near, yet it might as well be on another planet. She longed for her comb that would untangle the matted mess of her long hair, the pins that would fasten it neatly out of her way. She wanted a bath to rinse away the salty stickiness that pervaded every pore.

She crossed to her father's dressing table and picked up a shell comb. Bailan had used it, she noted with disgust, and removed several short black hairs that wrapped about two of the teeth. A few of her father's long silver strands twined near the base as well, and these she set aside gently. They might form her last link to him.

She swallowed back the ball of emotion that threatened to choke her, and blinked away the tears that she wouldn't let fill her eyes. She couldn't believe he was dead. Not yet, not until she'd actually seen his body or spoken with someone who had. Until then, she would not let herself grieve.

Agathas returned before Dia had finished working out the knots. The woman clucked her tongue, took charge of the comb, and in short order had braided Dia's thick black hair and coiled it around her head. It took an army of pins to hold it in place, and it dragged Dia's head back with its weight, but at last, the housekeeper arranged the maid's cap and attached it with still more pins.

The uniform was a one-piece sarong of light-weight violet synth-fiber, knotted over the left shoulder with one full length sleeve that gathered at the wrist. It covered most of her rys-bracelet, and the part that showed looked like every other Kerrinian's arm ornament. The coral no longer sat in the tracery of wires to betray her as a ruling rys Pauaia. It sizzled away in the tiny implosion chamber, its vibration humming in her inner ear a constant reminder that she was not defenseless.

She looked up to find Agathas studying her, a deep frown on her sharp features. "Well?" Dia allowed her shoulders to droop and walked across the room, shortening her long stride.

A deep sigh escaped the housekeeper. "Mind you, don't stick your chin out, and you'll do well enough. Just duck out of sight if you see any of your father's people."

Dia looked up quickly. "Are there any?"

"I've only seen one, so far. Old Connri. I checked his rooms to make sure he was all right."

"He's too ill to get out of bed." Dia frowned. "But if Bailan forces him to make an appearance, it'll provide a convincing display of the old regime supporting the new for the ambassadorial parties. Clever of someone." Which made it less and less likely Bailan managed to stage this on his own.

She picked up the tray Agathas had brought as part of her disguise, and strode out the door into the corridor. No one. Still, her nerves tensed as she struggled to keep her steps slowed, her posture casual, as of a menial in no hurry to be about her chores.

She almost started down the ceremonial main stair, but caught herself just before Agathas murmured a warning. Silently cursing her lapse, she crossed the gallery toward the wing which contained the rooms reserved for visiting dignitaries. The service lift stood just beyond, screened by an elaborate panel mosaicked in shell and several varieties and shades of common coral. All very touristy, and the visiting officials loved it.

Except, Kerrian was undergoing an image change.

A door opened to the second of the elaborate guest suites, and a tall man emerged into the corridor. He wore a uniform of dark hunter green, crossed with a dull gold and white sash, and rows of military ribbons indicating status. The ambassador from Gavin-Secundus, no less.

Dia's gaze narrowed, studying him. He strode toward them, his long, sandy brown hair secured at the nape of his neck, his expression grim. His harsh features—

Jarrod.

Chapter Three

Jarrod tolArvik strode down the ceremonial main stair of Kerrian-Isla Palace taking mental stock. A show place, designed to give tourists the maximum entertainment return on their vacation credits spent. Like the rest of the floating town, picturesque, almost too cute for words. A people—a government—intent on catering to off-world visitors and completely unprepared for warfare.

So many innocent, helpless people— His jaw tightened. That girl, Dee, haunted him, with her huge, frightened violet eyes that had seen too much horror last night. She'd seen her cousin die. Had she lost other family or loved ones in the fighting, as well?

He'd searched for her after she'd vanished from his room, but had found no trace. He could only hope no one else had spotted her, either. He'd feel better about her if he'd been able to see her home, know her safe.

Damn it, he'd wanted to see her home for another

reason, too. He'd wanted to find out where she lived, learn more about her, get to know her a little better. She'd intrigued him. Never had he encountered such an appealing combination of inner strength cloaked in desperate vulnerability. Before he left Kerrian, he vowed, he'd find her again.

He paused to massage the aching throb at his temple. He needed something stronger than the tablets he'd taken last night. But taking a headache, no matter how bad, to a med center that would be crowded with war casualties seemed ridiculous.

He reached the main hall and came to an abrupt halt. Someone had laboriously tiled the floor in a mosaic tapestry of underwater sea creatures, rendered in a brilliantly colored variety of crushed sea shells, then covered in plasti-clear. Even the damned uniforms of the so-called Royal Guard were nothing but sarongs. And as for weapons! Nothing more dangerous than knives existed on the planet—or so he'd been told. All visitors supposedly checked their sidearms, their laser pistols, especially their cell imploders, into lockers at the space ports. Yet, he'd seen any number of lethal weapons last night.

He hesitated, frowning at the five closed doors that let off this hall. One, to the left of the stair, would take him back to the courtyard through which he'd entered almost an hour before. The other four offered no clue as to which led to the audience chamber. There should have been someone posted here to direct him.

The slapping footsteps of sandaled feet hurried along a corridor behind him, and Jarrod turned to see a soldier in the purple sarong of the Royal Guard approaching. He wore his fair hair sleeked back from his squared, pale, very non-Kerrinian face. His turban-shell styled cap bore the insignia of a lieutenant. The man came to a halt and snapped off a very military salute.

"Ambassador tolArvik?" The bright green eyes took in every detail of Jarrod's official dress uniform. When Jarrod responded with an acknowledging half bow, the lieutenant held out a folded paper. "This arrived for you during the night. My apologies, sir, it was supposed to be delivered to you immediately upon your arrival at the palace. And this," he handed over a portable recorder, "came through just a few minutes ago." He gave another salute, did an abrupt about-face, and retreated back the way he'd come.

A *written* message? Jarrod tore it open and focused his blurring gaze on the formal opening identifying the communique as originating from Merylar Citadel, the tharl's capital on Gavin-Secundus. The greeting, more formal than Tharl Dysart's normal cryptic style, commanded the recipient's obedience and homage to his warrior-ruler. This Jarrod skimmed, and moved on to the transcribed text. He read it, his fingers tightening on the page, and his heavy brow snapped down as he scanned it once more. His temple throbbed with renewed vigor.

"You are hereby relieved of your position as ambassador," he murmured. No mistaking that. *Ordered to leave the palace of Kerrian-Isla upon the instant, return to the space port and board the next ship.* No explanations, nothing. Probably old Dysart's response to this Kerrinian revolution.

Yet this wasn't the response Jarrod had expected from him. No one understood rising to power through combat better than a Gavonian. The title of tharl, itself, meant "warrior-ruler." Of course, on Gavin, the aspirant to the throne issued a formal challenge for witnessed single combat, a duel. He didn't hire mercenaries to murder his closest relatives. Dysart, like all Gavonians, valued honor, and honor played no role in this revolt. The house of rys Pauaia had committed no wrongs. Greed alone drove these rebels.

So his tharl ordered him home. The honorable response, perhaps, but not the practical one. Dysart, as Jarrod had good cause to know, valued practicality as highly as he did honor.

Practicality. If the entire house of rys Pauaia had indeed been killed, then the other planetary governments had little choice but to recognize the victor as the new ruler of Kerrian. For the tharl of Gavin-Secundus to refuse to negotiate with the new head of state boded ill for future relations between the planets, despite their centuries old friendship. And they needed good relations. They needed coral.

Still frowning, he rubbed his aching head, then tucked the message into a pocket of his uniform coat and turned his attention to the recorder. He flicked it on, and a time imprint of less than ten minutes ago blinked at him. Apparently old Dysart was feeling the frustration of being so far away from the center of activity.

The screen presented an image of the white block walls of Merylar Citadel, then blinked to Dysart himself, sitting at a console. "Glad it's you there as ambassador, Jarrod." The tharl ran a hand through his thinning hair. "For once, honor be damned. Deal as you must with these rebels, only secure that coral and Gavin's place as their advisor." The screen blinked to static, then went blank.

Jarrod stared at the recorder and swore softly and steadily. He drew the paper from his pocket, re-read it, then tapped the crisp sheet against the side of the recorder. One ordered him to abandon his mission immediately, the other ordered him to continue at all costs. Dysart wouldn't send two contradictory messages, one printed only, the other by personal vid. Kerrian, it seemed, wasn't the only planet having a touch of internal difficulties.

He checked his chronometer. Already time for his meeting with this upstart Bailan. His lip curled. *Honor be damned for once,* the tharl had said in his message. That was easier to contemplate than do.

Trouble brewed on his home world. The tharl, and the implied treachery he faced, couldn't wait. The little Kerrinian upstart could; he was no rys Pauaia. Jarrod turned on his heel and strode down the corridor where the lieutenant had disappeared only a few short minutes before.

A long corridor, it turned out. Doors lined both sides, indicating they led into small cubicles. Offices with neatly lettered metal name plaques. He'd left the tourist portion of the palace and entered the efficient business operation that ran it.

Ahead, another corridor crossed this one, and a guard stood before the passage to the left. In spite of her purple sarong, the woman didn't look Kerrinian. Fairhaired, a firm chin—more Ceres Alphian, he reflected with a shudder of long-standing hatred. The cell-imploder she held diagonally across her body was no local weapon, either. This she shifted slightly so it pointed at Jarrod as he approached.

"Where is the communications center, corporal?" he snapped.

The woman held her ground. "Back there," she indicated with a jerk of her head, "but there's no admittance. Sir," she added grudgingly.

"Get me whoever is in command. Now. I don't have time for this nonsense."

The woman tapped the comm-unit on her shoulder with her thumb. "Lieutenant, the Gavonian ambassador is here."

So, she knew who he was, did she? Interesting. And this lieutenant was scurrying to come? Good. He crossed his arms and glowered at the corporal, and took perverse pleasure in watching her growing discomfort.

A door slammed along the corridor, and a man, tall and fair but with the slanted, ridged forehead of a Bertolian, strode toward them. The rolled cuff of a gray uniform pant leg just showed beneath the Kerrinian sarong. A mercenary officer should be more flexible, Jarrod reflected, more able to slip into a covert role.

"What may we do for you, sir?" The voice held a heavy accent—and very little willingness to help.

"I'm sending a message." Jarrod shouldered his way past both mercenaries, then turned with raised eyebrows toward the gaping lieutenant. "Are you coming?"

The Bertolian belatedly raised his imploder. "I have orders no one is to enter."

"Orders?" He spun on the hapless Cerean corporal. "I told you to get me the person in charge, not some useless underling."

Something—it might have been enjoyment—flickered in the corporal's eyes, to be immediately masked. She straightened to attention. "Sir. He's the best we've got. Sir."

"The best." He allowed a sneer into his words. "You'll have to do, then, lieutenant. I'm sending a message to the tharl of Gavin-Secundus. You will see to it that it goes without delay. Surely it was your *orders* to block only supporters of the house of rys Pauaia?"

At the mention of Gavin-Secundus, the man looked uneasy. He cast an uncertain glance at his corporal. "By whose authority—" he began.

"By the tharl's, himself!" Jarrod snapped. "Haven't you studied your uniforms, man?"

"He's the tharl's ambassador," put in the corporal. A touch of smugness crept into her words, as if it pleased her she knew something her commander did not.

"Which one?" the lieutenant shot back. The two mercenaries exchanged uncertain glances.

Which one? Jarrod straightened, thrusting out his chin to disguise his growing uneasiness. "As far as you are concerned, the only one that matters. If you doubt me," he held up the recorder, "you may look at this yourself. *Are* you coming?" And with that, he spun on his heel and marched down the hall. Sandaled feet hurried after him.

The best they had. His lip curled again. Bailan must have hired the cheapest mercenary force he could find. With coral power to bargain with, he could have afforded the best. But why waste money and promises when even this token army could do the job? The house of rys Pauaia had not been prepared to defend against even this. It was no wonder the tharl had sent Jarrod to his old Kerrinian friend to serve as advisor for the negotiations. Jarrod wished he'd arrived days earlier.

Two more guards stood at attention before the communications room. They stepped quickly aside to allow the lieutenant to palm open the door. Jarrod strode in, noting the neat rows of terminals and the giant screen on the far wall. Sophisticated. Probably had to handle complex reservations. After all, it would never do to allow R and R for rival armies at the same time. Bad for business.

The comm-tech—a Kerrinian native and little more than a teenager—cast him a nervous glance.

Jarrod smiled at him. "I want a line open and ready for relay to Gavin-Secundus. As quick as you can."

The tech glanced uneasily at the lieutenant. "Yes, sir."

Jarrod laid a steadying hand on the youth's shoulder. The lad reminded him of Dee. Not just the thick black hair tied back from the face, but the expression of shocked horror, of disbelief that any of this could have happened. How could he find her, when he knew nothing about her but her first name?

"Sir?" The youth's glance slid sideways toward the frowning lieutenant, then back to Jarrod. The vid screen flickered with the image of Merylar Citadel, then shifted to show the Gavonian tech seated at a console.

Jarrod stepped in front of the vid and willed himself to ignore his aching head. "Put me through to the tharl. At once."

"Sorry sir." The Gavonian's features remained impassive. "He's left orders he's not to be disturbed. Not for anything."

Jarrod glared at him, which produced no discernible effect. After a moment, he said: "All right, record the following message for him." He waited for the Citadel tech to signal readiness, then straightened, thinking fast. "My greetings, Tharl Dysart. I have received both messages, but the sender on the first was not noted. I remain your obedient Ambassador tolArvik." That formality, even if the carefully worded message failed, would alert Dysart to trouble.

The Gavonian tapped a button on his console. "The tharl's message indicator has been activated. Anything else, sir?"

A warning sent. But would it be received? He hesitated, then nodded. "What about Lomax tolDysart? He's at his business complex outside the Citadel." The tharl's son had returned to his headquarters in a violent fit of temper after his latest entrepreneurial venture failed. The man might be self-absorbed, but he could be counted on to support his father.

The Citadel tech keyed up something on his vid that Jarrod couldn't see. "Not now he isn't, sir. You can leave a message for him, too, if you like."

Jarrod's jaw clenched, but he nodded. Damn it, where was Lomax? With Dysart? Planning how to deal with this Kerrinian mess? That might explain why neither was available to take communications. But, he'd have expected them to request any and all news from here.

The Gavonian signaled for him to begin, and Jarrod recorded a similar message to the one he'd already left for the tharl. This accomplished, he thanked both techs, nodded curtly to the lieutenant, and strode out of the room and back down the hall.

The corporal saluted as he passed. He winked at her but continued without stopping. It might come in useful having someone not actively antagonistic toward him around here. He might need access to communications again. Though he would have preferred anyone to a Ceres Alphian.

But that was a war of his idealism, of his youth, over now these five standard years, though never forgotten.

He turned his thoughts to the more immediate, the more pressing matter of coral negotiations, and their possible implications for his own planet. Some treachery had occurred at home, that much he could guess from the messages. His first impulse, to return to support his tharl, he checked. That, after all, had been the jist of that written communique, to return. Thereby—Thereby what? Preventing Gavin-Secundus from taking part in the treaty negotiations by removing the ambassador? Or preventing that ambassador, a trained negotiator, from assisting the Kerrinian ruler in obtaining a fair bargain?

Where lay the threat? To the power at home or the power here?

He found himself very interested in meeting this Bailan bor Alleia.

Back at the main hall, a saronged official—a trumped-up doorman, Jarrod reflected—directed him across the elaborate mosaicked hall to the audience chamber. Jarrod stepped within, and the unexpected grandeur washed over him. The ceiling loomed high above his head, vaulted in a series of delicate arches supported on columns. Painted stars glittered in this artificial sky, clustered into unfamiliar local constellations.

Plasti-clear formed the entire far wall, offering a view of undulating purple waters and a sky of the palest amethyst-blue. Puffs of white clouds drifted along the horizon. Numerous boats of varying sizes, from luxury passenger liners down to fishing trawlers and kayaks, dotted the sea. A beautiful, peaceful scene, without a trace of the violence and death of the night before. How many people out there even knew their government had fallen over night? And, how many would it really affect?

His gaze swept the padded chairs that lined the chamber. Behind them, extending from the mosaicked floor to the star-painted ceiling, someone had worked murals of more undersea scenes. Beautiful in rendition, he reflected, if somewhat repetitive in theme.

When his survey reached the wall opposite the view of the ocean, he encountered a raised dais on which sat a throne designed in the shape of a giant cross-sectioned nautilus. Its subtle amethyst and amber tones gleamed, hinting at prestige and ceremony. Behind it rose a mural depicting a variety of giant, human-sized jell fish, swimming amid a school of porpoise.

Every detail of design subtly reinforced Kerrian's primary industry. This room stood as a monument to tourist-trapping. Perhaps the people of this planet possessed far more business acumen than anyone gave them credit for.

He had to admit, they knew how to make the most out of what they had. They'd taken an economically-classed "F" planet—as low as the scale went for habitable worlds—and supplemented its expected fishing potential with a thriving tourist industry. For their sakes, he hoped they'd prove as clever with their handling of the coral.

A panel of painted sea turtles to the right of the throne swung wide, revealing a concealed doorway. A young man stepped into the room, his slight figure enveloped in flowing purple robes made for a taller and heavier person. On his head rested a crown designed in the elaborate shape of a trunculus murex shell. About his neck hung several strands of amethyst pearls.

He strode forward three paces, then halted and raised his chin in an imperious gesture that didn't quite disguise the weight of the crown. His lavender eyes held a haunted, almost frightened gleam. He straightened, but his voice quavered as he pronounced: "I am Bailan, king of Kerrian."

Jarrod fought back a flicker of contempt. This posturing, uncertain child, to face the seasoned diplomats for the coral negotiations? Perhaps this explained the inefficiency of his mercenaries. No seasoned army would work for him, disbelieving in his abilities to make good on his promises. Well, if he were here to act as advisor, he'd begin at once.

Jarrod folded his arms across his chest. "Someone should enter before you, blowing a conch shell." Well, that suited the touristy atmosphere in here. "Never announce yourself."

Bailan flushed. *"I'm* king. I decide how things will be done. You—" He broke off, eyeing Jarrod with a touch of uncertainty. "You are a supplicant for the coral. I would advise you not to forget that."

"Perhaps your predecessor failed to inform you." Jarrod allowed the irony to linger in his tone. "I have been sent by the tharl of Gavin-Secundus to serve as your advisor during the negotiations. How much experience do you have with treaties?"

Bailan turned his back on him, mounted to the throne, and sprawled in the great seat. "I'm king, aren't I? And I wasn't yesterday at this time. That ought to prove I can make arrangements."

"How much are you paying your army?" came Jarrod's immediate response.

Bailan's heightened color deepened even more. "I came to power because I have the support of my people."

"If you want that believed, then make sure your mercenaries wear better disguises." He rocked back on his heels, eyeing Bailan with distaste. Honor be damned, all right. He'd rather deal with a straight-forward criminal than this little weasel. Perhaps he would. Bailan wouldn't last long in power, at least as anything other than a puppet. He looked to be a follower, not a leader. He lacked any vestige of charm or charisma, anything that might bring him support. A canny mercenary leader would have sized up the situation at a glance, and have take-over plans already under way.

Jarrod didn't owe Bailan anything in the way of warning. Yet his conscience reminded him of the ties between their planets. This Bailan should not have the right—he certainly didn't have the abilities—to speak for Kerrian in the matter of treaties. Still, he at least was a native of the planet. With the true king and princess dead, there was no one else at the moment.

Bailan straightened on the throne, drawing himself as tall as his meager frame allowed. "You say you were sent here to advise my uncle. Very well, you may speak your advice. I don't say I'll take it, but I'll listen."

"Before you accept an offer, make sure you know what's expected in return. And make sure it's a price you're willing to pay."

"Oh, your planet already—" Bailan broke off, his face a mask of consternation. "They—they all want the same, don't they?" he forged on. "Coral and acid, and giving me as little in return as possible?"

His planet already what? Jarrod stored the question for later contemplation. "How rare is the coral? And the acid? It's produced by the Columbine jells, isn't it? How do the jells feel about it? Does your government have to buy it from them?"

Bailan hunched a shoulder. "We're working out the details."

"If you don't know your own position, how can you expect to negotiate? You—" The door through which Bailan had entered opened once more, and Jarrod broke off.

An aged woman of small build, garbed in the violet sarong of the household staff, strode into the room. The housekeeper. He'd encountered her earlier, when he'd arrived. What was her name? With a frown, he realized it had slipped his mind. That wasn't like him. Damn this head.

The woman carried a tray which bore a thermal decanter, two fluted cups and a napkin-covered plate. Her gaze flickered across Jarrod with a piercing, calculating intensity before she turned to Bailan. "You did not send for refreshments."

"I didn't want them!" Bailan flared at her.

"Mistake." Jarrod took the tray from the woman and placed it on a low table beside the elaborate throne. "Consider it a bit of political foundation work. It places your visitors in the position of having accepted your hospitality."

"Lesson number one?" A sneer curled Bailan's upper lip, but his eyes no longer held that sullen look.

"Basic training," Jarrod agreed. "Bear in mind yesterday's events. You need to present yourself as being in complete control. So much so, that you can attend to the civilized niceties."

A muffled snort sounded behind him. Jarrod spun about and caught a glimpse of a saronged figure in the shadowed doorway. It retreated deeper, vanishing from sight, and the sound of running sandaled feet drifted back to him. The housekeeper, who stood near the throne, bowed to Bailan and exited the audience chamber with stately tread, closing the turtle door behind her.

Jarrod's gaze rested on the almost indistinguishable panel for a long, considering moment. Where did the loyalties of the household staff lie? Would they seek Bailan's overthrow for causing the destruction of the house of rys Pauaia? Or would they support him as being the closest relative of their ruling house, albeit by social rather than blood ties? Bailan bor Alleia was the king's nephew-by-marriage, the son of his late wife's sister. The princess's own first cousin.

And Bailan had ordered them slaughtered.

Or had he? Young, unsure of himself, brazen— no, Bailan had neither the strength of will nor the charisma to bring about this revolt. He had to be someone's puppet. And Jarrod intended to discover whose.

Chapter Four

Dia paced across the inlaid floor of the kitchen and slammed her fist against the tiled counter-top. "He's helping him! That damned Gavonian ambassador is helping Bailan! Tharl Dysart *must* be behind it."

None of the eight other people in the room looked at her. Two young staffers, both men, exchanged uneasy glances, and the head cook stirred the contents of a sauce pot with a concentration that defied interruption. One of the maids slipped out the door.

Dia crossed to the large window that looked out over the dock where the fishermen delivered their fresh catch to the palace. "How could Uncle Dysart have done this? He's a friend!" Pain stabbed through her forehead, and she pressed the heels of her hands against her eyes to block it out.

Agathas, who stood in the corner near the hydroponics room, frowned. "You really think the coral means more to him than his ties with your father?"

"*Damn* the coral. It's turned our closest ally against

us! And Dad's closest friend, at that." Her voice sank. "Thirty years of friendship. Exploded." She gave a short, mirthless laugh.

"I don't know, a man just doesn't order his best friend killed like that," Agathas declared.

"For greed, he does. Bailan didn't object to his whole family being wiped out, remember. Have you any concept of the value of the coral? We're sitting on a credit factory, here. And there's an entire galaxy out there ready to kill anyone and everyone to get their hands on it. So because we trusted Uncle Dysart, he beat the others to it. By the Great Net, we made it easy. All he had to do was kill my father and me, then set up that idiot cousin of mine as a puppet ruler. What chance has mere friendship against a prize like coral power?"

Agathas shook her head. "The more I think about it, the less I believe it. I don't think you should be so certain of it, either."

The cook took the pan from the burner. "What do you know of it? Just try thinking what *you'd* do to get your hands on more money than you could dream of."

"I wouldn't kill." Agathas glared at him. "And neither would the tharl. You've never seen much of him, but I have. All of us who work upstairs have. He finds out the names of anyone who waits on him, and remembers them from one visit to the next. That's the kind of man he is. Thoughtful. I'll bet he doesn't know anything about this. You just think about it, Lady. You call him uncle, and that's what he's always been to you."

Dia closed her eyes. "We trusted him with our lives. He promised to help, to send us advisors. And all we got were his mercenaries."

"And how do you know they're his?" Agathas snapped back.

Dia stared at the housekeeper. "Oh—Nets! I'm *not* thinking clearly, am I? Of course, Uncle Dysart wouldn't do such a thing. But it has to be someone else with power, familiar with our situation. Someone like—" Her hands clenched. "Like that ambassador. That—" She broke off, unable to think of words suitably vile to describe him. "Ambassador Jarrod whatever-his-filthy-name-is, and may he rot in the depths of the sea. He must be betraying Uncle Dysart's trust, as well. So much for Gavonian honor."

She paced to the other side of the large chamber. "I wish I'd known last night." She turned back to Agathas. "I had the perfect chance to kill him, and by the three moons, I'd give anything if I had! Well, I'll do it now, and I'll send his body back to Gavin-Secundus with a recommendation they pick their advisors with a little more care. And as for Bailan—"

A junior cook looked up from his filleting of a giant zori fish and cleared his throat. "If you think it best—"

"None of this is best!" Dia threw herself down into a chair.

The junior cook swallowed. "I—I could slip a little saltash grass into your cousin's—"

"No!" Dia looked up, appalled. "No," she repeated, striving for a calmer note. "No poisons. I don't have my family members murdered—no matter how much they need it. Besides, it wouldn't do any good. Bailan's not the force, here. It's that Gavonian." Her fingers drummed on the curved arm of the plasti-chair. "I need to get back in control. Until then, I want that Gavonian watched." She turned to

Agathas. "Find out if he sends or receives any messages. Do we have anyone loyal in communications?"

Agathas directed a questioning glance around the gathered servants, and encountered only uncertain shrugs. "We'll find out, Lady. Merris, take a cart of beverages—"

"I'll do it." Dia sprang to her feet and strode toward the pantry where the serving carts were stored.

Agathas reached the doorway first and blocked her way. "Lady, we don't know who'll be in there. Someone might recognize you."

"And betray me." She drew a shaky breath. "Yesterday at this time, I would've said that was impossible."

"Greed," Agathas reminded her.

"Greed," Dia repeated. "And we're the perfect victims. By the Great Net, we've got to be the most naive planet in the whole damned galaxy! If only we'd learned about negotiating treaties instead of catering to tourists."

A gleam lit Agathas's eyes. "Are you sure they're so different?"

Dia's lips twitched. "We've never been cut-throat. And the stakes have never been so high. We're going to have to look strong. Much stronger than we are."

"There are planets out there who won't wait for negotiating," Agathas reminded her.

Dia winced. "Good old Kerrian, good for nothing but entertaining a bunch of drunk tourists. Do you realize we're probably the only planet in this quadrant that doesn't have even a basic military fleet? Here we are, the greatest prize in the galaxy, floating here like a giant kubo fish, waiting to be scooped up in anybody's net. Well, there's nothing I can do about getting a battle fleet, or negotiating skills, for that matter, until after I've regained control. And that means I've got a vermin ambassador to exterminate.''

''You don't need to do it yourself—'' Agathas began.

''Oh, but I want the pleasure.'' Dia's brow lowered, and she worked her lower lip. ''Let's make some serious plans. I want to know where the mercenary guards are stationed. How many there are, that sort of thing. We should be able to find out by going about simple cleaning duties. And I need to find out who's in communications. If news of this revolt hasn't gotten out yet, I want to make sure it doesn't.''

Agathas stared at her as if she had gone insane. ''But someone might come to help—''

''You mean someone might come and take us over themselves. I'd rather deal with only one invading force at a time, if you don't mind. We map out the guards, close down communications, and I remove the ambassador. In any order that presents itself. Any questions?''

Agathas shook her head. ''You can't just kill the ambassador. If you're caught—''

''I won't be.'' Dia ran restless fingers along the tracery of metal that made up her rys-bracelet. It hummed with latent power. ''I'll wait 'til we're ready to take control, then do it silently and out of sight.''

She studied the uneasy faces that clustered about the long prep table. Only one of the assistant cooks had shown the initiative to join in the discussion, and his suggestion hadn't thrilled her. The household staff, she admitted with regret, was no substitute for the palace guard.

''Merris.'' She singled out the oldest of the kitchen help. ''Can you wheel a cart to the comm room, talk your way in there, and look around without acting suspicious? Just see if there's anyone we can trust still on duty."

"I'd be too nervous!" the woman protested.

"That's all right," Dia assured her. "You have every right to be as jumpy as you like, considering what's been going on here. I'd say they'd only be suspicious if you acted relaxed."

Merris opened her mouth, shut it again, then nodded. "I guess I could look around. As long as I don't have to shoot or stab anyone. That I couldn't do."

"You only have to remember my father and I are dead, and act accordingly. Help her stock the cart, will you, Agathas? Good luck, Merris."

Agathas folded her arms before her. "What are you planning to do?"

"Take a tray and look around. See which areas they've got guarded." Dia frowned. "I wish the tourist industry required bugs and scriers. I'd like to plant some in a few quarters. If we—" She broke off, possibilities racing in her mind. "The other ambassadors won't be here until late this afternoon. If we can find just one comm person we can trust, we might be able to make a bug or two."

Merris looked worried. "I wouldn't know—"

"You don't have to do anything. Just let me know if you recognize anyone. I'll—" She broke off at Agathas's quick glance. "Okay, *one* of us will make the contact."

Agathas sniffed. "You just keep yourself out of sight, Lady."

"Don't worry." Dia's mouth tightened. "I'm not letting myself get caught until I've killed Ambassador Jarrod whatever-his-name-is. After that, I'll be too busy regaining control. Let's get going." She threw Merris a grim smile. "It's show time."

She saw the woman off on her errand, then poured some hot stimi into a cup. The rich aroma filled the room, pungent of the sea lily from which it was brewed. Even the steam seemed to carry the heartening stimulant effect. She swished it around, then decided no point in wasting it. She swallowed the contents, her nose wrinkling at the bitterness. Should have added a measure of rubas sugar, a local product which was beaten by the harvesters from the roots and stems of the plentiful sea tuber.

She set the dirtied cup on a tray, along with a huge sponge and towel, and set off to roam the halls, ostensibly in search of other used dishes. No one would recognize her. She repeated that, over and over, though her nerves quivered as she hurried along the corridor. As long as she stayed away from Bailan, she should be safe. Still, she'd feel better if only she could have pretended to be one of the palace guard—in full ceremonial dress, of course. The helmets kept for special occasions had a band of chased metal that extended from the forehead to the tip of the nose. That provided a far better disguise than a change of hairstyle and smear of makeup to blur her cheekbones.

No revolutionary soldiers along the service corridor, at least. Apparently, Ambassador Jarrod didn't think the staff posed any threat to him. He'd learn. Oh, he'd learn. Pity he wouldn't live long enough to benefit from the lesson.

She reached the junction with the main hall, stepped onto the tiled mosaic, and saw Bailan coming out of the audience chamber. She ducked back, her heart pounding in her ears. By the Great Net, why did he have to be the first person she encountered? Don't, she prayed, let it be an omen. And don't, she added, let him come this way. She didn't want to kill him, but if he recognized her, her only other choice would be to take him captive, and that she was in no position to do—yet.

The steady tap of his sandaled feet drew closer, then changed in tone and cadence. The stairs, she realized, and relief flooded through her, leaving her faint. She could delay dealing with Bailan a little longer. Buoyed by this reprieve, she set off once more to map the mercenaries' positions.

Only a single guard stood on duty before the audience chamber. An off-worlder. She did no more than direct a casual glance at him, but she identified his planet of origin. Bertol. Her jaw set as she strode past. She preferred off-worlders in their proper place—as paying guests, not an invading force.

As she continued through the public portion of the ground floor, she spotted two more off-world soldiers, both garbed as Kerrinian palace guards. Why the pretence of uniforms? she wondered. To make Bailan feel less threatened? One had only to look at the varied facial features to know the truth. Not one possessed the fine bone structure, honeyed skin or thick black hair of a native.

She circled back to the audience chamber to collect the tray Agathas had brought earlier. Bailan and Ambassador Jarrod had drained the pot of stimi, she noted. Did that mean they'd held a long, serious discussion? Or had the vile ambassador sought strength in cup after cup as he realized how limp was the puppet with which he hoped to lull the other treaty negotiators?

She stacked the dishes and slipped through the private door, heading once more for the kitchen. She had seen only off-worlders on duty, even here, in the unimportant areas of the palace. Apparently none of her own guard remained. That sent a sharp pang through her, as if she personally had failed them.

They must be dead. Kerrian possessed no extensive prison facilities, certainly nowhere to confine a large number of guards except in their own quarters. The worst their planet dealt with were drunks and disorderlies, an occasional poacher. This was a *recreation* planet, damn it, a tourist trap, not a world where violence and lawlessness reigned. That would be bad for business.

Only at the moment, it was *not* business as usual.

Maybe Merris would have news from the comm room by now. That hope quickened her step.

She burst through the door into the kitchen, her gaze darting about. Only a couple of the cooks remained; everyone else had vanished. Probably on purpose, to avoid her, she reflected. Anger flickered in her, to be replaced the next moment by compassion. They weren't soldiers, and technically, she supposed, they owed her no allegiance that would endanger themselves. She couldn't expect it of staff sworn to do no more than care for the family. They'd served that function well over the years.

Agathas emerged from the hydroponics room, wiping her hands on the apron that covered her sarong. Following her came Merris, bearing a tray of leafy green vegetables.

"What did you learn?" Dia shoved her own tray toward a table, barely making the connection. The tray teetered on the edge, and she gave it an impatient shove.

Merris came to an abrupt halt, her face working with her distress. "I couldn't!" Anger sounded in her voice. "They wouldn't let me in. I was afraid if I insisted—"

"It's all right," Dia said quickly. "So they wouldn't let you in. Well, I guess that tells us something, too— though not quite as much as I'd have liked." She turned away, frustration gripping at her. Why couldn't it have been simple? Why couldn't just one thing have been simple?

Everyone in the kitchen concentrated on the food they prepared, studiously avoiding looking at her. If Merris couldn't get in, there wasn't much chance she would fare better. Still, she had to try. She couldn't just sit and wait and do nothing. Somehow, she had to contact her ministers at Waianoa and summon the reserve guard while there was still time to regain control of the government. Driven more by nerves than by a practical plan, she snatched up her tray once more and headed out the door and through the corridors leading to the comm room.

Someone stood at the junction ahead, a tall, solidly built man in a hunter green uniform crossed with a gold and white sash. Ambassador Jarrod, himself. Beside him stood a small woman dressed as a palace guardsman, but nothing about her appeared native Kerrinian. Ceres Alphian, Dia realized, and came to a halt. Now, why would a Gavonian—particularly one of military age—chat in such a friendly manner with someone whom he must still regard as an enemy? On his last visit, Tharl Dysart talked long and bitterly of the war between Gavin-Secundus and Ceres Alpha, of the mines where the prisoners of war worked as slaves, where his own brother had died.

And here stood the Gavonian ambassador, apparently flirting with a former enemy.

How much more proof did she need that in him she beheld a traitor? His tharl was innocent; *this* was the man who betrayed them all.

The hum of her bracelet filled her, until her entire body vibrated with it. She balanced the tray in one hand and raised the other, refusing to acknowledge the aching stiffness of her muscles after last night's endurance swim. She had a clear shot. She only had to move closer, perhaps twenty meters or so, to assure the tiny weapon's accuracy. He would be dead, her planet saved. Bailan would be no contest for her.

Ambassador Jarrod's mercenaries would be another matter, though. She studied the two as they stood together, the woman giving a short, derisive laugh at something the ambassador said. If she killed him, as every instinct urged her to do, she would have to kill this Cerean soldier, as well, and that gave her pause. Killing someone who merely followed orders, who was an inconvenience rather than an instigator, Dia could not justify. Yet the woman was, after all, a soldier, and this was war. If she grasped this opportunity to kill Jarrod, her choice would be to either kill this woman as well, or be killed by her.

The Cerean must have said something, for the ambassador turned his head to glance at Dia. Dia hesitated, her arm trembling with fatigue; at this distance she had no chance of hitting either target. She took hold of the tray with both hands again, not sure whether common sense or cowardice dictated her decision. No, not cowardice. She would seize a better opportunity to kill him when it would not be a wasted gesture.

The ambassador's eyes narrowed and he studied Dia with a frown. "Dee?" he called. A question sounded in his voice, as if he weren't quite certain.

He said something to the mercenary which didn't carry, and started toward Dia.

She froze. *Opportunity* part of her mind screamed, while the rest clamored with questions of how he could have recognized her. She'd been disheveled, her hair loose and matted. Now it was pinned up, and she wore a servant's uniform. She took an unsteady step back.

Jarrod stopped. "Dee?" he repeated. "Yes, it is you." He closed the distance between them. "Don't you remember me? Jarrod, from last night?"

"I—" She swallowed. He had no idea who she really was, she reminded herself—no more than she'd guessed about him last night. She could play along, *make that opportunity*. Show time.

She forced a hesitant smile to her lips. "I didn't expect to see you here."

"I tried to find you." His gaze ran over her, as if checking for injury. "That was a crazy stunt, running out the way you did."

She straightened, meeting his frowning scrutiny. "I made it home all right, just like I said I would."

"No one bothered you?"

"I swam," she admitted. Damn the man, did he have to look so concerned, as if he really cared what happened to one insignificant girl in the midst of all this chaos and death he'd created? And did she have to glow all over from the way he studied her, from the way a slow, predatory smile lit the depths of those gray eyes?

A predatory smile that just might be used against him.

"Your family? Were they all right?"

She lowered her lashes, thinking fast. What had she said last night? Only that she didn't know about them. "Not everyone reported to work this morning," she said with complete but misleading truth.

His brow lowered. "After a day of peace, they'll probably come out of hiding. Do you live at home with them, or here?"

Polite concern cloaked the question, but something just beneath the surface tugged at her, intrigued her. Something in the tone of his voice, in the way his gaze strayed from her face to linger on her body, then returned to study her mouth. Too damned intriguing by half! Certainly for her own good.

Opportunities, she reminded herself. He seemed inclined to flirt with her. So be it. She'd turn it into the opportunity she needed.

She looked down, her nervousness very real. "It's kind of you to be concerned, considering how busy you must be."

"Part of my job here." He brushed a wisping tendril of hair from her cheek. "I'm supposed to help protect the interests of Kerrian."

His touch, brief as it was, sent a thrill of awareness racing through her. *Damn* her attraction to him. She couldn't let it get in the way of what she had to do.

She stepped back a pace, needing the distance between them. "I don't need protecting now."

"Don't you?" His voice took on a husky, tantalizing note.

"Only from you," she said with real sincerity. Nerves raced through her. Did her fears show in her eyes? In her expression? Could he read her determination?

A slow smile tugged at the corners of his mouth. "Am I dangerous?"

In more ways than one, she reflected, but she kept

that to herself. She merely shook her head. "Is your head better?"

The gleam in his eyes acknowledged her abrupt change of subject. "The med center will be too full for anything less than a missing limb. Have you got anything useful in the kitchen?"

The under cook's mention of saltash grass sprang to her mind, to be dismissed at once. It might be the easy way to get rid of him, but poison was a coward's approach. When she killed Ambassador Jarrod, it would be an execution—direct, face to face, clean—though that was not the death this traitor deserved. She ignored the part of her that wanted him to live, to touch her again.

"I think we could find you something," she said, knowing it would be, in fact, a harmless but effective remedy.

The smile lines about his eyes deepened. "That would be a kindness."

A kindness. If only he knew, he'd just handed her the opportunity she'd needed. She would fix his remedy. She would bring it to him. Herself. Alone. To his room. She forced out a lone, lingering regret. For what he had done to her planet, her family, he must die. And by her hand.

"You owe me one for last night," he went on, "for running out on me like that. I'd intended to find out where you lived so I could see you again."

She looked up quickly, all too aware of the attraction radiating between them. She made a dismissive gesture. "The Gavonian ambassador and a maid?"

His eyes darkened from the gray of the Merlin oysters to that of the massive thunder clouds that rolled across the seas. "What about Jarrod, the man, and a very fascinating young woman?"

This time, his tone caressed her, with a strength and sincerity that for a moment robbed her of both breath and words.

"After what's happened around here, do you think anyone would mind—or even notice—if you took a couple of hours off from work? To show me around?" Both curiosity and a deeper, more urgent note colored his voice. "Other staffers don't seem to be at their posts."

"What do you expect?" Her jaw clenched. "They're probably dead. Or hiding in fear for their lives."

His brow clouded. "Didn't they support the revolution?"

"Is that what you think? That any true Kerrinian— aside from my—from Bailan—could have been involved in anything like this?"

"Bad for the tourist business," he agreed, his tone dry. "Bailan couldn't have done it alone, though."

"Oh, no. Someone from off-world planned this. Someone—" She broke off. Someone like him, she'd been about to say.

"Does the staff know anything?" he asked quickly. "Or have any guesses?"

"How many systems out there would like to control the coral?" she asked, avoiding his question.

"Too many." He rubbed his head as if it ached. "Well, it's done, and now we have to minimize the damage. Will the staff support Bailan?"

She caught the changed note in his voice. No longer flirtatious, he was all business, all concern. Did he worry that the weak link in his takeover chain would snap and fail him? Her lip curled. "He's no rys Pauaia."

"No!" he agreed with surprising force.

Well, he'd probably like his puppet to be stronger, but he should be glad he didn't try to manipulate a member of her own house. Little did he know he'd shortly have to face one, though, and a vengeful member, at that.

"If you want your planet to survive, you're going to have to present a united front for these negotiations," he went on.

"We will. We owe our king that much, and we owe it to ourselves. It's not just the ruler of Kerrian who's going to benefit from the coral treaties. Do you think any of us want to see part of our planet thrown away? No true Kerrinian is going to accept domination, or any attempt to gain control of our assets."

Jarrod's eyes gleamed. "I'm glad to hear it. Your best chance will be to at least *seem* to support Bailan and make these negotiations run as smoothly as possible. If the ambassadors have cause to complain about their accommodations or treatment, I think there's every chance your Bailan will grovel and give in on their treaty demands."

"Bailan—" She broke off the comment she'd been about to make. With Jarrod's sentiment, at least, she had to agree. Kerrian had to present as much of a united front as they could muster. Only it wouldn't be under Bailan.

Still, she could use his concern about the running of the palace to her advantage. "The staff—" She paused, searching for the right words, how Agathas might explain it. "We need to go about our normal duties, to preserve that feeling of *being* normal. Sir."

"Jarrod," he said quickly.

She studied the tray she held, not wanting him to see the calculation that must show in her eyes. "I need to finish my rounds. It bothers me when there's something not completed. It just reinforces the fact that everything's up in the air and unsettled."

"You find comfort in returning dishes to the kitchen?" A smile sounded in his voice.

She glanced up, met his eyes, and saw the touch of amusement there. Did he really think she worried over something so insignificant in the wake of his invasion? So be it, then. "I've really got to make a tour of the comm room," she said. "But when Merris tried to bring the morning stimi to the crew, she said no one would let her in."

"I think I can arrange something for you." He turned back, and with a tilt of his head indicated she should follow.

It was working? She couldn't quite believe it. He could be such a fool, playing the gallant, that he would actually betray his own interests without realizing it. That disappointed her—but her purpose was not to admire him, but to bring about his downfall.

She followed a respectful pace behind him along the corridor, until he stopped, once more challenged by the Cerean mercenary.

"She needs to collect dishes," he told the woman.

The mercenary glanced at him, her gaze holding scorn. "Probably not enough in there to matter yet."

He shook his head. "The surest way to collapse things around here is to let the staff feel unsettled. I hear you've already refused to let the morning stimi cart in."

The woman shrugged, but a touch of uncertainty flickered across her features. "I got a cup, at least."

Dia clutched her tray. A knockout powder. Why hadn't they tried to drug the mercenaries? But no, she realized with regret. It would work for one person, but not a group. Any of them who didn't drink their share would realize what had happened to their unconscious comrades, and retaliate.

"I don't see where letting that maid in would have done any harm," Jarrod pursued.

The mercenary shook her head. "What if she's a spy? My orders are not to let anyone through."

"So what's in there for a spy to see? You can't tell me there aren't enough of your people in there to stop someone from sabotage or sending messages."

The woman grinned. "Orders," she repeated, making a face to show how little she thought of them.

"You could have summoned your prize lieutenant to escort her," he pointed out.

That brought a sudden grin to the woman's face. "She should be glad I didn't."

"How about if I escort the bus-girl?" he offered.

The woman considered a moment, then shrugged. "Go ahead. As long as you keep an eye on her, that should keep them happy." She touched her comm link. "Two to come through. Ambassador tolArvik and a maid."

TolArvik. Dia burned that name into her memory. TolArvik. Forevermore she would equate it with betrayal—his, of his tharl and his honor, and hers, of her own yearnings that there might have been something between them.

Dia bobbed a quick curtsy as she passed the corporal in Jarrod's wake. One aspect of their exchange puzzled her. Didn't the mercenary know who had ordered her army's services? Jarrod—Ambassador tolArvik—asked permission, he didn't order. Or did he keep his role quiet, maintain his power in the background? To openly declare himself might well defeat his purpose.

At the door to the comm room, they encountered two more armed soldiers. One—a Rualdan, Dia thought—looked them over, then stepped aside and gestured for them to enter. Jarrod waved her in ahead of him.

Dia glanced around quickly, spotting the unfamiliar officers in their familiar uniforms. Did *none* of her people survive? The thought broke off as she encountered a boy sitting at a comm unit, staring at her open-mouthed. Her stomach clenched, and only with difficulty did she control her expression. With her heart pounding in her chest, she gave the slightest shake of her head and moved away.

Would he betray her? Whether he did it on purpose or by accident would make little difference to the outcome. For that matter, *she* could betray herself, too, if she weren't careful. She forced herself to draw in a calming breath, then another. Casting a seemingly random glance about the room, she saw that the boy now studied his comm screen as if oblivious to her.

Did that mean she was safe from him? Who was he, anyway? She didn't really know him, not even his name. He was new to the service, he'd come from—where? She closed her eyes. He'd come from the—from the far east. A family—something about a volcanic mountain, a waterfall. Details evaded her. Why couldn't she remember now, when she needed to? His name, any part of his name. If she could just speak to him, call him by name, it might tie him to her, summon up that touch of loyalty. But even if she knew who he was, she didn't dare make betraying contact.

She glanced back. He still studied his screen, ignoring her. Could he perhaps be loyal to her? *How could she enlist his help without being caught?*

Frustration left her sick. Here she was, in the comm room. Five minutes alone with that boy, and she could contact her ministers, summon her reserves—even call up the personnel files to discover where her people should be, if any of the missing ones could have run for the safety of distant families and survived the horrors of last night.

She shoved a glass on her tray, then moved on, past a mercenary whose planet of origin she couldn't place. She collected a plate and a set of dirty utensils, and kept walking. The room showed traces of having been occupied by a large number of people throughout the night. She should have brought a larger tray, but these concerns had never come her way before.

She stacked another dish with care on top of the others, turned to scan the room, caught the young Kerrinian boy's eye. Quickly, he looked away. Had that been just a touch of a smile? She searched the room for Jarrod and found him talking quietly in a corner with a lieutenant, whose gaze remained fixed on her. Dia flushed and gathered several more cups.

The last of the dishes stood on the far side of the room. She headed toward them, deliberately passing the young Kerrinian. She couldn't really look at him. The lieutenant watched her too closely, probably to see if she did try to contact the boy. It would be his loyalty questioned, his life jeopardized, she realized, as well as hers.

She added the last of the dirty plates to her pile,

gave the counter top a quick wipe with the sponge she carried, then turned to Jarrod. "Thank you, sir. I'm done in here." She started from the room.

To her surprise, the ambassador fell into step beside her.

"You promised me a headache remedy," he said as the door to the comm room closed behind them.

"Yes, sir."

"Probably what we all need is just some peace and quiet." He winked at the Cerean mercenary as they reached her, and shook his head. "Obviously this one's a spy," he announced. "Just couldn't wait to get in there and get her hands on the equipment. See? She's got a load of vital components she's smuggling out."

The Cerean laughed. "I'll bet the lieutenant thinks she has," she said, and waved them past.

If only she *did*. "They won't be expecting someone like you in the kitchens," Dia said to divert his mind from thoughts of sabotage. "Is that common on your planet? For someone like you to drop into the kitchen?"

"For field officers. We prefer the practical to the protocol." He walked for a minute in silence. "Do you know," he said abruptly, "I think I preferred it last night, when I was just Jarrod and you were just Dee."

She shook her head. "We'd have found out soon enough." She still feared he'd find out—too soon. "Illusions rarely last."

"Illusions." He stopped abruptly, placed his hands on her shoulders and turned her to face him. The tray kept him at arms length. "Some things aren't illusions." His gaze held hers. "Some things are true.

It's an old cliche that the eyes are the windows to the soul. That's where you can read truth or falsity.''

For a long moment she stared into his eyes, those clear eyes that burned with purpose. No, that couldn't be honor.

He held her gaze, but a frown creased his brow. "Dee?" His quiet voice probed, puzzled.

His eyes. . . .

Your eyes don't lie, damn it! her mind screamed.

Yet, they told her the opposite of what she knew to be true.

Chapter Five

Jarrod paused in the doorway of the kitchen, his quick glance darting about the well-appointed, no-nonsense interior. Stainless steel. Plasti-clear. Touches of tile. Easily cleaned, no surfaces that might trap harmful microbes. Like the comm room, not a place for the tourists. A place for business. These people knew when they could abandon the picturesque image.

The slightly built housekeeper stood by one of the long, shining tables, talking to a large, aproned man who held a chopping blade in one hand. Before them lay an assortment of tubers, partially prepared. What, by the fires, was the woman's name? Irritation flashed through him; he *should* remember.

Dee stepped into the room behind him. "Agathas?" Her soft voice carried easily.

The housekeeper looked up at once. "Yes, La—" She broke off, staring at Jarrod, her expression one of consternation.

Dee advanced further into the room. "It's all right. This is Ambassador tolArvik, from Gavin-Secundus. He needs something for a headache."

The woman's eyes screamed questions, which she didn't voice. Jarrod's gaze narrowed, but he remained where he stood, pretending to look around with mild interest. Mild, nothing. The people, not the room, pricked his curiosity. Dee—a lowly maid—bore no traces of subservience in the presence of the house-keeper. Did they work together on terms of equality on this planet?

Maybe there'd be no problem getting Dee assigned to wait on him. He'd like having her around—and not just because she'd become someone familiar in this alien, revolt-torn world. There was something about her that attracted him, something that went beyond the brilliance of the huge violet eyes that dominated her fine-boned face, and the slender curves that her tattered sarong had failed to cover fully last night. She fascinated him, with her loyalty to her former ruling family, her spurts of temper, her underlying intelli-gence—and the pain of last night's revolution, the sense of heavy burdens she couldn't share. He wanted to shelter her, provide a safe haven where she could forget the tragedies. Desire stirred in him, emphasizing this last thought. Yes, he wanted her in his bed.

Agathas still watched Dee. "A *special* headache rem-edy?" she suggested, though she sounded uncertain.

"No!" Dee shook her head. "A regular one."

"Don't I rate a special?" Jarrod asked.

"It would make you too tired for the afternoon's negotiations," Dee said quickly.

What was in that special concoction, anyway? He'd have to find out—and discover why it was to be denied him.

The housekeeper. Agathas. He committed the name to memory. Agathas went to a cupboard and ran her finger along a line of bottles. She drew one out, started forward, then glanced at Dee.

"A single dose." Dee crossed to another cupboard and brought out a cup of Forezian china. "Let's see if it works for him."

Agathas shot her a swift glance, then measured out a small amount. She handed the cup to Jarrod.

He took it, glanced at Dee, then swallowed it in one gulp. At first, nothing happened. Then sweet liquid fire burned down his throat, warming his entire body. Blood seemed to race through his veins, and his hands and feet tingled. For a moment his head spun, then it settled. The throbbing ache, which had plagued him since the night before, faded.

He handed the cup back to the housekeeper. "That was fast."

The woman nodded. No trace of friendliness touched her features. "It's a good remedy." She returned to the cook's side.

Jarrod watched her, frowning. She seemed to regard him as if he were an opponent; but what battle did they fight? He'd sensed something different about Dee, today, as well. The shock of finding her life altered, he supposed. Or was there something more? A banding together of those who had served the royal house? These were the people who would find it the hardest to accept the changes brought by the revolution.

The level of tension in the room seemed to be rising. Brought about by his presence, Jarrod realized. It hit him like a wave of malevolence, as if he were the target of intense hatred. He glanced around. Only the cook, the housekeeper, and Dee. For one moment, he had the uncanny sensation he'd walked into a trap filled with deadly enemies. Even Dee, lovely Dee, into whose strained, frightened eyes he had gazed, and sensed her desperate need for strength.

The door burst open, and Bailan strode inside, his robes swirling about him, fury etched deeply on every fine-boned feature. He glowered at everyone indiscriminately. "Why is no one answering the comm link?" he demanded.

In a tone that dripped indifference, Agathas said, "It hasn't sounded . . . sir." She added the title after a pause just long enough to turn it into an insult.

"I've been pressing the damned thing for the last half hour." He fixed his glare on the woman, but his features bore more resemblance to a pout.

Agathas gave the matter a dismissive shrug. "Then obviously it was damaged in the fighting last night. You should complain to your mercenaries."

Bailan straightened. "It wasn't *my* doing that the people of Kerrian revolted against my uncle's house and chose me as their new king."

Agathas made no response. She merely stared at him, her expression forbidding. The cook resumed his chopping as if his newly made king were not in the room, and Dee— Jarrod glanced around, looking for her. Dee had vanished, probably into the room next to the cupboard. The door stood slightly ajar. He'd guessed her contempt for her new ruler already, though he hadn't expected her to refuse to face him. Insults to his face, like Agathas delivered, seemed more Dee's style.

Bailan hunched a petulant shoulder and turned

from the housekeeper. Ignoring the cook, he settled on Jarrod. "You're supposed to be here helping me," he complained. "So help. Get the comm link fixed."

Jarrod propped one shoulder against the wall, folded his arms, and regarded the young man through hooded eyes. "My role is to advise you. So I advise you to ask your staff—politely—to see to it that it's fixed. As quickly as possible. The other ambassadors should begin arriving at any time, now. Broken comm links might seem to you like a minor inconvenience, but they'll be seen for what they are—evidence that you don't have your house in order. You may be very sure they'll take advantage of that fact."

Bailan opened his mouth, snapped it closed, then with reluctance returned his attention to the housekeeper. "Who's in charge of fixing things like that?"

"One of the techs—but I haven't seen any of them this morning. It's possible your soldiers killed them all."

"Why—" Bailan began angrily, then broke off, his face a picture of consternation. "Oh, right. We didn't trust them."

The cook stopped in mid–chop and stared at Bailan. "What have you done with them?" His gravelly voice held a growling menace.

"I don't know. Where's Captain Reebol?" Bailan looked to Jarrod. "He's supposed to take care of staff problems."

Jarrod shrugged. "I've no idea. But, I suggest you find him—and quickly. You'll need to be in the audience chamber—with no workmen anywhere in sight—in just over two hours for the formal welcoming of the ambassadorial delegations."

"Damn the delegations," Bailan flung at him. "I suppose you'll try to tell me how to dress, as well? And what to serve for refreshments?"

"Very good. You managed to learn about refreshments. But since I'm not a Kerrinian, I don't know what would be appropriate. You'd better take that up with your housekeeper and head cook. Then you need to find that captain and arrange for the repairs. And Bailan?"

The young man, who had started toward the housekeeper, glanced back, his expression flustered.

"A king never enters his kitchen. You should have sent one of the staff or a guard to summon your householders to you."

Bailan spun on his heel and stalked out the door, slamming it behind him.

Jarrod shook his head. "A king also needs to control his temper."

"That's never been Bailan's strong point." Dee stood beside the cabinet as if she'd never been away.

"Ummm." Jarrod studied her flushed face for a moment, then turned to Agathas. "He seems to have forgotten to order the refreshments. I suppose you'd already made plans?"

Agathas sniffed. "The—the princess took care of everything. She was raised to the position of royal hostess."

A grim smile tugged at Jarrod's lips. "Well, we can't accuse Bailan of that, can we? Two hours," he said, eyeing the pile of tubers awaiting the chopper. "I'd better get out of your way so you can prepare." He hesitated, waiting to see what Dee would do, but she turned to the huge refrigerator and began unloading trays of already arranged delicacies.

As Jarrod left the room, though, he knew eyes watched him. He could feel them boring through his back, dissecting him. Distrusting him.

He couldn't blame them, he supposed; he couldn't

let them bother him, either. He had work to do, if
this planet were not to be decimated before the day
ended. Bailan, in his current pettish mood, was more
likely to retire to his room and sulk than take care
of necessary arrangements. Which probably left Jarrod to make certain someone made the repairs,
cleared the room and arranged the chairs.

As for preparing Bailan, Jarrod's mouth tightened.
He didn't see any way of teaching that little upstart
regal grace and manners in the short time allowed.
Still, he had to try.

At least he could leave the hospitality to the
housekeeping staff. That very peculiar and hostile
housekeeping staff. He didn't like feeling at odds
with Dee. It would make his job here a great deal
more bearable if he could come to an understanding
with her—if he could forge one real friendship in
this palace. One real friendship. Damn, he wanted
more than that with Dee. He wanted to get her alone,
break down that barrier she had thrown up between
them. The possibilities thundered through him.

Dee slipped into the banqueting hall, her tray laden
with platters of tubers and fresh greens from the
hydroponics room. So far, no disasters had befallen.
The ambassadorial delegations had arrived,
exchanged no more than veiled insults during the
welcoming reception, and now sat down to dinner.
Dee had remained out of sight, assuring herself she
recognized—and would be recognized by—no one.

Tonight, she would wait only on the lower tables;
that way she'd stay well out of her cousin's sight. The
plan had its drawbacks, though. Here, among the
lesser dignitaries, the assistants and secretaries from

the five systems that sent delegations to seek treaties, she heard nothing of any importance.

All five ambassadors, resplendent in dress uniform or their native formal attire, sat on plush cushions arranged around the head table, which rose a scant half meter off the floor. Bailan, in full regal robes and murex shell crown, reclined on a low, conch-shaped couch, alone on one long side of the table. Ambassador Jarrod tolArvik, still in his hunter green uniform, held the position of honor on Bailan's right.

Dia's satisfaction swelled. A dangerous mistake on her cousin's part. Why had his Gavonian advisor not warned him? Or did Jarrod—no, tolArvik, she renounced the use of his given name—did tolArvik enjoy the ostentatious display of favoritism over the others? It certainly set the tone for the upcoming negotiations—a tone fraught with tension and resentment.

Her mouth tightened. She should be the one seated on the dining throne, facing the ambassadors, making clear the strength of both her house and her planet. Bailan should be incarcerated in what passed for a Kerrinian prison, until she decided how to prevent his trying anything like this again. And tolArvik should be dead, not leaning along the table to listen to a comment made by his Rualdan counterpart.

She studied the back of tolArvik's head, with the thick waves of sandy brown hair that fell to his shoulders. He'd been busy all afternoon, closeted with her cousin. Not one chance had she found to bring him another headache remedy, to be alone with him long enough to tell him who she was and why she was about to execute him.

TolArvik glanced up and around, as if aware of her unwavering gaze. She moved on at once, offering servings from her tray to the lesser members of the delegation from Quy'dao. Tonight, she promised herself. Tonight she would even all scores.

She had much to do before then. She still hadn't learned anything of the young Kerrinian who manned the main comm console. He hadn't yet denounced her, but how could someone loyal to her have survived the obvious purge?

She cast a hate-filled glance toward the head table, to find that tolArvik watched her. She couldn't see his expression; too much distance separated them. Yet still he'd found her amid the other waiters. Had he been aware of her gaze boring into the back of his head? She would very much like to make him feel uncomfortable —but not at the expense of putting him on his guard.

She moved on to the next table, where more of the Quy'doans sat on their low pillows, and offered them the array of greens. What if tolArvik requested that she serve at his table? She wouldn't put it past him. She'd really be in a mess, then. She could just imagine Bailan's reaction on seeing her—and tolArvik's on realizing who she was. No, when he learned that, she intended to be alone with him, just the two of them—and her rys-bracelet.

She laid the platter on the center of the table, collected several empty ones and returned to the kitchens, seething with impatience. Perhaps Bailan would make himself so unpopular with the ambassadors tonight, they would welcome her when she took her rightful place in the morning. TolArvik, of course, would not be one of them; he would not survive the night.

She returned to the banquet hall once more, pushing a cart bearing platters of a pastry redolent of cinnamon and perri nuts, which were borne from the water trees that grew around the edges of the coral atolls. The rich odor filled the chamber, and a number of diners looked up to find the source. And well they should. She'd already eaten a piece in the kitchens, and the sweet-tart taste lingered in her mouth, the spices warming her stomach. A heartening dish, leaving her ready for the dangers of the night to come.

She settled the cart against the back wall and cast a quick glance toward tolArvik, who leaned in the direction of Bailan, listening to something his charge related. She wanted to get closer, to hear what they said. She'd be in a better position tomorrow if she knew what was discussed tonight.

A woman's deep voice rose, Quy'doan by its dialect, heavy with bitterness. Bailan waved an airy hand, then checked as tolArvik snapped a response. Dia inched along the wall, closer, straining her ears.

The Quy'doan ambassador, garbed in rich tones of deep blue and silver, her near-black hair echoing the blue tinge, slammed her fist against the table, setting the crystal glasses shaking. "Let us understand one another." Her voice rolled the words with her thick accent. "Is it your intention to *give* the coral and acid to Gavin-Secundus, then charge the rest of us more to make up for it?"

"Of course not!" Bailan turned first to tolArvik, then back to the Quy'doan ambassador. "This—your accusation—is an insult!"

Dia clasped her hands. "Yes." She barely whispered the word. "Oh, yes, start a fight with her."

"It is your obvious favoring of Gavin-Secundus that is the insult!" came the prompt response from the Quy'doan.

"I don't favor anyone." Bailan cast another anxious glance toward tolArvik.

His falsity pronounced itself clearly both in his tone and in his continual seeking of Gavonian guidance. Dia struggled to keep her countenance blank, not to betray her satisfaction at her cousin's blunders. The ambassadors would welcome her tomorrow rather than objecting to this second change of power.

"Gavonian puppet!" The ambassador from Ceres Alpha, an elderly man, surged to his feet, his deep maroon robe swirling about his ankles as he spun to glower at tolArvik. "My delegation will leave at once. We came to negotiate with the royal house of rys Pauaia. Instead, we find an upstart in possession of the throne. An upstart who is molded and coddled by Gavin-Secundus! Can this planet not even manage its own internal affairs?"

The appalled look on Bailan's face sent a ripple of pleasure through Dia. She deserved to revel in his discomfiture, after all the pain and anguish he'd caused, he and his Gavonian masters. Hadn't Bailan the sense to remember the recent war between Gavin and Ceres Alpha? Nothing could more surely anger the Cerean ambassador than Bailan's blatant reliance on a Gavonian advisor.

The Quy'doan ambassador rose, also. "An upstart, indeed, who has not even an idea of his own, but has to listen to his Gavonian master at every step. The people of this planet are not fit to control an asset as valuable as Dahmla coral and Columbine acid."

Not fit to control the coral. . . . Dia's enjoyment evaporated. She leaned against the wall, sick with shock at the implication of those angry words.

The Cerean ambassador gestured toward the lower tables, and the maroon and gold garbed members of his staff rose at once, knocking dishes and cushions aside in their haste. At a nod from the Quy'doan, more men and women, all wearing deep blue sashes, stood, too. Neither ambassador made any further acknowledgment of Bailan; they simply strode from the chamber with their people hurrying after them.

Dia hugged herself as horror dug in and took a firm grip. Those two ambassadors didn't walk out as part of a negotiating technique. They had analyzed the situation—all too correctly—and now left to alert their governments that Kerrian was a prize fruit ripe for the swiftest hand to pick. Her planet was about to face "protective takeover" attempts from at least two very strong powers.

She opened her eyes, then wished she hadn't. The Rualdan and the Bertolian ambassadors stood now, also, and the members of their staffs scrambled to their feet. Only men and women clad in hunter green remained. The Gavonians.

Four systems. Kerrian would soon be battling *four* systems, each of which would pretend it sought to annex Kerrian for its own protection from the other three.

And she couldn't forget Gavin-Secundus. Jarrod tolArvik would not allow his prize to be snatched from his fingers before he had a chance to take a good, hefty bite from it.

At the door, the Bertolian ambassador turned back. "This planet—you are a backward race, still indulging in your petty internal power squabbles. You need protection—and direction—from a strong world."

Dia sagged against the wall, her mind whirling. Unless she moved swiftly and effectively, her planet would never again be free from off-world domination.

She straightened and threw the towel she carried aside. She hadn't so much as a moment to waste.

Chapter Six

Hatred filled Dia, directed at— No, not at Bailan. How could one hate a creature so weak? Even the tiny puff jells, who drifted on the tides, showed more spine when confronted with trouble than did he. No, she directed her hatred where it belonged, at the person who planned this mess, at the man who betrayed both his own people and hers for personal gain. At tolArvik.

So far, Kerrian had already suffered unprecedented internal warfare because of his machinations. Now they would suffer attacks from without, from every system wanting to claim the coral while pretending to protect it. Had tolArvik expected this? Did he plan to plunge her planet deeper and deeper into war?

She had to stop him. Now, before things grew even worse.

Several members of the Gavonian delegation rose, casting uncertain glances toward the head table, where only Bailan and their ambassador remained.

TolArvik didn't move; Dia couldn't see his expression. Had he planned this, to force Bailan to acknowledge his need for a strong Gavonian military presence on Kerrian?

"Lady?" One of the waiters touched her arm.

She glanced at him, only to discover that the other members of the household staff stood in small groups about the room, all watching her.

She couldn't stay here. Her people would betray her. If that happened, she'd have to fight and the staff had no weapons, no training. They'd all be captured or killed.

For a moment, her anger told her that her own death would be worth it, if only she could destroy tolArvik. Common sense, though, had to rule. Without her, Kerrian would lawfully fall to Bailan's inept hands. That couldn't happen; she'd already seen the results. As inadequate as Dia felt herself to be, she was her planet's only hope.

She strode to the back wall, grabbed the pastry cart, and wheeled it from the room, forcing herself not to run, to look as if she merely did her job. She had to move quickly, now. And the first item on her agenda would be to get into the comm room and summon the reserve guard.

That, she recognized, was essential. She could—and would—kill tolArvik herself. But she and a few frightened cooks and staffers couldn't take on an entire mercenary army on their own. Of course, if she couldn't reach the reserve, she might be able to strike a deal with the mercenary leader, offering him double the amount of tolArvik's agreement with them. If tolArvik were already dead, they might not feel this to be a breach of contract. Damn, she hated the thought of dealing with mercenary scum.

Morning. She had until morning, but no longer. By then, the other systems would be ready to begin their own takeover attempts.

Once out of the banquet hall, she abandoned the cart and broke into a run. Why hadn't she and her father prepared for these possibilities? Why had they been so naive, so trusting? She slammed her fist against the wall, but it did nothing to relieve her anger and frustration. Rubbing the bruise, she swung the kitchen door wide.

The cooks looked up, startled, as she burst into the room. "We're not ready—" the head cook began.

"There's no need. The banquet's over." She grabbed up an empty tray.

"Lady," he protested.

"I'm going to the comm room." Ignoring his further protests, she hurried out.

This time a young man stood on duty at the hallway junction leading to the comm room. He, too, wore Kerrinian uniform, though his ridged forehead and green-tinged skin would fool no one into thinking him a native. Dia gave him a casual nod and strode past.

"Halt!" came the order. A rough hand, its finger tips ribbed, grabbed her elbow and jerked her around. "Where do you think you're going?"

She fixed her features into a mask of surprise. "To clean out the comm room. Like I did this morning."

His gaze narrowed on her. "You're Kerrinian," he accused.

She rolled her eyes. "Very good. What did you expect? Most of us on the staff are, for some reason."

"No admittance," he snapped.

"Look, you can't disrupt the basic running of this place. No matter who you think you are, you—"

Footsteps sounded along the hall, and she glanced back. Oh, damn, tolArvik. Would nothing go right for her this night? He was the last person she wanted to see—at least, until she could get him alone to kill him.

Or maybe she might have one last use for him. He'd gotten her in this morning. Maybe he could do it again. Her rys-bracelet hummed. If she had to, she could kill or disable two, maybe even three people before anyone realized she wore a weapon. If the room were nearly empty, she'd take the chance.

She straightened, her resolve firming. "He'll tell you."

The soldier gestured her back with his imploder. "Yeah? Who's he?"

"By the Net, don't you even know the Gavonian ambassador?" she snapped.

He cocked a ridge-brow above one eye. "So that's him, is it?"

TolArvik strode up to them, his scowl easing only a trifle as he glanced at Dia. "Trying again?" he asked her. "Come on, I'll take you in."

"That you won't . . . sir." The guard raised the imploder a suggestive few centimeters.

"By the Fire Devils," tolArvik snapped. "What incompetent idiot put you out here?"

Almost, Dia thought, she could have liked tolArvik. Even deranged mass murders had their moments.

"No one goes through," the mercenary stated. "I have my orders."

TolArvik glared down at the man from his superior height. "They don't apply to me."

"Tonight they apply to everyone. Sir."

"Summon your commander," tolArvik demanded. The man raised his chin. "I've been given my orders, and they were specific about you. You are not to be permitted in."

TolArvik took a step forward, and the mercenary snapped his imploder into position. For a long moment the two men glared at each other, then tolArvik relaxed. "Stupidity seems to be at a strong point on this planet." He turned on his heel and strode off.

Dia hesitated, but knew she hadn't a chance to get in. Well, she'd jump ahead to Plan B. TolArvik time.

The ambassador stormed down the passage several paces, then slowed. Without looking back at her, he said: "Is there more of that headache remedy, and can you make it a little stronger?"

"As strong as you like." She could use some too, for that matter. She forced a throaty, seductive note into her voice. "I'll bring it up to your room, if you'd like. Or will you be busy down here for a while longer?"

He came to an abrupt halt, then very slowly turned around so that his steady gaze followed her every movement as she caught up to him. She added a slight sway to her walk. A light kindled in the depths of his charcoal eyes, a smile that eased the tension in his set features, at last tugging at the corners of his mouth.

Dia swallowed. He had no right to be so damned attractive, so—so sensual. And she had no right to respond like this. She'd fallen under his unconscious spell at their first meeting—but to allow it to continue now, when she knew who and what he really was—It was unforgivable.

His expression clouded. "I have a couple things I have to take care of. How about in an hour? I should

be ready for . . . whatever you bring me." He touched
her cheek, his fingers lingering in a tantalizing caress.

Sparks raced through her as her rebelling senses
responded. Intellectually, she knew him to be a traitor
to his own people, an enemy to hers, but her body
refused to acknowledge it. Only the subtle messages
of the awareness that pulsed between them, of his
power and masculine aura, penetrated, and they
delved deep within her, threatening her resolve.

His fingers trailed down to her chin until he cupped
it in one hand. She stood very still, trapped in the
welter of sensations his touch created, her breathing
shallow, echoing the racing of her pulse. Slowly he
bent toward her, his warm breath teasing her cheek.
Her eyes closed of their own volition, and her lips
parted. His mouth brushed across hers, barely making
contact, more a promise of what might lie ahead. She
melted with the yearning for it.

"An hour," he whispered, and released her.

For a long, shattered moment, she remained where
she stood, unable to move. Not even the sound of
his retreating footsteps shook her from the grip of
longing.

Longing. For a man she had to hate. For a man
she had to kill.

One hour from now. In his room.

She blinked, trying to shake off the lingering
trance-like state he'd generated in her. By the Great
Net, was she doomed to fall to pieces—and into his
bed—every time they came near each other? Had
she no strength of will—or even common sense? Why
did she have to desire her sworn enemy?

One hour. What did he go to do? Probably consult
with Bailan. That wouldn't matter, now.

One hour. The thrumming of her bracelet over her hand increased, rising up her arm, leaving the hairs standing on end. One hour.

She strode into the kitchen and drew up short at the sight of seven of the staff gathered there. The excited humm of their voices filled the room, phrases reached her concerning the events in the banqueting hall. The conversation faded to silence as heads turned to look at her.

Agathas took a step forward, her gaze brushing across the empty tray Dia held. "They didn't let you in."

"They didn't even let tolArvik in."

"What do you mean?" Agathas's gaze narrowed. "If he's in charge—"

"I think the mercenaries' commander is planning a little takeover of his own. Either that or my cousin is trying to double cross tolArvik. Either way," she added, remembering the ambassador's mysterious errand, "I imagine the situation will be settled within the hour." She set the tray on a table, then leaned against its edge. "Getting rid of tolArvik and Bailan isn't going to be enough. We may have to storm the comm room."

The staff cast uneasy glances at one another. The head cook cleared his throat. "With nothing but cooking knives, Lady? Against imploders?"

"I hope not." She looked from face to face, noting the fear. "We're not fighters, any of us. If we work this right, all we'll have to do is *pretend*. And I may be able to hire the mercenaries myself. I'm going to try, at least. But I'll need a show of support to convince them I really *am* who I claim, and that I can really pay what I offer."

One young man, Eelam, who'd waited on tables

with her that night, raised an uncertain hand. "I'll go with you. If we can get weapons."

Dia nodded. "We'll have to steal them. Even one might be enough, though that guard at the corner isn't going to be easy to get past. The comm room—" She broke off, considering. "One imploder might do the trick in there, but I'd feel better with a backup or two."

One of the assistant cooks, Sorin, straightened. "I'll go. I've never handled an imploder, but I hunt gyro gulls every season. I usually hit what I aim at."

Two more staffers, a very junior cook and another waiter, also volunteered. Dia nodded and thanked them. Great. A five person army. Weaponless. They'd be a joke if they weren't so determined.

The waiter, Tomlin, cleared his throat. "When?" he managed to ask.

Dia drew in her breath, calculating. "An hour— no, better two hours from now. The more people who've gone to sleep, the better for us."

Her make-shift army she dismissed to their beds, to manage what rest they could. The rest of the staff she sent to investigate possible weapon sources. The mercenaries might grow lax in their sentry duties as the lateness of the hour took its toll. One dozing guard, knocked unconscious, bound, and stored in the pantry, might provide not only a cell imploder, but possibly even a backup weapon. It was worth a try.

"And what do you plan to do?" Agathas asked.

Dia turned to find the housekeeper watching her, arms akimbo. "I'm going to remove our major threat."

The woman nodded. "Want me to come?"

Dia shook her head. "I'll have a better chance if I do this one alone." TolArvik would certainly wonder at her arriving with a companion at what he obviously considered to be a tryst.

She broke off that thought, for it awakened her to longings that were best left buried. Instead, she concentrated on finding a glass, then on measuring out the dose of headache remedy from Agathas's store of bottles. She might as well bring him water, she reflected, for all the good it would have time to do him. He'd be dead before it could even begin to take effect. Possibly even before he had a chance to drink it.

But she couldn't count on him being alone, on everything running smoothly. And she couldn't count on herself to deal with more than one enemy. The prospect of killing a person—even such an enemy as tolArvik—left her feeling ill.

She placed the cup on a tray of inlaid shell, then added another glass and a decanter of brandy. Not Gavonian, but still the best obtainable in the kitchen. She glanced at the wall chronometer: still twenty minutes to go. She sat on one of the chairs against the wall, closed her eyes, cleared her mind, and tried to brace herself for the ordeal to come.

Deep, calming breaths . . . resolution of purpose . . . desired outcome clearly in mind . . . thoughts of peace, of certainty, of success. . . . Slow her breathing, calm the internal trembling, steady her hand. . . . The rys-bracelet thrummed gently, pulsing at a rate all its own, drawing her pulse to match it. . . . Calm, confidence, peace. . . .

With a sigh, she returned to the present and eased a stiffness in her shoulders. Now, she could do what she must. She glanced at the chronometer, to discover forty minutes had passed. Well, being late would be worth it; she'd needed the time to prepare and strengthen herself.

Besides, the extra time increased the odds of her finding him alone. Any personal servant would probably have left him, and tolArvik would await her arrival with impatience. And that, she well knew, tended to overcome caution.

She didn't hurry; not for anything would she sacrifice her current composed state of mind. He would wait. She would be ready. This would be a show to remember.

The service lift carried her unseen to the residential floor, where they had housed the ambassadors and their delegations. Second room on the right, she reminded herself as she emerged from behind the elaborate screen. If she needed an escape route. . . .

She cast a rapid glance about. The lift, the main stair—or perhaps she could bolt to her own quarters. Those of her father would be best, with their hidden stair that led down through the palace walls to the basements and the caverns below. But Bailan would be in her father's rooms. Well, she knew her options; she'd leave it up to circumstances where she fled. And if all went well?

One step at a time, she told herself sternly. First, tolArvik.

She stopped outside his door, drew a long breath to reassure her calm, then tapped lightly. Movement sounded within, footsteps crossing the deep carpet, and the next moment the panel slid sideways into the wall. TolArvik stood before her, robed in a dressing gown of hunter green. His thick sandy hair waved loose about his shoulders, framing his squared face. A striking face, full of character and experience—

and filled with something else. Desire, she realized, as it washed out to encompass her.

"You're late." His hand closed about her bare shoulder and he drew her into the room. The door slid shut behind her.

"Things are rather confused in the kitchens." The warmth of his touch sent a thrill of yearning through her, which she fought. She pulled away and set the tray on the nearest table. *Clear your mind, don't give in to him. Just bring up your hand and aim.* Gathering her courage, she turned to face him.

He caught both her hands and brought first one, then the other to his lips. His thumbs caressed their backs while his fingers worked a miracle of sensation on her palms. "You're tense. Is everyone upset down there?"

She couldn't take aim with her tiny pistol when he held her hands close against his chest. His lips brushed her curled fingers, and maddeningly, all sense of will and hatred melted from her. She wanted only to feel his arms about her once more, to press her face against his broad shoulder, to feel the rapid beat of his heart as she had when he'd carried her to safety last night.

As she might again if he carried her to his bed. . . .

"You're safe here." His voice sounded softly, urgently, against her ear. "There's no need for you to leave again tonight."

His spell lapped about her until her consciousness floated adrift in a sea of sensation and desire. His cheek brushed hers, then his lips found the hollow at the base of her throat. She caught her breath, swept along by its currents. A willing victim, she swam joyfully toward the spiraling whirlpool that would pull her under, drowning her in the depths of his passion.

How could anything feel so right, so perfect—yet be so utterly and completely wrong?

With a wrenching effort, she reminded herself who he was, who *she* was, what he had caused her to suffer. Why, of all the men she had met, must it be *he* who stirred her soul?

She struggled back to the surface of awareness to find herself clasped tightly against the length of his firm body, her arms about his shoulders, her fingers entwined in the long, thick waves of his hair. His mouth moved slowly over hers, exploring with what a moment before had seemed a sweetness so exquisite it bordered on the painful.

Pain. . . .

She needed to summon every weapon she possessed against Jarrod—against tolArvik.

Linore, she reminded herself. Edrick. The palace guards. She could add many names to the list of cruelly murdered victims. And her father. She still didn't know his fate, no one on the staff had seen any trace of him, could tell her anything. Her heart cried out with the uncertainty of it. His disappearance—whatever he suffered—it was by this man's design.

"Stay with me." TolArvik's breath teased the hairs about her ear. "Stay till morning. I want you here." Again, his lips began their sensual descent toward the base of her throat.

She planted her hands on his shoulders and gently pushed him away, back far enough so she could study his face. He had dimmed the room's lights, but she could clearly see the strong lines of his features, the burning intensity of his eyes. Who—*what*— was this man, that he could be both angel and devil to her, lover and murderer of all she loved?

"Oh, my sweet Dee," he murmured.

The smoldering glow of his gaze washed over her. She tensed, and her right hand closed about his shoulder, holding him away from her. Her left hand tingled with the thrumming from her rys-bracelet. Dad. Linore. Edrick. The names ran through her mind like a litany, arming her, strengthening her will. The hiss and humm of the coral as it continued to dissolve in its acid filled the silence of the room.

It took every ounce of will she could muster to raise her hand with the tiny laser. She should hate him— she *did* hate him, especially for tearing her apart like this. Her entire arm trembled, and she brushed his jaw as she drew back, positioning herself to fire.

He stiffened, his eyes widening in shock and disbelief. He grasped her left wrist, bearing her arm downward even as she fired. An exclamation broke from his lips, and the odor of scorched fibers and flesh surrounded them. With his free hand he clutched at his thigh, at a smoldering patch of his robe; with the other he twisted her wrist, half-wrenching the rys-bracelet from her arm. "Masters of fire—" The words tore from him.

Dia jerked her arm against his hold, breaking free. The pistol portion of her bracelet dangled useless from her hand, torn from her finger. She swung wildly at his head. He ducked, losing his balance as he lunged to grasp her.

If he did. . . . She raced for the door, knowing only that she had to evade capture.

A muffled exclamation of mingled pain and anger sounded behind her. She'd injured him, at least, she realized, as she palmed open the door and dove out into the hall. She'd lost the use of her weapon. She should have brought a second, a backup. Everything had gone wrong. She'd ruined her best chance.

But, she was still alive.

For now.

ANOTHER NAME   105

ahand rose through a fog and a feeling knowing
had come, telling her, a signal for breaking spate
She sat and still wide...
                                        Pat Rowe

Chapter Seven

Jarrod caught his balance on the back of a chair, clenched his teeth against the pain that shot burning through his thigh, and lurched toward the door. It slid open in response to his touch, and he dragged himself through. Nothing. The hall stood empty.

How could she have vanished like that? He hadn't been that far behind her. And he hadn't made such a stupid, near-fatal blunder of judgment since his first days as a soldier in the Cerean war.

His eyes closed as he leaned against the wall, fighting back the pain. Dee. Lovely, sweet, vulnerable Dee. An assassin.

But whose? Did she work for the Cereans? Or Bailan? Or—and the thought sent a chill through him—for some Gavonian who sought the overthrow of the tharl?

He limped back inside and closed the door behind him, then sealed it with the lock that could not easily be broken. Dee. An assassin. His mind cried out against the evidence. His senses still registered her presence in his arms, the sweet smell of herbs mixed with the tang of brine that clung to her luxurious hair. He could still feel the warm, firm curves of her body pressed against his as she clung to him, melding against him, her mouth as passionately eager as his.

Yet she'd drawn back, studied his face, then calmly attempted to murder him with a laser pistol.

No, not calmly. He sank onto the edge of his bed and pulled the robe aside to examine his wound. She'd trembled, though not with fear. He could have sworn she acted against her will.

Mind control? Drug-enhanced hypnotic suggestion? He couldn't have mistaken their mutual awareness, the attraction that pulsed between them. Only moments before her attack, he would swear their desire had flared from flickering fire to raging bonfire. *Not* his alone. *Theirs.*

He focused his attention on the burned flesh of his leg. He should be glad, at least, she didn't favor a cell imploder. He reached for the comm unit at the head of the bed, then drew back. He wasn't ready to alert anyone to this peculiar turn of events, not even his trusted man-servant. Trust, he realized with a grimace, was not a commodity of which he possessed a great deal at the moment. He'd tend this on his own.

Painfully, he pulled himself to his feet and made his way to the bath chamber. He checked the first cupboard, only to find a selection of fragrant but non-medicinal salts, oils, and lotions for adding to the giant conch-shaped soaker tub which stood at the far side of the tiled room. Luxuriant, if not downright decadent.

The next cabinet proved more useful, holding a

small emergency med-aid kit. He picked through the contents, checking labels, and selected a tube of numbing antibiotic cream. This he smeared over the wound, and moments later came welcome relief as the burning faded to nothingness.

He secured a large bandage over the area, then made his way back to the bedroom. An odd tingling enveloped his leg. Healing, he reassured himself, but the sensation disturbed him.

No, what bothered him was that he'd placed himself in a situation where he *needed* healing. He lay down on the bed and closed his eyes. She'd had no weapon—then suddenly, a laser pistol appeared in her hand. Only it hadn't. He concentrated, trying to remember. He'd sensed—no, he'd *heard*. He'd heard a hissing noise close to his ear as her bracelet brushed his chin.

A hissing noise. Her bracelet.

His eyes opened and he stared, unseeing, at the mosaicked ceiling above his bed. Her bracelet.

Almost every Kerrinian wore one of those decorative things. The tracery of wire looped over the fingers, criss-crossed in fancy patterns over the hand, connected with links at the wrist, then traced patterns up the arm to the elbow.

Only they weren't weapons.

His fingers tapped against the softly furred cover of the bed. He'd heard of ones that *were,* though. Something the tharl had mentioned. Something about the bracelet worn by his friend, King Harryl. Not just any bracelet, but a Dahmla-rys-bracelet.

He clasped his hands behind his head and stared straight up, every nerve alert, his mind racing. According to the tharl, only a member of the Kerrinian royalty wore a rys-bracelet. Dahmla, for the coral-power they possessed. Rys, for their link to the royal house.

Only three such bracelets existed. One the king wore. The other, which had belonged to the queen, now lay in a vault in the cellars. The third belonged to the heir to the throne. Princess Dialora.

For a long moment he lay still. Princess Dialora. *Not* Dee. Dialora.

He conjured the image of his little serving girl, his assassin, in his mind. Her exquisite bone structure, the proud tilt of her chin, the fire of determination in her huge, violet eyes. No, no servant. He had beheld—and held—Princess Dialora herself.

The memory of her in his arms raised his pulse rate. He'd wanted her from the first moment he'd seen her, when she'd dragged herself from the dark waters onto the ancient wharf. And he wanted her now, here, in his bed. He wanted her sweetness and fire and passion.

But she wanted him dead.

He frowned and moved his bandaged leg to ease the tingling of healing. In trying to assassinate him, she did no one's bidding but her own. But *why*? He'd been sent to help her father. The tharl had been as an uncle to her. Surely she'd know she had only to seek the aid of the Gavonian ambassador to be assured of his help.

But trouble brewed on his own planet, as well.

Someone sponsored this so-called revolution on Kerrian.

His mind spun with the possibilities, and reached the inevitable conclusion. Princess Dialora had reason to believe that Gavin-Secundus played a major role in her planet's upheaval. He doubted she'd blame the tharl she knew and loved. No, she'd blame the man who was here, who seemed in charge, whom she'd seen helping her traitorous cousin. She'd blame him.

He sat up. If she had proof of Gavonian interference, then he wanted it. He wanted to know what treachery occurred on his own planet. And he'd need to warn the tharl before it proved too late.

As for the princess herself. . . . The possibilities flooded his mind, intriguing—and distracting. He had no desire to be killed by her before he got this little misunderstanding straightened out. He reached for his clothes.

The lift had never moved so slowly. Dia leaned against the back wall, aware of the sinking sensation as she struggled to repair her torn rys-bracelet. She'd bungled it! She'd taken her one chance and made a complete mess of everything!

The lift slid past the level of the kitchen, down to the cellars. As soon as the door slid open, Dia burst out, running, driven more by despair than fear. She sought with fumbling hands along the line of casks where the brandy and wine aged, found the secret door, and let herself out into the volcanic caverns.

The panel slid closed, sealing her onto the cool, damp stairs. She leaned against the rail, breathing hard, furious with herself. How could she have blundered so badly? Had part of her—some traitorous, foolish, desire-driven part of her—wanted him to live? Had her weak, sensual body betrayed her honor?

She dashed her hand across her eyes, wiping away burning tears of frustration. He'd never give her another chance to come so close, to take her vengeance. He'd have her hunted and killed.

Or had she made matters worse than that? Had he realized who she really was? If he knew anything about her planet, he'd be able to figure it out. She had a healthy respect for his intelligence.

She should never have risked using her rys-bracelet. A dagger would have served just as well. Of course, he might think it was her father's, stolen from his body. No, if that possibility occurred to him, he'd dismiss it soon enough. No one but a member of the royal house would have such reason to hate him. And she'd given him enough of her name for him to make the connection.

She swallowed, trying to control her breathing, to calm her panic and think rationally.

All right, she'd blundered. She hadn't lost everything yet, though. But she had forced her own hand. No time remained for uncertainties or delays. She had to move now, swiftly, decisively—or acknowledge defeat.

So what did she do? She cowered in hiding! Chalk it up to panic, and put it behind her. She had work to do.

She slipped back through the door, emerging once more into the cellars. Two hours, that's what she'd told her army of four. Two hours. She'd used up all but twenty minutes of that time. She could only pray Jarrod tolArvik couldn't organize his troops much faster than that.

Every nerve alert for danger, she crept up the steps to the kitchen. No one. No alarms clamoring. Nothing. Perhaps she'd wounded him worse than she'd thought. That might give her time to implement Plan C.

The door to the kitchen stood slightly ajar. Dia paused on the dark steps and peeked through. TolArvik must realize the servants helped her. He might well send his mercenaries here, to trap her. Yet she saw no sign of danger in the large, brightly lit chamber.

Agathas sat in a corner, sharpening a long, thin knife. The head cook stood before the cutlery rack, studying the available blades. She couldn't see anyone else. Pushing the door open more, she stepped into the room.

Agathas's head jerked up, and she raised the knife to throwing position. She lowered it the next moment. "Lady, you were in the cellars? Did it go well? Is he dead?"

"Only wounded." All her self-disgust sounded in her voice. "But we don't have time to dwell on mistakes. Has anyone found any weapons?"

"Not yet." The housekeeper watched her with narrowed eyes. "I don't see how——"

"We'll just have to be creative. Things have gone wrong around here before, and we've always managed to pass it off as a special show for the tourists."

Agathas set down the knife and selected another. "This isn't the same sort of situation." She struck it along the surface of her whetstone.

Dia studied a bowl of fruit and tubers on the countertop, then selected a couple at random. These she stacked on top of one another half a meter from a tiled wall. She stood back, raised her arm, and fired the bracelet. The topmost fruit split in half, and the spicy-sweet scent of baked paffa melon filled the room.

"Very impressive." Agathas rose and inspected the damage. "Next time the ovens aren't working, I'll beg your help."

Dia rubbed her hand, which tingled with the power

that still grew within the tiny implosion chamber. "TolArvik nearly tore it off my arm. I wanted to make sure it was working again."

The woman's gaze narrowed on her. "You shouldn't have been close enough to him for that."

Dia shrugged. "It won't happen again." The pang that realization caused troubled her. Some day she'd find another man, one worthy of sharing her love, one who stirred her senses every bit as much as did tolArvik. Someday.

But now she had her work cut out for her, and it didn't include wasting time on regretting a lost dalliance.

"We're going to need rope. I don't want to kill anyone if we don't have to. If only we had just one stunner!" Dia flung open the cabinet behind her and ran her fingers along the trays, then back. With a soft exclamation of triumph, she drew out one of heavy, gleaming metal. She hefted it in her hand, then made a tentative swing with it.

"Lady!" Agathas took it from her.

"Don't you like my primitive stunner?" She grinned, though it was a fleeting expression. "Emergency backup. We may have to knock someone out. Will you wake up my poor volunteers? And bring me a nightrobe, will you? I'm getting an idea."

"Moons preserve us," Agathas murmured, but left the kitchen.

Dia entered the hydroponics room, and a wave of vitality washed over her, generated by the endless rows of living, greening entities. The air smelled rich and heavy, of mulching, of the nutrient tubs, of the lushness of each plant. She loved it in here. She stopped to touch the tendrils of a nyad vine, which quivered as if in delight at her attention. Its berries ripened toward fullness, tempting her with their deep ruby color and honey-cinnamon scent.

She opened the storage cabinet and rummaged through the shelves of buckets, pruners, and chemicals, until she found the cord used for rigging trellises for the twiners. Good, stout cord. Perfect for tying up someone.

When she re-entered the kitchen, the first member of her makeshift army, Sorin, already stood by the counter, downing a mug of steaming stimi. Then Eelam shuffled in, followed by the junior cook Vester and Agathas bearing the requested robe. Dia dragged this on, shoved her feet into the slippers the house-keeper had thoughtfully included, then unfastened her hair so it fell, still waving from its tight braids, below her knees.

She eyed her reflection in the shimmering stainless wall. "Do I look like I couldn't sleep?"

Sorin eyed her with a frown. "How close will you have to get?"

Some vote of confidence. "About four meters for a straight shot. But the guard won't believe this is a weapon—" she gestured with her braceleted arm "—unless I prove it, and I'm not entirely sure of my aim. I'd rather just hit him over the head."

Tomlin, who straggled in last, regarded her uneasily. "You're planning on going in there alone, Lady?"

"Only to the guard on the corner. If I can take him out, we'll have his imploder. And *that's* a weapon no one will doubt. So all of you," she looked from one to the other of her uncertain soldiers, "stay out of sight until I've dealt with the guard. If things go wrong, there's no need to throw away your own lives." She turned to Agathas and managed a lopsided smile. "Thanks."

Tears filled the woman's eyes. "May the Great Sustainer go with you."

Dia picked up her tray, set several mugs and a pot of hot, fragrant stimi on it, cast one last glance at her companions, and forced a bright grin. "It's show time," she said and swept out through the door Agathas opened for her.

Her make-shift army kept just behind her until they reached the corridor where the guard stood on duty, protecting the hall on which the comm room stood. Dia gestured for the others to wait, then gathering her courage, paced around the corner. Nothing. No response. The mercenary—was it the same one she'd seen earlier, who'd refused tolArvik admission?—leaned against the wall, his posture slumped.

Not asleep, or he'd never remain erect. She doubted she could reach him before he noticed her, and she'd rather not startle him back to full awareness. He might react first, then be embarrassed about shooting a harmless servant. She shuffled her feet in their warming slippers and allowed the tray to rattle.

He stirred, bringing his weapon back to its "on guard" position. A moment later he raised his head, looked around, and started visibly. "Halt! What are you doing here?"

Dia halted. "I was getting desperate for someone to talk to." She started toward him, and to her relief he made no menacing gestures. "Everyone's asleep. Except us. I—I just can't, and I was pacing the floors until I remembered you'd be on duty, and probably bored."

His weapon lowered a trifle. "Aren't you the one who was here earlier? When Ambassador tolArvik came?"

"This is my area to clean. Which I guess is why I

came down here." Only eight meters from him, now. Almost within firing range, if he caught on. "I don't know if you're allowed to drink any stimi, but I brought some just in case."

"You've probably had too much today." His gaze roamed over her, as if the length and thickness of her hair fascinated him.

The drawbacks to her plan began to dawn on her. The moment she started to swing her tray, he'd stop her, probably by shooting. Just over a meter from him, she set the tray on the floor, then ran her fingers over the metal tracery on her hand. Looking up at him, she asked, "Have you ever heard of a *rys*-bracelet?"

"Pretty." He glanced at it, following it up her arm as she drew back her sleeve. "Most of you wear 'em, don't you?"

"Not like this one. This is a *rys*-bracelet." She raised her arm so that her index finger pointed at his shoulder. "This one's a weapon."

He laughed. "What do you do, hit people with 'em?"

"No." She fired a short burst. The sleeve covering his upper arm smoldered, and the imploder dropped from his hands.

"You—" He stared at her, then transferred his gaze to his shoulder. His hand covered the wound, cauterized by the laser so that no blood seeped from it. "You—"

"Kick your imploder over here. I'd rather not kill you, but that's up to you. Now, please."

Footsteps sounded behind her. She moved so she could see both the guard and the corridor along which she'd come, and relief filled her as she saw her four-soldier army hurrying to her aid. She'd never been so glad to see anyone.

Dia plucked the comm link from the mercenary's collar. Sorin drew the cord from his pocket, and, with the aid of Vester, secured their prisoner. Tomlin clutched their captured imploder as if not quite sure how to hold it.

"Now what?" Eelam asked.

"Lock him in one of the offices." Dia, her hand with its laser pistol still pointed at the man, indicated the line of doors with a nod of her head.

Her companions, buoyed by their initial success, marched their prisoner down the hall and into one of the little rooms. Dia followed, her weapon at the ready, but the hapless guard made no foolhardy escape attempts. He sat in glowering silence while Sorin bound him to a chair and Vester shoved a kitchen towel into his mouth and secured the gag in place.

Sorin looked up from admiring his handiwork. "We did it, Lady. Let's get the rest of them!"

"This isn't a game." She took the imploder. "Who knows how to use one of these?"

Eelam cleared his throat. "My brother served on an off-world freighter for awhile. He showed me how his worked—though it was a sprayer we used for shooting practice."

Dia glanced at the others, who gave a variety of negative responses. "You're it, then. Don't kill unless you have to."

Eelam took the weapon, made a show of checking it over, then gave her a short nod. His face had taken on an unnatural pallor, and his mouth looked pinched. "Let's get it over with."

They moved silently along the corridor to the inter-
section beyond the guard's station, where Dia signaled her followers to wait. Eelam, shaky but
determined, started forward, but Dia caught his arm.
"It'll make enough noise to warn anyone inside,"
she hissed in his ear. "This one has to be mine."

For her father, she told herself. For Linore and
Edrick. For Kerrian. She raised her arm and rounded
the corner.

The guard snapped to the ready, but her first shot
seared his hand. The imploder hung limp in his grasp
as he stared at Dia in bewilderment. "What—?"

"Set that thing down—softly! And don't reach for
your comm link." She took a shaky step forward.

Behind her came Eelam and Sorin, followed by
Vester and Tomlin. Sorin produced his cord, and
with Vester's help shortly had a second prisoner ready
to join the first. Sorin picked up the second imploder
and eyed it uncertainly. Eelam pointed out the sight
and firing mechanism, then Sorin, looking somewhat
more confident, accompanied Vester and Tomlin to
stow the second mercenary into another office.

Dia stood before the comm room door, with Eelam
slightly to one side. Both held weapons ready. If someone came out before the other three came back. . . .
No, she didn't want to think of that possibility. Two
people, one without an obvious weapon, would not
seem intimidating. She needed the others if they were
to accomplish this with the minimum of bloodshed.

Minutes dragged by, and every moment her nerves
tensed more. What if a relief guard came? What if
tolArvik came? What if—

Footsteps approached, and she spun about,
trembling, but it was Tomlin who rounded the corner,
followed by the other two. She let her arm drop to

her side and drew a deep breath, trying to calm herself, trying to reclaim her inner peace from which she drew her reserves of strength. Trying to keep from screaming from too many hours of fear and strain.

She glanced at her companions, saw the two with their imploders at the ready, and palmed open the door.

Chapter Eight

Dia and her make-shift army burst through the door. Three men looked up from their various stations about the room. Three. It took a moment for their number to sink into Dia's tired mind. Three. She'd feared half a dozen or more.

"Get against the wall." She indicated the left with a nod of her head. "Sorin, guard the door. You three—" She waved her hand at the mercenaries. "This is a laser. I'll be glad to demonstrate it on one of you if you give me any trouble. Put all weapons on the floor. Now," she added as they complied, warily, "your comm links. Good. Okay, tie these guys up."

This time, Vester took the cord, and Tomlin helped in securing wrists and ankles. Dia watched, her gaze studying each of their prisoners. A Cerean, a Tauran, and a Gavonian. She didn't remember seeing any of them before.

Leaving Eelam to stand watch over their prisoners,

she went to the nearest computer terminal. She'd never investigated more than the basics of the comm system, and it dawned on her that establishing the needed link with Waianoa might prove tricky. She wasn't about to risk sending messages that might be monitored or intercepted by the mercenaries. To be safe, she needed a trained tech.

At least, she could access the personnel files. She keyed up the data, then scanned the most recent additions to the comm room. Three possible names turned up, but none of them struck the right chord in her memory. She brought up the information on the first, rejected it, then tried the second.

Lyacles Atoll. That was it. The boy had come from Lyacles. Got him. Darmin vis Ellis. Vis Ellis. She repeated the name, committing it to memory.

She glanced over her shoulders. "Where are the Kerrinian staff being held?" she asked of everyone in general.

"The ones who don't normally live in the palace are in the gymnasium," Vester called back.

"I want Darmin vis Ellis." She hesitated. "Eelam, go with Vester in case you run into trouble. I'll keep an eye on this lot."

Eelam moved away from where he leaned against the long counter. "Your power, Lady—?"

"I could take out their entire army. That kind of power's what this mess is all about. We'll be fine. Just hurry. I want messages sent as soon as possible."

The two men left. Dia sank into the terminal's chair and watched her prisoners. Only one looked back. The others stared into space, their faces set in grim lines. Tomlin paced uneasily to the door to check on Sorin, then returned to her side.

Dia ran her fingers over her bracelet. It hummed,

sounding in her inner ear, awakening every part of her. So much power—but she needed more than that. She needed the will to use it, and the aim to hit her target.

Which brought her thoughts back to tolArvik. Where was he? She should have stayed nearby, finished him off when he tried to pursue her. Only that hadn't been an option. Her bracelet had needed repair.

What was he doing now? Nursing his wound? Unwanted concern for him lanced through her, which she blocked at once. She'd *tried* to hit him, damn it. She'd wanted him dead. But with the way he'd deflected her aim, she couldn't have hurt him seriously enough to have prevented further action on his part.

So why hadn't he countered? Why—so far—hadn't he interfered?

Tomlin cast her a sideways glance. "Have we won, Lady?"

"Yes," she said with more certainty than she felt. "Once those messages are sent, it won't matter what the mercenaries try to do."

The one mercenary, a sergeant, eyed her with skepticism. Dia ignored him. She had a message to compose.

Before she'd finished its wording, the door slid open and Eelam and Vester entered, accompanied by the young man who had worked the console earlier. Darmin. She threw him a bright, triumphant smile. "Thank you."

He strode across the room, dropped to his knee before her, and grasped her hands. "Lady, they said you were dead. When you came in here—" He shook his head, and moisture blurred his bright, lavender eyes. "Forgive me, I nearly gave you away."

"So did I," she admitted. He still clasped her hands, gazing up into her face, his expression reminding her forcibly of a lost otter youngling reunited with its mother. "You have no idea how glad I was to see you, that you were all right—and here. Will you work the comm station for me?"

"Anything, Lady." He rose and made his way through the room to the terminal where he'd sat earlier. His fingers danced over the board, then he looked up. "What's first?"

"First, we get this lot out of here." Eelam sounded cheerful as he waved his imploder toward the three prisoners. "Come on, Vester. You, too, Tomlin. We'll put them in separate offices." He swung his weapon into a ready position and herded his captives out the door.

Dia returned her attention to Darmin and the comm console. Raising the government center at Waianoa proved surprisingly easy. Finding someone with any authority was another matter. It would be six hours before dawn there, Dia realized, not just two like it was here. Not exactly normal business hours for either place.

The sleepy tech on duty in Waianoa stifled a yawn and shook his head as if to clear it, then blinked at the comm screen. "Sure it's an emergency? Everyone's asleep. They're not going to like it if I wake them."

Dia sat down beside Darmin, taking over his position on the vid. "There's been a coup attempt by my cousin. I want the captain of the guards on line within twenty minutes. Any of the ministers you can rouse, as well. Twenty minutes."

"Lady—" The Waianoa tech swallowed. "You—"

"Twenty minutes," she repeated. "That's not much time. If I'm not available, Darmin vis Ellis will explain the situation. You might warn the captain I want the reserves down here within four hours."

"Four?" The tech's voice quavered on incredulity. "They'd have to get a shuttle ready to leave at once!"

"Very good. You know your time tables." She turned from the vid. "Darmin?"

He broke the contact, then keyed up channels to give them simultaneous contact with each of the four ambassador's ships that remained in orbit about the planet. Dia faced the screen and silently cursed herself. She should have dressed for the occasion—yet it hadn't been safe to fetch robe and crown from her room. She'd just brazen it out.

The vid screen blurred, and one quarter of it cleared to show a communications officer dressed in the deep maroon and gold of the Cerean uniform. Darmin signaled him to stand by while each of the other three ships responded to the call. The last barely had time to acknowledge the connection before Dia demanded: "Have the ambassadors arrived on board their ships?"

"Ambassador Xar is in his quarters," came the neutral response from the Cerean.

"Madam Chevika is on rest cycle," the Quy'doan informed her in his heavily accented speech.

"Who would disturb him?" demanded the Rual-dan, and the Bertolian echoed his words.

Dia straightened, tilting her chin upward. "Very well, if they cannot be bothered, you will give them this message. Any move whatsoever toward this planet will be treated as an act of war, and Dahmla coral-powered weapons will be used in retaliation." That they didn't possess any, she considered irrelevant at the moment. As long as the ambassadors *thought* they did, it would be sufficient. "You will remove your ships from orbit within one half standard hour from now. Any further contact with Kerrian must be directed through proper channels to Princess Dialora rys Pauaia at Kerrian-Isla."

She signaled Darmin to break contact. As the screen went blank, she sagged in her chair, drained. One should never make rash threats one wasn't prepared to back up. She'd learned that as a child. She had the sinking sensation she'd just declared war on four planets.

Darmin shifted in his chair. "Well done, Lady."

"Was it? Well, we've bought ourselves a little time, at least. I'm afraid I'm dumping this on you for awhile, though. There's some more unfinished business I've got to take care of. If the ambassadors check in, make sure they've taken their ships out of orbit. If they give you any argument, tell them we're perfectly capable of managing not only our internal affairs, but our external ones, as well. They'll know what you mean."

"They'll want to talk to you."

"Tell them they can wait. But most likely they'll pull out to give themselves a chance to think. They won't know who really sent this message, whether it has any validity or not. They'll want to determine who actually *is* in control here."

"They'll find out soon enough," Darmin assured her.

"Look—" Dia broke off, studying the young man whose worshipful gaze rested on her. "They're all willing to fight a war for control of our coral. We have to convince them it's not worth the effort to fight each other over us, that they'll come out ahead leaving us in possession of our own planet. Think you can imply all that without saying it directly?"

Darmin grinned at her. "I'll just play 'em off each other a bit. Hint that no one can win a five-way war, and imply we're looking for an ally we can trust."

"Play up the five powers all fighting each other at the same time. If only they would, and destroy each other and leave us in peace." She stood. "Back as soon as I can. Keep them groveling."

She slipped out the door, and Sorin snapped to a sort of attention. "All well, Lady?"

"Sent the messages. Do you need help out here?"

"Wouldn't mind company." He cast an uneasy glance down the hall, where Eelam, Tomlin and Vester's hushed voices could be heard as they returned. "No sign of the Gavonian ambassador—yet."

"No." It made her uncomfortable, too. When the other three men reached them, she directed Eelam and Tomlin to stay with Darmin in the comm room, and Vester to stand watch with Sorin. That unlikely pair of guards resumed their soldierly duties as if trained to them.

One last step remained before she could concentrate on tolArvik. She had to cut his puppet's strings. Trusting in the hope that her small retinue would retain control of the comm room, she returned to the kitchens. The few servants who waited there greeted her eagerly, demanding news.

"We've got the comm room," she assured them. "Will someone take stimi down there? No, no fighting. No need. Each one of them played his part perfectly. Agathas?" She drew the housekeeper aside, leaving Merris to brew the hot, stimulating beverage. "I'm going to visit my cousin. Can you convert some room into a jail for him? I'd rather not take him into the caverns if I don't have to. He doesn't know any of the entrances.''

The woman gave a short nod. "Best to keep it that way, Lady. We'll have something for you.''

"We've got other prisoners, too. Four mercenaries. They're currently locked in offices, but we'll need something better.''

The woman pursed her lips. "There're more mercenaries than that.''

"I know." Dia's courage wavered, then revived. "There can't be that many. They must have smuggled themselves in as tourists, because none of the invasion warnings sounded.''

"You're right." Agathas rubbed her chin, her expression thoughtful. "I don't think I've seen more than about two dozen. At least, that's about the number that've taken over the guard's quarters.''

"Two dozen," Dia mused. "Maybe three. To take over a whole planet." She'd be insulted if she weren't so relieved. "I suppose a small commando force was the right approach, under the circumstances. If I'd been killed according to plan, that's all they'd have needed.''

"But now?" Agathas watched her through narrowed eyes.

"I have an idea," Dia said slowly, the details still hazy. "Get our people out of the gymnasium. Quietly. I don't want the mercenaries hearing anything, and the guards' quarters open right into it.''

"*Very* quietly," Agathas agreed. "Then?''

"The gym will make an ideal holding tank for the mercenaries. We'll just herd them in and seal it off.''

"Very neat." Agathas folded her arms, her expression skeptical. "*How?*''

"We'll deal with that when we get to it. First, I've got to put my cousin out of the picture.''

Agathas sniffed. "Do you want help?"

"Against Bailan?" Dia smiled. "I'd rather keep this a—a family matter. I need a dagger. I've lost mine."

"Your bracelet—?" Agathas looked in alarm at the tracery of wire.

"It's fine. But my cousin is more likely to respond to the weapon he can feel."

Agathas bent and unstrapped a seal-skin sheath from about her lower leg. Dropping to one knee, she fastened it on Dia, then checked the fit. "A bit snug, Lady, but it won't slip."

"Thanks. If I'm not back in half an hour—" She hesitated. "I'm not likely to be. Look, give me that half hour, then create a diversion. There's bound to be a guard at the door, and I want to bring Bailan out that way. Do you think you can get someone to run up there yelling emergency?"

Agathas frowned, considering. "Eelam or Sorin, I think. They tend to show the most initiative. I'll send someone to relieve them in the comm room. Half an hour, Lady." She turned to her waiting staff.

Dia let herself into the cellar, opened the secret door, and once more stood on the landing between the cavern and the palace wall. She mounted the steps, moving slowly. Less than twenty standard hours ago, less than one Kerrinian day, she'd made this climb. She still had much to accomplish.

Once more, the door into her father's wardrobe opened on silent hinges. She eased herself through his collection of garment bags, across the open space, and placed her ear against the door to the room beyond. Nothing. Complete silence. And darkness.

She touched the opening mechanism and the door slid back into the wall. Rhythmic deep breathing reached her, broken abruptly by a short nasal snort. The pattern resumed at once.

Not complete darkness, here. Pale light from the setting moons seeped through the heavy drapes, creating a pattern of shadows against a vaster darkness. She could make out shapes, the positions of the heavier pieces of furniture. And the man-shaped lump jumbled in blankets in the middle of the great bed.

Bailan. Her awareness centered on her rys-bracelet, and her arm tingled, vibrating with the power. Unless this were a trap. . . . She longed for a drink to relieve the dryness of her mouth. Gavonian brandy would be nice, but water would do. She wouldn't get either.

A short snore emitted once more from the depths of the pillows. Someone lay in there, at least. Whether or not it was her cousin, she couldn't tell.

How much of her half hour had she used up? She'd lost her chronometer during the course of events. She'd better hurry.

Still, she remained where she stood, every nerve alert for some other presence in the room. Nothing, no betraying whisper of fabric to indicate some hidden being's making an unwary move. Only a shifting on the bed as the occupant stirred in his sleep.

Bailan lacked subtlety. He'd rely on a guard positioned in plain sight, outside the door. He didn't know about the other way into this room; nor had he the imagination to extrapolate the probability. He slumbered in secure ignorance.

She stooped and grasped the dagger that fit in its sheath against her lower leg. Cool steel met her fingers, and she drew it out. Moonlight cast only the slightest of glints off the polished blade. Knowing Agathas, it would be deadly sharp.

She slipped forward through the darkness until her outstretched hand found the edge of the fur-covered bed. She eased along it until she stood beside the blanket-swathed lump, then rested a knee on the mattress. In one swift move, she leaned forward and dragged back the covers. The point of her dagger pressed unerringly against the neck of her victim.

He jerked in her hold, then froze. His shoulder trembled against her hand that pressed there.

"Wake up, Cousin." She couldn't keep the triumph from her voice. "Your revolution is over."

"My— Dia?" He choked on her name and fell silent.

"It's about time." From barely a meter behind her, from out of the shadows, Jarrod tolArvik's deep voice sounded in deep satisfaction. "You can have no idea how I've waited for this moment, Princess."

Dia spun about, searching for that commanding face in the darkness. Her heart pounded in her throat, but the point of her dagger never wavered. It pressed against her cousin's neck. It might well be her only hope to live.

She should have known. Anger flared within her, directed at herself rather than him. She should have known he'd guess this move.

His dim shape groped to one side, and soft light sprang to life as his hand encountered the plate on the wall. Bailan, in his tangle of furs and blankets, blinked at the sudden glare, and Dia's dagger glinted. Jarrod tolArvik stood before them, legs spread slightly, a cell imploder pointed at Dia.

Chapter Nine

Dia's fingers clenched as her mind raced. She could drag her cousin in front of her, use him as a shield. She could throw him against tolArvik, try to escape back through the wardrobe, down the secret stairs to the caverns. She could. . . . Her gaze met his, and her frantic thoughts faded.

She stared at him, unable to look away, unable to move. He, too, remained still except for the steady rise and fall of his chest as he breathed. An even, unafraid breathing. A man capable of great feats, in complete control. His gaze held her, compelling her to look, to sink under his power. Her world swayed and seemed to focus somewhere within those swirling oceans of his eyes.

"Lady." His deep voice sounded soft but clear, mesmerizing in its intensity.

It robbed her of breath. If that dagger in her hand weren't her lifeline, she'd let it fall, go to him. . . .

Slowly, his gaze never faltering from hers, he

dropped to one knee. He clasped his imploder in both hands, then allowed it to rest on his palms as he extended his arms, holding the weapon out to her in offering. "I should have paid proper tribute to the rightful liege of Kerrian upon my arrival. Forgive me for being late in this courtesy."

"What?" gasped Bailan from the bed. He started to move, but subsided at once as Dia didn't slacken her hold.

Jarrod tolArvik's expression clouded. "Lady, I have been sent by my tharl to offer you every assistance. I hope you'll forgive my misunderstanding of the true situation, and accept my services."

She shifted, still holding her cousin's shoulder with one hand and her dagger with the other. "Misunderstanding?"

"You know I thought you dead," he reminded her. He didn't move from his kneeling position. "You neglected to correct that little bit of misinformation. A great deal of trouble might have been spared if you had."

"You expected me to trust you? You expect me to trust you *now?*"

The tiny lines about the corners of his eyes crinkled in sudden amusement. "Dee, if I'd wanted to, I could have killed you just now." His voice softened. "Your death is the last thing I want."

She swallowed, fighting the wave of yearning that washed over her. *Damn* the man, by every great fish in the everlasting seas! She wanted to believe him, to know the security of his arms about her. He *could* have killed her. Or did he seek to trick her into releasing her cousin?

She could find out in only one way. Give him that

chance. Or at least, let it *seem* that she gave it to
him.

She dropped her hold on Bailan and slid away from
him on the bed, her sandaled feet seeking the floor.
The dagger she lowered, but she kept her left hand
in front of her, the muscles of her arm tensed, her
finger ready to fire the tiny laser pistol at the first
sign of treachery. If Jarrod tolArvik moved, he would
die.

He didn't, except for his expression. His slow smile
twitched at the corners of his mouth, tugging at her
heart. She stood, then moved back to where she could
see both her cousin and tolArvik.

His eyes glinted in the subdued glow that surrounded the bed. "Well, princess? Do you accept my
weapon—and allegiance?"

"I . . . accept them." Keeping her left hand toward
him in firing position, she reached out with her right.
He released the imploder to her, and her arm sagged
with the weight.

"I think we have a few things to straighten out
between us. But they'll have to wait—I don't believe
they're any of your cousin's business." TolArvik rose
and turned to the bed.

Bailan had crawled a meter and a half away, his
terrified gaze resting on them. He opened his mouth,
then offered them a sickly grin. "It—it's awfully late
for talking."

"Long overdue, you mean." TolArvik sat on the
edge of the mattress and reached across with a long
arm to grasp Bailan by the shoulder. He dragged the
erstwhile king back to his original position. "I think
you have a few things to tell us."

"I—I don't know what you mean." Bailan turned

from him, glanced at Dia, then looked down at the fur covers. "It's not my fault."

"You hired an army to take over your planet, didn't you?" TolArvik's voice held nothing but contempt.

Dia held the imploder by its butt, letting its barrel dangle toward the floor. "*Why,* Bailan? Whatever made you think our people would accept you?"

"I *didn't* hire anyone." He looked back to Dia. "They told me I had to go along with it, or I'd be killed, too. They needed a member of the Kerrinian royal family as a figurehead on the throne. They thought they'd be able to control me, but they wouldn't have! I'd have taken care of our people."

"Who is 'they?'" tolArvik demanded before Dia could voice the question.

"The Gavonians. They planned it all."

"They." Dia's hand clenched on the weapon. "The tharl, do you mean?" She couldn't believe that. If Bailan tried to confirm it, she'd know he lied.

A puzzled frown creased her cousin's brow. "I—" He shook his head. "I don't think so. *You* know Dysart. He's Uncle Harryl's best friend."

"Then who?" came tolArvik's sharp question.

"I don't know." Bailan straightened, and for the first time met the ambassador's piercing gaze. " 'Factors representing the government of Gavin-Secundus' is what I was told. I only learned of it all two days ago, on the morning it happened. A man came to me, said he represented the ruling interests on Gavin, and if I wanted to live I'd better cooperate." He cast a sideways glance at Dia. "That's why I didn't come to Linore and Edrick's party. They wouldn't let me see anyone. Then they told me you were all dead and I had to take over and run the negotiations. But they promised they'd arrange everything."

"Who came to you? You know that at least, don't you?" tolArvik demanded.

Bailan shook his head. "I never got a really good look at him. He wore a cloak with a hood that covered his face. It slipped a bit, but I don't think I'd ever seen him before."

"And you wouldn't know him again," Dia muttered.

TolArvik drew in a deep breath. "Are you sure this person really was Gavonian, or just claiming to be? Could it have been a Cerean, perhaps?"

Bailan's eyes narrowed. "You mean trying to throw the blame on Gavin?" He considered. "No, I got a glimpse of him, and the features were Gavonian. Like yours. Coarse and hairy. Not as pale as a Cerean."

Coarse and hairy. Not quite the way she'd describe Jarrod tolArvik, Dia reflected. She liked the implied strength in his rugged features and the thick, waving hair that framed his face when it escaped from the tie that held it back. But Bailan's words did imply a Gavonian.

TolArvik rose and paced—limping—the distance to the wall, then turned back, frowning. "A Gavonian, and someone with enough money or power to hire a mercenary army. And someone in a position to send messages from Merylar Citadel in the tharl's name."

Dia looked up. "What do you mean?"

He explained about the communique he'd received, which contradicted the tharl's recording. "I tried to contact Dysart and Lomax myself," he added, "to warn them. But that was before I knew the extent of the plot."

"You mean you do now?" Dia asked.

"By the Sacred Fire!" His hands clenched. "I wish I did!"

"You were supposed to be sent back to your planet," Bailan offered from the midst of the covers.

"I doubt he'd ever have gotten there." Dia met tolArvik's frowning gaze. "You'd have given the whole thing away to Uncle Dysart."

He resumed his pacing. "I think it's too late for that to matter. It's control of the coral that's at stake, not the tharldom. But whoever is behind this must know me, and knows I'd never go along with this takeover plot." He came to a halt in front of Dia. "We'll find out who it is. That I swear." He rubbed his temple.

"Does it still hurt?" Dia asked. "You should have taken the remedy I brought you."

His sudden smile flashed. "You mean it wasn't poisoned?"

She shook her head. "I trusted my aim. Wrongly, as it turned out."

"Rightly, you mean. I think I'll be of far more use to you alive than dead."

She grinned suddenly, the heaviness that had gripped her heart since the night before easing. "Does your leg hurt much?"

"I still have the use of it. A word with you, princess?" With a touch on her arm he drew her aside, where the subdued lights cast heavy shadows into the darkness. "Have you thought what you intend to do about your cousin?" he asked softly.

"I already took care of it." She looked up at him, studying the harsh planes of his face. "And no, I don't plan to have him killed."

"Of course not." His eyes gleamed. "That's reserved for me."

"You've won a *temporary* reprieve." She let that sink in a moment.

"Learning not to give your trust too easily?" he shot back. "Good for you. Do you plan to leave him in here?"

A slight smile tugged at her lips. "Just because Bailan's a fool doesn't mean it runs in the family."

"No." He studied her for a long moment. "You're no fool. Merely innocence coming of age. I'm sorry it had to happen."

She shrugged, pretending to make light of it. "It's the natural progression of life. Say rather it's a shame it was torn from me." Her cousin stirred on the bed, recalling her to her unfinished labors. "We'd best get him downstairs. The guard outside the door—"

"Taken care of," Jarrod assured her. "That's how I got in."

She nodded, though she remained unsure. TolArvik didn't need to trick her, he'd had his chance to kill her if he'd wanted. She'd risk it—but she'd let him go into the hall first. "Get dressed," she called to Bailan.

"It's the middle of the night!" He folded his arms before him in a stubborn gesture of refusal. "Whatever you want can wait 'til morning."

"Never keep a lady waiting." TolArvik limped to a bedside chair and picked up a robe that lay flung across it. "She has excellent aim with that bracelet."

Bailan directed a resentful glare at Dia. "Her *rys*-bracelet. Don't see why I didn't get one, or even Linore. But no, Uncle Harryl locked up my aunt's after she died. He should have passed it on to me."

"Maybe he had a premonition," Dia shot back.

Bailan's chin came up. "None of this is *my* fault. I'd be dead, too, if I hadn't gone along with it."

"I heard what you said to Ambassador tolArvik in the audience chamber. I—" Dia broke off. Bickering with her cousin didn't help anything. She needed to appear strong before tolArvik, a woman in complete control rather than a frightened child. Supreme confidence in her own abilities, she reminded herself. If he guessed, for a single moment, the absolute terror that raged within her when she thought of the immediate future, that she hadn't the faintest idea how to go on, that she was a frightened child wanting desperately to cry for her father, he'd have her in his power.

"Now, Bailan." She strode to the door, then turned back. "I've put up with too much in the past twenty hours and more. Move it!" Yet what would she do if he called her bluff?

Bailan's lip curled. "You think *you've* been having it rough? Come off it, Dia. You don't have to impress anyone with that 'important princess' routine. All we have to do is find the man who approached me, and—"

"*We* aren't doing anything. You're under house arrest, Bailan. And don't think it's just me. I have a—a small army, and we've already taken the comm room and summoned more guards. They'll keep you safe until we've sorted this mess out."

"An army?" Bailan paled. "Damn it, Dia, from *where*?"

"Now, cousin." She raised her left hand and felt the unsettling thrumming of the coral power building within the tiny chamber.

Bailan scrambled from amid the sheets and covers and grabbed the robe that tolArvik held out.

"Have you really taken the comm room?" TolArvik glanced at her, his expression one of respect mingled with doubt.

"And sent messages. The guards are already on their way from Waianoa. And the other ambassadors

must be bombarding the poor tech I left in charge
with demands to know what's going on.''

"Lady, you impress me."

"Thank you. Will you lead the way, Ambassador?
Cousin? After you." She gestured for them to precede
her from the chamber.

TolArvik emerged into the corridor. Bailan, a step
behind him, gasped and halted, and Dia pushed him
ahead so she could see. No sign of her diversion yet.
All this must have taken less time than she realized.

Only one man waited in the hall, a Bertolian,
garbed in palace guard uniform. He sat propped
against the wall, his head tilted back as if in sleep.

TolArvik stooped to check his pulse, then lifted
the man's eyelids to inspect the pupils. "He'll be out
for another two standard hours, I should think."

"My turn to be impressed." Dia eyed the ambassador with wary respect. "What did you do?"

"It's all a matter of pressure points." He straightened. "I didn't want to attract attention by killing
him or tying him up. The mercenaries seem rather
lax in their security."

"Let's take the service lift, anyway. I don't want to
run into any of them on the stairs." Dia directed
them toward the door behind the elaborate screen.

TolArvik slowed to walk at her side. "This isn't the
way you came," he remarked, but in a tone lowered
so Bailan wouldn't hear.

She gave him a deceptively sweet smile. "We're not
quite as naive as you think."

"That you aren't," he agreed, and ushered her
into the lift.

Bailan met her with a sulky glower. "There isn't
any need for this. If you'll just let me help—"

"Oh, you've done your part." Dia palmed the controls. "Now you get to lie around and rest while I clean up the details."

He shot her a darkling glance, but held his tongue.

"Do I get to meet this army of yours?" Amusement sounded in tolArvik's voice. "Or are you turning *me* over to them, as well?"

A touch of longing rippled through Dia, and she made a show of considering her answer to cover it. If she'd met tolArvik under different circumstances, if she had nothing more pressing on her mind than to indulge in playful verbal sparring with him, perhaps even mild flirtation— She broke off that thought. There'd be nothing mild about it.

"Consider yourself on parole," she told him as the door slid open, letting them out in the hall leading to the kitchen.

Eelam and Sorin stood in front of the lift door, clasping their imploders with uneasy determination. Sorin stepped toward them, raising his weapon, then hesitated. His anguished expression passed from Dia to the two men accompanying her. He took a step back again, then seemed to brace himself.

"It's all right, I didn't need the diversion after all." Dia prodded her cousin forward. "Tell Agathas her guest is ready. Ambassador tolArvik is—" she glanced at him, "—helping us. For the moment."

TolArvik flashed her an infectious smile, but before he could speak, the kitchen door swung open and Agathas herself emerged. The little woman directed a piercing look at them, then nodded. "You will be our guest for a little while, Lord Bailan. If you will come with me? Eelam? Sorin?" She signaled for the uneasy guards to escort them. "You will be quite comfortable, Lord," Agathas continued as she directed the man's faltering steps toward the storage rooms.

"Will he?" tolArvik asked.

"For now. And if he really is innocent of all this." Dia rubbed her arm where the tingling of the bracelet continued unabated.

"And what about me?" The amusement still sounded in his voice. "Am I likely to be shot by some over zealous protector of yours who sees us together?"

She directed a sideways glance up at him. "Who knows? Guess you'll just have to be careful."

"You might tell them I'm on your side," he pointed out.

"And so you *might* be."

He grinned, an unexpectedly boyish expression that caused her heart to skip a beat. For a long moment he gazed at her, still smiling, and warmth seeped through her. If only it were all over. . . .

She shifted her shoulders, easing the tension. Still another task remained, one she had to accomplish now, before morning. Before she lost everything she had gained. She had a mercenary army to roust.

"What—the mercenaries?" he asked, as if reading her mind.

She nodded. "It'll take my guards four hours to get here. If I wait for them—" She grimaced. "As soon as the mercenaries wake up, they'll figure out what's been going on and take over again."

"Time for some stimi." TolArvik drew her into the kitchen. For once, the vast apartment stood empty.

Dia checked the brewing pot, found it near full, and poured two steaming mugs. "I've arranged for a secured spot to store the mercenaries 'til we can get them off planet. The problem is getting them into it. There's no way we can overpower them. Any ideas on how to make them surrender of their own accord?''

"Only by cutting off their pay. But since we don't know who hired them—''

Dia sighed and took a scalding sip of the bittersweet liquid. "I could offer them more than what they're currently getting. They don't strike me as being very loyal. But it goes against the grain to pay them, and who's to say they won't take what I offer, then finish the job for their original employer?''

"From what I've seen of them, that sounds likely.'' He inspected the counter, opening containers at random until he found one holding sugar. He added a hefty dose to his mug, stirred it, and took a swallow. "That's more like it. I think we should have a talk with the mercenary commander.''

Dia sank into a chair. "Oh, good. Let him know I'm still alive. He'll be glad to take care of that little oversight, I'm sure.''

TolArvik awarded that sally a singularly disarming smile. "There are four war ships up there, thinly disguised as ambassadorial vessels. Do you think he wants to pit his army against that?''

She opened her mouth, then shut it again. "War ships?'' she managed.

"They're just as likely to fight each other as you, remember. And who says we have to consult them? We—'' He broke off, and his eyes gleamed. "Do you have visual contact from the comm room with the commander of the guard's quarters?''

"Yes. With everywhere in the place. You've got an idea?''

"I think so. Let's get over there.'' He set his unfin-

ished mug on the counter and swung himself lightly
to his feet.

She smothered a yawn. "I have to get back there,
anyway. There'll be any number of messages coming
in I'll have to handle."

"Good. Maybe we can make use of some of them."

She didn't feel up to questioning that cryptic utter-
ance. She'd been too many hours without sleep, running on nerves stretched too thin. If she didn't get
some rest soon, she feared she'd collapse. And that
was *not* the way she wanted this Gavonian ambassador
to see her.

She started along the corridor, and he slipped his
hand under her elbow to give her support. Did she show
how tired she was? Disgusted with herself, she tried very
hard not to lean on him—and not to enjoy the pleasur-
able warmth caused by the contact. It wasn't easy.

Vester and Tomlin stood on guard outside the
comm room, nerves obviously vying with the exhaustion that threatened to overcome them. Vester
stepped forward as Dia and tolArvik approached, his
face pale as he swung his borrowed imploder to the
ready. Tomlin followed suit.

"Lady?" Tomlin asked, eyeing tolArvik with uncertainty.

"It's all right." Dia gestured for them to lower their
weapons. "My cousin's safely locked away, and the
ambassador here seems to be helping us. Any trouble
while I was gone?"

"Only keeping awake, Lady," Vester admitted.
"Seems like everyone must be asleep except us."

"You will be soon," she promised, and could only
hope she told the truth. At tolArvik's gentle urging,
she entered the comm room.

Darmin sprang to his feet as the door slid wide, his eyes wary and shadowed. "Lady—" he began in relief, then broke off as tolArvik followed her in. His eyebrows rose, but he made no comment. "I'm glad you're back. I've never been very good at acting haughty."

"Sorry you needed to." She wended her way amid the consoles to his station. "How bad has it been?"

"The messages have been coming in steadily." He grinned suddenly. "Those ambassadors don't know what to think, that much's clear."

"As long as they don't decide to open fire on us, then pick the coral and acid out of the pieces." She leaned over tolArvik's shoulder where he stood before the next console, keying up the message file.

The screen flickered, and the Quy'doan ambassador, in full ceremonial dress, appeared. "Message to be recorded begins," she said. "Princess Dialora, we are pleased to learn that in spite of what we have been told, you are indeed alive and once more in control of your planet's affairs. We regret that you seem to have misunderstood our intentions, and look forward to beginning treaty negotiations with you at the earliest opportunity. Recording ends."

"I'll bet she's looking forward to it," Dia muttered. She keyed up the message from the Cerean ambassador, and viewed a similar transmission. The other two followed almost identical lines, except the Bertolians ranged their entire diplomatic delegation behind their ambassador.

"Nice touch." TolArvik brought up a fifth message, once more from the Cereans. Five more followed, one from the Quy'doans, another from the formal Bertolian delegation, then two from the Cereans and another from the Rualdans. "Do you think that last one had a touch of groveling about it?" he added.

Darmin grinned. "Are you here for them when they call again? It's been nearly five minutes since the last message. One of them should be checking in any time now."

"I don't think so," Dia said. She cast an uncertain glance at tolArvik.

"No," came his quick response. "Let them wait 'til after you've rested, Lady. It's too easy to make a mistake when you've gone so long without sleep. It won't hurt them to sit for a while longer. And we've got another little job to do."

"I don't want to provoke the ambassadors." She eyed her self-appointed advisor with uncertainty. "Just because I told them we had coral-powered weapons doesn't mean we do."

"We won't let matters go that far. I think you could use some rest and a little coaching before any of them try to back you into a corner."

With that, Dia agreed. "We should give the ambassadors some sort of an answer, though." She thought for a moment, then turned to Darmin. "Tell them I've received their messages and I'll speak to each of them, personally, in the morning. Tell them I'm going to sleep."

"Good touch." TolArvik frowned at the notes Darmin jotted down rapidly. "Use her full title, and present the message with her compliments. They'll know she means the exact opposite."

Dia allowed his corrections to stand. Too bad high level treaty negotiation techniques had never been considered a priority in her education. Recreation opportunities were all any other planet or system had ever wanted from a world with a surface of almost nothing but water. Now their entire existence as an autonomous government was threatened. Instead of catering to tourists, she had to overwhelm these people with pomp and majesty. She could only pray she had sufficient acting ability within her.

TolArvik drummed his fingers on the back of a chair. "Can you put the visuals of all the ambassadors on the wall screen, then freeze them?"

Darmin considered. "Each one in quarter screen, or superimposed so it looks like they're all in the same room?"

"Quarter screen. Can you send an in-house message with that as the backdrop?"

"A show of power?" Darmin grinned. "Sure can. Lady? Will you take the seat over there?"

Dia crossed to the elaborate chair where her father had occasionally recorded travel ads, with scenes of watersports playing on the huge screen behind him. Her father—

No, not yet! She was alive. He would be as well, somewhere, and she'd find him when all this was over. She clung to that. Believing anything else right now would be more than she could bear.

TolArvik joined her, taking up a position behind her chair. "Get us the commander of the guard's quarters—and block him from communicating with anyone else. Lady? Do you want me to do the talking?"

"That would make it look like I'm *your* puppet." Which she could only hope wasn't the actual case. "I'm ready, Darmin. Show time."

A console sprang to life before her, its screen remaining dark. After a moment, it cleared to reveal a sleepy Bertolian face. "What do you mean by disturbing me?" his gravelly voice demanded.

Dia straightened. "I believe I'm the one who should be asking you that. Do you command this—this farce of a mercenary squad?"

The man rubbed his eyes and glared at the screen. "Who are you?"

"Dialora, Princess of Kerrian." Princess, not queen. She *would* find her father. "I've reclaimed my planet. There's already been sufficient bloodshed, so I'm granting you the opportunity to surrender. If you refuse—" She broke off, and indicated the screen behind her. "The ambassadors are no more pleased than I am that some unauthorized person is trying to take over the coral. There are four warships currently in orbit around Kerrian, each with a full compliment of soldiers. I don't believe *that's* the force you were hired to tackle. You will not, I'm afraid, be able to communicate with your people."

A look of cunning passed over the face on the screen. "Are you desirous of hiring us yourself?"

Dia gave an almost convincing laugh. "With this support? Don't be ridiculous. Are you being paid enough to make this a suicide mission for your squad?"

The man worked his lower lip between his teeth. "What're your terms?" he asked at last.

She glanced over her shoulder. "Ambassador tolArvik?"

"As you wish, Lady." He stepped forward and faced the screen.

Dia remained erect in her chair, her expression stern. TolArvik's deep voice rolled about her, commanding, yet her exhausted mind didn't take in his actual words. She should make the effort—yet, it was all she could do not to close her eyes. She hadn't thought it would be this easy. *He'd* made it that way. Without him, she might have risked her four weary supporters in a suicide mission of their own. She might have . . .

"Princess?"

She blinked and looked up to find tolArvik leaning over her.

He smiled. "How can you look so alert, yet be so asleep?"

"Long practice at dinner parties. What happens now?"

"Now we oversee the turning in of weapons and the withdrawal of the mercenaries to your holding tank. Unless you have any staff you can trust with the job? I doubt it'll be hard. That captain wasn't expecting any resistance. He's ready to cut his losses."

Dia went to the door and opened it. "I've got a job for you two," she told Vester and Tomlin. "Find Sorin and Eelam, will you? The mercenaries have agreed to hand over their weapons. All you have to do is herd them through the door from the guards' quarters into the gymnasium and keep them secured there. Agathas has been preparing it."

The triple tone announcing an incoming broadcast sounded. She left tolArvik filling her people in on the details of the surrender and returned to Darmin. The Bertolian ambassador's chief of staff, she noted. She remained out of visual range while Darmin delivered her message. He closed the channel and looked up at her.

"Good work. Now, will you contact Waianoa for me again?" she asked as tolArvik rejoined her. "I'd rather not have the entire guard here—just in case we need more backup later. Half of them should turn back, I think. That should leave us enough to deal with unarmed mercenaries." She avoided looking at tolArvik to see what he thought of her plan. It shouldn't matter to her, yet it did. She turned to him. "How do we get those mercenaries off planet?"

"Let your guard deal with it when they get here. We'll keep them locked up 'til then. Four hours shouldn't be any problem. Show them vids—just not war shows. They look as if a little entertainment will keep them from planning escapes."

She succumbed to a cavernous yawn and turned toward the door, so tired she could barely keep her eyes open. Reaction, she realized, but that didn't help. It only made her look weaker in tolArvik's eyes. And that she didn't want.

"Lady." TolArvik joined her at the door, keeping his voice low.

She drew a deep, strengthening breath before turning to face him. "Thank you for your assistance, Ambassador."

The deep gray of his eyes clouded to the charcoal of storm clouds. "It's the least I can do. Someone from my planet has caused you a great deal of trouble. Allow me to continue offering my services to you, as partial repayment." He palmed open the door and ushered her into the hall.

"What else tonight?" She stretched her back, easing the tension in her muscles, and swayed with weariness.

He caught her arm. "You and I have a lot to talk about, but it'll keep a bit longer. Have you slept at all since I saw you at my inn?"

She shook her head. "I lay down a couple of times, but for no more than an hour or two. There's been too much to do."

"You won't be doing anything if you don't get some sleep. Come on, I'll take you to your room. You can send for me when you've rested."

"But—"

"When you've rested," he repeated. "Don't worry any more tonight. We'll see you trained in negotiations, and your people in the uses of the coral."

"Your planet probably owes us at least that," she agreed. She couldn't let him think he put her in any way in his debt, no matter how grateful she felt at the moment. Strength. Why did she need it the most when all she wanted was to hide somewhere and sleep and sleep and sleep?

"You're under no obligations to us," came his gentle, amused assurance.

He understood her. She accepted his escort along the hall, trying not to stumble. It would be too easy to lean against him, to rely on his strength. His presence comforted her, made her feel secure, made her—

She straightened and moved away from him, dismayed by the reactions of her body. He attracted her, she couldn't deny that. She looked up at him sideways, through her lashes, allowing herself no more than a glimpse of his rough-hewn, capable features. A man of strength and decision, swift in action because of his familiarity with the political intrigues of Gavin-Secundus's checkered past.

He could have controlled Kerrian if he'd wanted. He could have killed her. Yet he'd shown himself to be a man of honor. Somehow, through the tortuous happenings of the last couple of hours, he had won her respect.

Or was it more than that? Certainly he was an ally worth having. And a man worth having, as well.

She hugged herself. If this were not a time of danger and unrest, she might find herself falling in love.

Chapter Ten

How many hours had passed, Jarrod had no idea. He stretched in the large bed and discovered far too many stiff muscles. His left thigh blazed with pain as if all the fire demons of Mt. Beleron had gathered there for their Vortris Eve bonfire.

Another fire burned within him, as well. His bed, comfortable as it was, was far too empty. Dee—

Only she wasn't Dee. She was Princess Dialora. And what he wanted was out of the question. The situation was already too complicated.

He rolled over and slammed his fist into the mattress, which provided about as much relief as the scent of food to a starving man. Maybe he should take something for his leg. It might quench the other aching in him as well.

He rolled out from beneath the covers and set his feet on the thick carpeting. His wound—a present from his princess, he remembered with a slight smile. At least he carried something of her with him. He stumbled to the bathroom and eased off the bandage he'd applied hours ago.

What time was it, anyway? How many hours since he'd seen her? Longing for her wrenched through him.

Zero nine twenty hours, standard time, the wall chronometer flashed at him. He groaned. He'd left Dee—Dia—at the door to her room shortly before five. Four and a half hours of sleep. Four and a half hours without her.

He wished she'd summon him. Off hand, he couldn't think of a more pleasant way to pass a few hours than in her company. Right now, he'd settle for just looking at her, watching the play of expression across her open countenance. He'd prefer it, though, if the circumstances were less tense. Once she'd established unquestioned control—

He paused in the process of pulling on his uniform. He'd like to see her relaxed, laughing, at ease. He'd like to take her to his favorite place, a mountain glen a few short kilometers outside Merylar Citadel. The crystal clear lake there gleamed in the summer sun at this time of year, and a waterfall tumbled into it over boulders in a cascade of frothing white water. And the ancient, majestic trees with their rich, pungent aromas— By the Sacred Fire, he missed trees on this planet. And the deer and smaller animals which came to his glen to drink and feed on the waving grasses heavy with seed. He'd like to take her there, sit on the rocks watching the ripples caused by the fish, lie in the tall grass. . . .

He broke off that dangerous line of thought. He could think of something else he'd like to do with her among the tall, soft blades.

He fastened his jacket. The pills he'd swallowed had eased only one of his aches. He forced his mind from the one activity that might help the other.

As he re-entered his room from the bath, a message light blinked on his console. He keyed it up, and Dia's image filled his vision as her voice surrounded him.

"Good morning, Ambassador." She looked calm and damnably beautiful. "I hope you've rested. Please join me for breakfast in my apartments whenever you're ready."

The screen blinked into blackness and silence filled the room. He touched the save key; he'd use that image to drive himself insane looking at her again and again during the long hours of the night to come. More fool he.

For several minutes he stood before the mirror, straightening his sash, tying back his unruly hair. She might not even like him, he reminded himself savagely. She could well have put on an act for his benefit, to gain her chance to kill him last night.

But could she have faked the way she'd melted into his arms when he'd stolen that kiss in the corridor, then again here, in his room? There was one way to find out, his baser self whispered in his ear.

He caught himself eyeing his reflection, and turned from the mirror in disgust. He never concerned himself unduly over his appearance. She had an unsettling effect on him. Fighting the urge for one last glance, just to reassure himself, he exited the apartment and strode down the hall.

A man stood before her door, one of the ones who'd helped her take the comm room the night before. He stiffened as Jarrod approached, but though his fingers seemed to clench the imploder with loving wistfulness, he remained at attention. Only the man's dark violet eyes betrayed his distrust.

Jarrod stopped a meter away from him. "The princess sent for me."

"She told me." He pressed a recessed panel at the door's side, then grudgingly moved out of the way.

A soft bell sounded within. Jarrod waited, and a minute later the panel separated in the middle and slid softly into the walls. Dia stood just inside, her hand still pressed to the locking plate.

"I hope I didn't wake you." She started across the room.

For a long moment, Jarrod simply stared at her, at the swirling folds of her deep purple sarong with its edging of downy feathers in shades of pink and silver. They clung to her lithe body, enhancing every supple curve. Her loose hair tumbled below her knees in a waterfall of black silk. A soft, exotic scent clung to her. One of the water lilies, he remembered. It played havoc with his self control.

What would she do if he took her in his arms and kissed her, and not just a quick pressure of the mouth but the way he wanted to kiss her. Fully, lingeringly, savoring. . . .

"Thank you, Loris." Dia touched a middle-aged maid on the shoulder, her smile warm. "Go get some more sleep. We'll finish my hair later."

"Your breakfast—" Loris began.

"It'll be here any minute now. Agathas will have known the moment the ambassador left his rooms." Her smile broadened. "You've done more than enough. All of you have. I'll be needing you in a bit, though, before I face everyone."

Loris cast a darkling look at Jarrod. "If you need me for anything, Lady—"

"I have Sorin right outside. Go to sleep and stop worrying. We still have work to do, and I'm going to need coaching."

Loris let herself out, but not before glaring once more at Jarrod. He returned the stare, his own features void of expression, his mind assessing. Loyal, he decided. But in what way did the woman consider him a threat to Dia? Politically or personally?

Dia stood before a side table, a pot of steaming stimi in her hand. "You like it sweetened, don't you?"

"Straight in the morning." He crossed the room to join her. A large chamber, and not her bedroom. A sitting room, designed for the informal receiving of guests. One plasticlear wall looked out over the harbor; the others, painted white, displayed tapestries and murals in the muted underwater tones of blue violet and silver. A gleaming bronze brazier, built low to the ground, stood in the middle of the room, circled by comfortable chairs, sofas and low tables. Thick fleecy carpets covered the floor, and everywhere the exotic fragrance of water lilies filled the air.

He took the stimi and swallowed a mouthful. Energy seeped through him as the hot liquid burned down his throat, clearing the vision he hadn't realized was blurred. He shifted his shoulders, and the stiffness eased. Damned potent brew they served on this planet. It beat the more conventional stimi they produced on Gavin. He'd have to take a load of these seaweed berries home with him.

She stood before him, her attention concentrated on the mug she held in both hands. She didn't look at him—had she at all, since he came into the room? Deep shadows showed under her eyes and she gulped at her drink as if it were all that kept her on her feet.

"Did you get any sleep?" he demanded.

"Some." She managed a brief smile, but moved away rather than look at him.

"Not enough, obviously."

"You couldn't have, either," she countered.

"At least I went to bed. It looks like you've been working all night."

At that she did turn back, though she didn't quite meet his gaze. "Do I look that bad? No, don't answer. I don't need my confidence undermined any more than it already is."

"You look beautiful," he said with complete honesty.

"Ever the diplomat, aren't you? Great Net, what a—a ridiculously mundane conversation. There's so much we *have* to talk about. My guards arrived."

"And the mercenaries?"

"We're keeping them right where they are, 'til we figure out how to get them safely off planet. My guard captain has been muttering about ransom for them, but I don't want the rest of their army staging a rescue raid."

"Wise. Though I doubt they'd try it with those battle cruisers in orbit."

She shook her head. "I don't want to take chances. And speaking of battle cruisers, the ambassadors have been calling already."

He set down his empty mug with a thud. "Have you spoken with any of them?"

"No, don't look so alarmed. Darmin is still at his post, and he's holding them at bay. I'm not seeing anyone until I look more regal."

His lips twitched. "The loose hair? It looks—" He broke off, watching the way the thick waves drifted about her shoulders, allowed glimpses of her arms. Erotic, that was the word. Sensuous.

"A mess. I know. I—"

The bell sang out its hushed musical note, and a moment later the door slid open. Agathas herself wheeled in a cart laden with covered trays. She cast a searching glance at Dia, then nodded to herself.

Dia hurried forward. "You're supposed to be asleep, too, you know." Her voice sounded both resigned and affectionate.

Agathas sniffed. "There's more chaos downstairs this morning than there was yesterday. Some of the missing ones have come out of hiding, and they're all so busy claiming they're completely loyal to you and never would have served your cousin that they're not doing their jobs."

"Tell them there'll be some shifts in positions. That'll get them back on their toes. I've got to have everything running smoothly before the diplomatic invasion gets underway."

Agathas fixed her with her unblinking regard. "I've got a few suggestions myself, if you're serious about promoting a few people."

"Very serious. No, leave the cart with me. You've got to get the staff under control. We've still got the Gavonians—" She broke off, the delicate color in her cheeks darkening.

Very becomingly, too, Jarrod noted. He merely smiled. "You've got the Gavonians under foot, already, and it won't do to show any sign of weakness or disorder in front of them."

Dia glared at him. "That's not what I was going to say."

"No, because I'm here. It's the truth, though." He pushed the cart away from her and positioned it in front of the huge window. "Lady? I believe you invited me for breakfast. I'm damnably hungry."

"Sorin is still outside," Agathas told Dia in a hushed whisper that carried to Jarrod every bit as well as she'd undoubtedly intended it to. With a nod of satisfaction, the woman let herself out.

"None of your people trust me." He placed a chair for Dia, holding its back and waiting for her to sit.

"Can you blame them?" She settled before the table. "Last night they were helping me plan to kill you."

He set a chair for himself. "I hope you've taken that off your agenda for the moment."

"For the moment," she agreed. She lifted the lid from the first of the dishes.

The most heavenly aromas wafted forth, reminding Jarrod of how very long ago had been the interrupted banquet of the night before, and how busy had been the intervening hours. She served them both, a small portion for herself and a heaping one for him, full of various tubers, sea bird eggs, cheese from some ocean mammal, and seasonings unique to this water planet. The next dish contained rolls made from various flours, some containing chopped fruits or jams. For several minutes he concentrated on eating, relishing the contrasts of tart and sweet and tang.

At last, the worst of his hunger sated, he slowed to savoring each mouthful. Dia, he noted, picked at her plate. A fine mist filmed her eyes, which held an expression of infinite sadness. How hard did she struggle to contain her grief? he wondered. Her father, the female cousin blown up with the outrigger—that made her only close living relative Bailan.

She wouldn't welcome his intrusion, he guessed. He turned to the window, allowing her time to master her emotions. Outside the morning shown bright and clear, the only clouds on the distant horizon toward the north, where winter lay heavy on the floating cities. Here, the warm sun held sway, enticing the vessels from their moorings. A steady stream of them flared outward from the mouth of the harbor, like expanding rays. Business, it seemed, continued as usual.

Beyond the line of tiny ships, trawlers and kayaks, a pod of giant cetaceans swam by, their great heads just breaking the surface in a continual series of graceful arcs. Beside them, smaller shapes leapt from the waves into the air as if dancing at their sides. Giant reeka gulls dipped and spiraled, their three-meter wing span and their bright ruby-tinged feathers making them visible from kilometers away.

He glanced back at Dia, to find her gaze resting on him, her expression troubled. "Don't worry." He offered her a smile of far more confidence than he felt. "You'll be every inch a head of state—every inch who you are."

She nodded. "It'll go well. It has to." She added the last under her breath so it was barely audible.

The poor girl was terrified, he realized, and trying desperately hard not to show it, even to him. She needed confidence, to appear intimidating. He needed to relax her, make her proud of herself, of her planet, of her heritage. Besides, he needed a few questions answered.

He selected another roll and took an appreciative bite. "Tell me about the coral," he directed around his mouthful.

She twisted her napkin with nervous fingers. "I suppose all this was inevitable. We—our family, at least—have known about its power for generations. Since the time of Symon the Mercenary's grandson, in fact."

He nodded encouragement, not wanting to interrupt her. He knew enough of her planet's history to know about the man with the keen business sense who purchased Kerrian back in the days when buying an uninhabited planet and making oneself a king was still possible. When she remained silent, he prodded her gently. "It took its name from someone, didn't it? A Doctor Dahmla?"

She blinked as if her mind had wandered from the topic. "Doctor Frankl Dahmla," she agreed. "A marine zoologist. One of the Columbine jells guided him to a tiny patch of the coral. No one had seen that species before, it's incredibly rare." A slight smile touched her full lips. "The jell did it on purpose, according to the story. It urged Doctor Dahmla into hiding, herding him the way they do when they want someone to go somewhere. Then it released a tiny stream of its jellactic acid onto just a fragment of a coral branch. Doctor Dahmla reported that the water spouted ten meters into the air."

Jarrod raised his eyebrows. "Dahmla didn't go yelling about it all over the place?"

"Apparently, he went to the king first. Jaesom, that was. He took after old Symon, and decided that common knowledge of a potential hazard would be bad for business. Since the jells obviously knew enough to avoid the coral, he decided to ignore the problem and let it go away." She picked up a clear goblet filled with an amber liquid. "Jaesom the Shortsighted, that's what later generations called him—and they didn't even know about the coral decision."

Jarrod rubbed his finger along the line of his jaw. "Can't be easy being the king of a planet-sized tourist attraction."

"No." For a moment she stared at her plate, then went on. "Several more generations passed before Maroc the Shrewd came across a mention of the explosion in the old records. A wily old guy, by all reports. He decided to harness the power—for his own personal protection. And so we have these." She held up her left arm, turning it slightly to display the intricate wire tracery that made up her rys-bracelet. "Only three of them, for the ruler, his or her consort, and the heir to the throne."

"What about the plain ones? The ones everyone else wears?"

"Easy enough. You yourself said it, we're a planet-sized tourist attraction. Maroc only had to drop a hint that the bracelets were just another affectation for the delectation of the tourists. Like the sarongs and the shell beads and my hair and the rest of the nonsense. No one complained when he reserved the right for the royal family alone to wear the rare amethyst-colored coral. Made it more quaint and touristy. No one else knew about the power of the coral."

"Lucky he never had to use his bracelet. That would have given away the trick."

"Oh, he was prepared. Or someone in the family was, at any rate. There were rumors over the years about them, but everyone seemed to think it was just nonsense, another tourist gimmick, an attempt to imbue a simple piece of jewelry with a magical aura. It was only with the disclosure of the coral power that we let the secret out." For a long moment, she stared at her bracelet in silence. "I wonder what epithet

they'll add to my father's name? Foolish or Great?"
She tilted her head sideways and looked at him.

"Great, I should think. Any major change always
has a few minor glitches, but they get straightened
out. Now." He folded his arms before him. "Address
me as if I'm one of the ambassadors."

"You are," she pointed out.

A slight frown creased his brow. "I—" He broke
off. He could hardly tell her he hoped he was much
more to her than that. He turned his expression stern.
"Is this how you deal with an ambassador?" he
demanded.

She straightened, her own expression taking on
just a hint of haughtiness. She rose, offering him her
hand in a gesture that defied him to do other than
bow over it. "Ambassador tolArvik. You will forgive
the slight irregularities we have experienced." It
wasn't a question so much as a command.

"Lady," he murmured, retaining his hold on her
fingers. Cold fingers that trembled slightly.

She withdrew her hand with only the slightest raising of her eyebrow to indicate he had overstepped
the boundaries of the permissible. "I believe we will
do best to forget the recent past and start anew. If
that is acceptable to you?" Again, her tone didn't
leave the matter open to discussion.

Jarrod folded his arms and grinned. "Very good—
Lady. Did you learn that manner to impress the tourists? It'll do very well." More than very well, he
acknowledged, but only to himself. Her sudden aura
of power and importance had taken him by surprise.
She was every inch a princess, a head of state. Not
his little maid Dee anymore.

But to his surprise, he found himself pleased. Dia,

with all her fears, her bravado, her acting a part—it was Dia herself, the woman she truly was, that he wanted with an aching need that threatened to destroy his concentration.

Chapter Eleven

Dia tugged at her ceremonial cape, shifting its position so it no longer scratched her between the shoulder blades. The spine of one of the feathers must have punched through the soft fabric of the lining. Again. Why couldn't they wear simple military-style uniforms like the other two remaining royal families in their quadrant? But no, not them. Feathers from the colorful sea birds impressed the tourists as exotic and picturesque.

The giant audience chamber stood empty except for Dia and Ambassador tolArvik. That didn't mean she could relax, though. It was as important to keep up appearances for his benefit as for anyone else's. Still, she'd have been glad of some distraction, someone else to talk to. She was far too aware of him, of his every move, even of the play of emotions that flickered across his countenance.

He offered her his hand, and with a slight inclining of her head in acknowledgment, she permitted him to lead her up the shallow steps to the elaborate nautilus throne. She needed the assistance; the murex shell crown perched precariously amid her mass of braided and pinned up hair, throwing her off balance. She settled on the cushioned seat with a distinct feeling of relief.

"Just remember how angry you are with them," Jarrod tolArvik told her. "Be imperious. They planned—and may still be planning—to wrong you. You have the right to be indignant and make demands."

"And they have the option to join forces and take us over."

He shook his head. "Not with the threat of coral-powered weapons protecting the planet."

A short laugh broke from her. "We'll have to see about getting some, won't we?"

"It's not what you have, but what they *think* you have, that matters."

"Let's hope they go on thinking it." She touched the comm link in the side of the throne. "Are you ready, Darmin?"

A sound that could have been a yawn came over the unit. "Whenever you are, Lady. They're on standby, waiting for the vid-link."

"Show time." Her heart rose in her throat. "Proceed," she managed to choke out around it. "Ambassador?" She glanced at Jarrod.

He moved away, out of line of the vid camera that would transmit her image to the ships that had just re-entered orbit. He could cue her if needed, but the representatives of the other systems didn't need to know she'd accepted his aid. That sort of thing caused the charges of preferential treatment flung at her cousin last night.

She keyed a command into the throne's control panel. A screech, as of the hushed tearing of metal, sounded, and the bottom step of the dais separated. From the exposed gaping hole rose a large vid console. It halted in front of her. She drew in a steadying breath, then touched the power switch. The screen flickered while Darmin, away in the comm room, established the connections; then it split into four quadrants.

The ambassadors stared at her, even as she studied each of them. She took her time—*keep your expression haughty*—though she'd studied each one covertly the night before as she crept about the edges of the banqueting hall. She didn't know any of these four personally. Whether that would be a hindrance or a help, she wasn't certain.

She allowed another half minute to pass while she concentrated on controlling her voice, on keeping out the note of panic she felt swelling within her. "You have all had a chance to identify me by now." She kept her expression cool, emotionless. That would make a flash of anger more impressive later.

The Rualdan ambassador answered first. "You are indeed Princess Dialora, last of the house of rys Pauaia."

"That would make me *Queen* Dialora. But as to my being the last of my house, that isn't certain. There is no proof of my father's death."

All four of the ambassadors glanced off-screen, toward their own consultants. Dia sat impassive for a slow count of ten, then addressed them again. "It is me you will deal with in these negotiations. Unless my father returns, no one else has the right to speak for my people."

"Lady Dialora—" The Cerean ambassador leaned

forward in his chair. "Before we go further, I require your personal assurance that you are not under the control of Gavin-Secundus."

"You *require?*" She had to force the flash into her eyes and the indignation into her voice. Whimpering with nerves would be disastrous. To her amazement, the Cerean flushed. She stole rapid glances at the other three images, and discerned a speculative gleam on the Quy'doan woman's face and expressions of pleasure on those of the Rualdan and the Bertolian. Rivalry was strong between these four. That decreased the chance of their joining forces against her.

"Lady," the Cerean hastened into speech. "I only meant—"

"To offer me an affront?" From the corner of her eye, she caught Jarrod's nod of approval. She made a dismissive gesture with her hand, turning pointedly from the Cerean to include the other three ambassadors as well in her next comment. "Do not think—" damn, this formal language was hard to maintain, "—your comments of last night went unnoticed. I am fully aware that each of you have harbored thoughts of placing yourselves in the position of 'protector' of Kerrian."

"Lady—" The Bertolian lurched forward, barely catching himself before falling out of his chair.

"There was never any such idea!" the Quy'doan protested.

The Rualdan looked frantically toward his advisors, but the Cerean leaned back, a slight smile just touching his lips. "It appeared your planet had been deprived of viable leadership. Someone obviously had to step in to prevent further internal warfare until the quadrant's council could step in to administer affairs."

"Of course." Dia managed a sarcastic twist to her lip. "Such altruism will not be forgotten, I assure you." Nor would the Cerean's cleverness, to accept her claim rather than try to deny it, as did the others.

The Cerean met her steady gaze. "The coral, Lady, is too valuable—and dangerous—a commodity to be left without a guardian. Weapons powered by it, as you must know—" he allowed the hint of a question to enter his voice, "—would be a formidable threat."

He guessed! But it was *only* a guess that she'd lied about their level of coral technology. He couldn't know. She stared back, unblinking. "Indeed they are. As anyone unwise enough to test us will quickly find out."

The Cerean regarded her through half-lidded eyes. None of the other three ambassadors said anything for several moments. Dia tried to catch a glimpse of Jarrod without appearing to look away from the screen, and failed.

The Rualdan, who had been consulting with his advisors, straightened in his chair and raised his arms before his chest, palms facing the screen.

"Rualdan sign he's opening formal negotiations," Jarrod hissed. "He won't speak until you acknowledge him."

"Ambassador Pieral?" She added the name Jarrod hissed at her. She should have memorized them, been more prepared. Still, she'd gotten away with it— thanks to Jarrod. Pieral, Rualda; Pieral, Rualda. She wouldn't let herself make such a mistake again.

"Lady of Kerrian." Lord Pieral bowed, and a hint of smugness touched his features. "I am relieved to see you alive and well. You can imagine, I am sure, what the failed usurper told us. I can only be glad it isn't true. With your permission, my delegation will return to the surface of your planet to pay our formal respects to you.''

"And ours, Lady." The Quy'doan smiled on Dia in a benevolent manner. "I feel certain you and I will be able to come to terms profitable to us both. I look forward to meeting you in person."

"The motherly approach," muttered Jarrod.

"Lady." The Bertolian beamed at her. "Our delegation stands ready to depart the moment it is convenient for your people to receive us."

"Though they'd prefer it if you weren't ready," Jarrod stuck in.

Dia rose in a rustle of silks and feathers that she found impressive. She could only hope the ambassadors did, as well. Her chin tilted upward, and she managed a properly haughty stare at the images on the screen. "You will arrive at your own convenience. I will receive you this evening. Darmin?" She swept from the dais, hoping like mad the comm tech would cut her image before the crown toppled from her head or she missed her step and took a tumble.

To her relief, the screen went blank. She dragged off the pearl-encrusted murex shell and sank onto the throne once more. With a quick touch of the controls, she sent the vid screen back into its cozy nest beneath the dais.

Jarrod moved forward and leaned against the side of the throne. "That should have given them the right impression."

"One problem dealt with—for the moment." She rubbed her tired eyes.

"Have you been trained in protocol? This lot likes to keep things formal."

"Enough." She hoped. "I know better than to insult them—or let them insult me. I've been my father's hostess since my mother died, and we've entertained any number of heads of state.''

His eyes narrowed. ''But that was in your role of head caterer. Now *you're* in control.''

She inclined her head, hoping he wouldn't realize how crippling fear crept up her spine, winding its paralyzing tendrils about her heart and mind. This all applied to him, as well. He mustn't know how badly she wanted help, how ill prepared she was. Within the next day or two, she might be tricked into bargaining away her planet's security, its future. That possibility—that *probability*—terrified her.

She desperately needed someone to trust. And she desperately wanted it to be Jarrod. It *felt* right, turning to him. Or did her heart misguide her? She couldn't deny the physical desire that enveloped her at the mere thought of this man. Physical desire, she knew, could block out logic, make one behave in foolish ways, blind one to the true nature of the one you wanted. Did she fall prey to that great deceit? Would Jarrod's be the biggest—and cruelest—trick of all?

She looked away, busying herself unnecessarily with the control panel, closing it up, wiping it clean. Had he gauged her desire for him, calculated his opportunities, and spared her life as the first step in a plot to gain control over her, over her planet? Did he hope to set her up as his puppet, the way some traitor from his planet had set up Bailan?

Not now! her mind screamed. She'd remain wary, try to retain some measure of logical thinking. Surely the fact she suspected treachery on his part should prepare her, arm her against running willingly into his traps.

She rose once more and dropped the crown onto

the abandoned seat. She'd retrieve it later, when she again needed to look regal. Now, she had work to do.

Jarrod watched her with his steady gaze that seemed to miss nothing. "What next?"

She straightened, meeting his look with a calmness she didn't feel. "Prepare for the ambassadorial invasions. We—" The chime of her comm link interrupted her, and she touched it. "Yes?"

"The vale boat has returned, Lady," Darmin's somber voice announced.

Her heart seemed to still. "Did it find them?"

"Both, Lady." His tone held a note of apology, of sympathy.

"Very well. Tell them I'll—" She caught her lower lip between her teeth. No, she wouldn't treat this as just another chore to be completed as quickly and simply as possible, but with the full honor Linore and Edrick deserved. "Have them prepare the bodies. I'll go with the torch boat, myself."

The sound of Darmin clearing his throat preceded his hesitant words. "Is that wise?"

"It's proper. Turn your post over to someone else and get some sleep." She tapped off her unit and stared unseeing at the mosaicked floor.

"A funeral?" Jarrod asked, though his tone held little question. "They've found the bodies of your cousin and her fiance?"

"I sent them to look this morning." She hugged herself, chilled more internally than without. "I guess I've been hoping I was wrong, that it was all just a nightmare. That—" She caught her lip between her teeth and fought the pain of loss that flooded through her. "They were so—"

"You cared for them," Jarrod said with a simplicity peculiarly his own. "Grief is natural and should be expressed."

"Tonight—" She swallowed back the lump in her throat. "I want them to share their funeral barge, so they can be united in death, at least. I'm going to light the fire myself." She threw the words at him, like a challenge.

Instead of arguing, telling her it might not be safe, that she had other duties here, he merely said: "Do you want company?"

"I—" She blinked rapidly, refusing to give in to the tears brought on by his gentleness. "Thank you."

He looked away, down the long chamber to the clear wall with its view of the never ending seas. "They haven't found your father."

"No." The word barely escaped on a whisper. "Until I actually see him, I don't think I can accept his death."

"Then don't." He laid a hand on her shoulder.

She fought the urge to turn toward him, to know the shelter of his arms, to feel the strong beat of his heart. He was so solid, so real, so . . . alive. She moved away. "There's a lot to be done before the delegations arrive."

"And I can't be seen to be your advisor. With your permission, I'll withdraw with my delegation to the space port and arrive with the other ambassadors."

"I suppose you'd better." She'd much rather he remained—which made all the more reason for him to go. Still, she couldn't help but add: "Let me know when you get back."

"At once." He took her hand and bowed over it, then raised her fingers to his lips. "Be at ease, Dee.

You'll get through this ordeal very well." He turned and strode from the chamber.

Dee. He'd called her Dee. She could still feel the brush of his lips on her fingers, which raised other memories in her, of his mouth covering hers, of his hands coiling in her hair.

Enough of that, she told herself savagely. She had any number of duties to occupy her. She returned to her rooms, which only reminded her of the breakfast she'd shared with Jarrod. She changed into one of her regular sarongs and, to take her mind off the Gavonian ambassador, she went to pay her cousin a visit.

She found Bailan in a windowless storeroom, but didn't experience so much as a pang of pity. He lounged in his robe on a couch covered in furs, blankets and pillows. A bowl heaped with a variety of fruits, and a plate of sweet breads and biscuits, stood at his side. The scent of an aromatic spiced wine filled the room. Someone had arranged a vid screen on the opposite wall, and a variety of entertainment disks lay scattered across a low table.

"Roughing it, I see," she said when he didn't look up at her entrance.

That brought his head around. He studied her for a long moment, and his eyebrows rose. "Where's your puppet master?"

She selected a grape from his abundant supply. "I sent him back to the space port. Just because he claims to be a friend is no reason I should trust him."

"He could have killed you," Bailan pointed out.

She looked around, but saw no other chair. With all the ceremony of one who had been brought up from infancy with her cousin, she dragged one of the pillows from beneath his feet, tossed it on the floor and sat cross-legged on it. She took another grape but only held it.

"Visiting the prisoners?" He rearranged his cushions. "If you've got something to say, then say it. You're interrupting my vid."

"You've seen it before. And you only like it because of how little everyone's wearing. Did you see my father's body?" she demanded abruptly.

"His—No, I didn't. The captain told me you were all dead. I—I didn't ask for the proof."

"He was right about one of us, at any rate. I'm going with Linore and Edrick's barge tonight."

Bailan remained silent for a long moment, his mouth compressed into a tight line. His eyes glittered with a fine mist. "She's—she was—a good kid. It shouldn't have happened. Throw some perri blossoms on for me, will you?"

Dia nodded, not trusting herself to speak. She pulled herself to her feet and started for the door.

"Dia?"

She stopped, but she didn't look back. If she did, she might start crying.

"I admit, I did think being king here would be a lot of fun, especially with all the other systems begging for coral. But I didn't plan any of this. Linore—" His voice cracked, then he got it under control. "If you were dead already, then I *was* king. But I didn't *want* anything to happen to any of you."

Dia nodded, a response he could take any way he liked. She let herself out into the hall, avoided looking at the guard who stood on duty, and hurried down the corridor. She didn't know what to believe. It didn't seem possible her own cousin could have contrived for the deaths of his family—yet she'd heard his bravado bragging to Jarrod. Let him remain in comfortable custody for the time being. That way he wouldn't be a temptation for anyone who might like to try again.

She needed to check on dinner preparations. Not a banquet again, she decided as she headed toward the kitchen. A simple meal. Austere elegance. That would be quite a change from blatant tourism. Maybe it would make an impression.

Agathas, to her mixed surprise and relief, had indeed retired to her room to sleep. So had most of the staff, who had been up during the long eventful hours of the night. She discussed the menu with the assistant cook, the only one present who looked like he might know what she was talking about, but recorded the conversation for those who would come back on duty when they'd rested. Satisfied all would proceed well, she set forth to check with the chamber staff's assessment of the rooms allotted to the diplomats.

Half way to the housekeeping office, her comm link brought her up short with its soft, melodic chime. She tapped it. "Yes?"

"I'm sorry to bother you, Lady." A woman's uncertain voice came across the unit. "Darmin left instructions to notify you of all incoming messages, though why he should, and why you'd want to know—"

"He's following my orders." How many of her people had no real idea of what had occurred during the last forty-odd hours?

"It's from Charis Atoll. There's been fighting there, and one of the Columbine Liaisons is missing." She still sounded uncertain.

Charis Atoll. Dia's stomach clenched. Karla innis Mecca had her floating lab anchored near the coral mass. Of the few marine biologists empathic enough to communicate with the Columbine jells, hers was the strongest talent. Her shared understanding with the beautiful, intelligent sea creatures never ceased to awe Dia. And she was missing.

Kidnapped? Or had she disappeared of her own accord? Whichever it proved to be, it must have involved an attempt on the mercenaries' part to secure jellactic acid.

More mercenaries,ones their captain hadn't bothered to mention.

She had more internal affairs to deal with, it seemed. Fighting in one of the outer atolls. Nothing like it had ever happened before. Her people would be confused, frightened, not knowing who controlled their planet.

She slowed her steps. Someone had to go to Charis Atoll. Someone had to contact Karla's family, see if they knew anything, break the news to them if they didn't. That would be an unpleasant job.

She drew a deep breath. She'd have to go herself. That would be the only way to convince people that normalcy would soon be restored, to squelch any lingering rumors of her death and the fall of her house.

And here she was—or shortly would be—with a palace full of ambassadors to entertain. She couldn't walk out on them, no matter how much she'd like to. She'd have to take them with her.

The idea took root, appealing to her. A goodwill tour of the planet, show the visitors a little of Kerrian's beauty—and incidentally show her people she had the support of the representatives of several other systems in their quadrant.

She had to visit the capital city of Waianoa, anyway,

for only there could she be formally crowned. But not queen. Regent—at least, for now. She would not accept full rule until she had tangible proof of her father's death. She hadn't thought of it before, with so much chaos to deal with, but her crowning was necessary to legitimize the treaty negotiations. It would also provide the excuse for dragging the ambassadors from the tropical haven of the winter resort of Kerrian-Isla into the frozen depths of the north.

She turned her steps toward the comm room. She would request the loan of a luxury liner to carry her guests in sufficient comfort. Some wily captain out there would be only too glad to place her in his debt.

Favors for favors. Was that what ruling a planet was all about? The web of diplomacy seemed to be expanding about her, like ripples in still water, invading every aspect of her interactions with other people. Life, she realized with a sinking heart, might never be simple and straightforward again.

Chapter Twelve

Jarrod brushed a fleck of dust from his uniform sleeve and glanced over his shoulder to where the five members of his diplomatic team waited with stoic patience. A familiar routine, rarely varying, never demanding, this presentation to the head of state. Only they'd gone through it all the day before when Bailan sat on the great nautilus throne. Now Dia sat upon it in full majesty. Already her *major domo* had announced the Rualdan and Bertolian delegations. Gavin would be next.

The door stood wide, allowing him a clear view of the proceedings. He could barely see Dia, for a visored guard flanked her on either side. The Bertolians stood in a small group before the raised dais, bowing in turn as their ambassador introduced each member of his team. The Rualdans, first to be presented, stood about the room, partaking of the refreshments offered by various staffers in their violet sarongs.

In front of the wall-window sat a five piece orchestra. Two members played classically styled violins, and one blew into an elaborate reed flute. The other two produced a haunting melody and counterpoint on curled shells, one lap-sized and the other resting on the ground. Over this rose the soft babble of voices, some with clipped accents, others with rolling ones.

The *major domo* tapped the end of his staff, which was shaped like the curled up tail of a porpoise, and announced, "The delegation from Gavin-Secundus." He inclined his head and gestured with the top of the staff—the upper body of the porpoise—for Jarrod and his assistants to enter the audience chamber.

The Bertolians bowed themselves backward, to find themselves presented with trays bearing glasses filled with pale wine or a variety of Kerrinian delicacies. Bailan hadn't bothered with so many niceties yesterday. Jarrod repressed a smile. Dia made abundantly clear her rightful status as head of state.

He reached the purple carpet runner that led to the nautilus throne and turned to look fully on Dia. She sat slightly forward, one foot ahead of the other, her hands resting on the curved arms. Never had he seen her look so regal. Pride welled in him, though she'd needed none of his coaching. She looked fragile, too, which brought his concern to the forefront. She must be under an unbearable strain, yet she didn't let it show.

He reached the dais and bowed deeply, granting her full status. As he straightened, he caught the flicker of relief in her eyes. Her two guards remained motionless; he couldn't even see their expressions, for their decorative visors revealed little of their features. "Well done, Lady," he murmured, then stepped to one side to introduce each of his assistants.

At the door, the *major domo* announced the Quy'-

doans. Jarrod and his staff backed away from the dais and at once received the offer of refreshment. Jarrod took a glass of sweet wine and resolutely moved away from Dia, from any position where he might give in to the urge to gaze at her, make sure she didn't need his support. She didn't need anyone today, he assured himself. Even if she did, for her sake he didn't want to raise talk of undue Gavonian influence.

Now the Cereans stood before the dais. The orchestra switched compositions, playing a livelier tune, and he strolled over to watch. A sixth musician had joined the others, adding an underlying rhythm with his gentle beating of a drum made from a skin stretched over a giant cowra clam shell.

A slight stirring behind him caught his attention and he turned to see the Cereans had retreated. Dia rose gracefully to her feet, and her guards stepped forward, offering their arms. She placed a hand on each and allowed them to lead her down the shallow steps to the floor. The Rualdan ambassador jostled the Cerean in an attempt to claim her attention.

Dia's calm manner and queenly demeanor would make anyone proud of her, Jarrod reflected. Not by the slightest sign did she reveal the unease he knew raced through her. She spoke to each of the ambassadors with a sweet smile, as if they had not threatened to take over her planet, as if she had not met that challenge with threats of her own. Yet not one of them, he wagered, would make the mistake of thinking she hadn't meant it.

She shifted her position, and her crown swayed on her head. It didn't slip, though; her maid must have labored for hours, securing it with innumerable pins. Or had locks of her hair been braided through it? Suddenly he wanted to find out. He wanted to get her alone, allow his fingers to caress her gleaming braids, explore their secrets. . . .

Dia's gaze swept the room, then paused as she spotted him. She raised her glass of wine, gave the slightest gesture with it indicating she wanted him, then continued the movement to take a sip. With every indication of interest, she returned her attention to the Rualdan ambassador who stood at her side.

Jarrod strolled over and bowed deeply to Dia, then with acknowledgement to the Rualdan. "Your musicians are remarkable. How many instruments are there unique to Kerrian?"

"Seventeen. So far." She awarded the Rualdan a dismissive smile, then looked up at Jarrod, her expression one of mere politeness. "And you, are your quarters comfortable? And those of your staff?"

"Your planet's reputation for hospitality stands unblemished." Out of the corner of his eye, he watched the Rualdan disappear. No one else stood close at the moment. "What is it?" he asked in a lowered voice.

"I just thought I'd scream if that man spouted any more obsequious pompousness at me." She kept her expression slightly bored, though a humorous glint danced in her eyes. "And this cape!" The feathers rustled as she shifted her shoulders. "Every time I wear it, I swear never again."

"It becomes you beautifully."

She rolled her eyes. "There's a quill poking me between the shoulder blades. And the crown weighs like a kubo fish."

He fought back a grin. "Concentrate on how good it'll feel to take them off."

"And burn them," she agreed.

A gong sounded, and a sigh escaped her. "Dinner. At least, it'll be harder for them to talk with their mouths full."

Jarrod shook his head. "That's the first lesson for ambassadorship. Learning how to talk under any circumstances."

She shot him a baleful glare. "Go away. I don't want to be seen laughing with you." She turned on her heel and swept toward the door to the banquet hall.

The Cerean ambassador gave her escort. Jarrod dropped back in the pack, letting her deal with each of these ambassadors as she thought best. The slight reservation in her manner became her, lending her a dignity she had not previously betrayed. She remained cool—yet willing to be persuaded. His pride in her swelled once more, though he realized he played no part in her behavior.

The staff, he saw as he entered, had changed the seating arrangements. The head table now stood in the middle of the room, where Dia would sit with the ambassadors. Longer tables radiated out from there, set for the other dignitaries. A comfortable arrangement, for each ambassador remained with his own people, yet received a place of honor.

Trays appeared, bearing platters of various seafoods prepared with simple sauces. Staffers served the guests from huge bowls of mixed tubers or greens. Nothing elaborate, yet all prepared and presented with simple elegance. After the upsets of the last few days, she followed a wise course.

"Lady." The Quy'doan—Madam Chevika—turned a motherly smile on Dia. "This must be a time of great strain for you. The negotiations—"

Dia held up her hand, stopping the woman's words.

"I must ask you not to speak of treaties just yet." She turned, meeting the ambassadors' gazes, which ranged from surprise to distrust.

Lord Xar, the Cerean ambassador, frowned, setting down his fork. "It is why we are here," he said with careful formality. "We should like to begin at once."

"So should I, but it isn't possible. No," she forestalled Madam Chevika's vexed exclamation. "The negotiations must be legal—mustn't they?"

The ambassadors cast sideways glances at each other, then towards the members of their delegations. Lord Pieral, the Rualdan, straightened, and his voice rose in anger. "We were under the impression that you have the right to speak for your house. If you have misinformed us—"

"Not in the least. But I must first be formally confirmed as regent for my missing father." She paused a moment, giving her words a chance to sink in. "Tomorrow morning I must depart for our capital at Waianoa. I thought perhaps you would all enjoy the trip. I have secured the use of one of our finest-appointed luxury yachts."

The Bertolian ambassador, Lord Feldar, looked up in pleasure. "I have heard of these, and the cruises through your kelp forests."

"I will arrange one for you before you leave," Dia promised. "This, though, must be a shorter trip. We can begin negotiations on the journey back."

Madam Chevika inclined her head. "I will be honored to attend your—confirmation."

"So will I." Jarrod met her glance with a bland smile. "My tharl has spoken highly of the Kerrinian luxury yachts, and his son Lomax is a frequent visitor to your planet for the voyages through the kelp and coral forests." Actually, for the notoriously decadent attractions offered by the more enterprising of the cruise lines. Those went a long way toward influencing the potential clients for the more questionable of Lomax's business ventures.

"Then it's settled." Dia bestowed her smile around the table. "I regret there'll only be room for each of you to bring two of your assistants, but perhaps you can all regard it as a brief vacation from duties. Those left behind may make free use of our facilities."

Lord Feldar leaned back in his chair, allowing his chief assistant to whisper in his ear in the Bertolian language. After a moment he straightened. "That will be most agreeable."

"For you, perhaps." The Rualdan glanced at his people. "I need my staff."

Dia's smile took on a touch of regret. "We'll miss your company, of course, Lord Pieral, but if you feel you must remain with all your people, I'll forgive you."

"I—" The Rualdan blanched. "No, I fear I gave you to misunderstand. I will be only too glad to go. It is just that it will be difficult to decide whom to reward by taking them with him."

Full marks, Jarrod thought proudly—and the possessive pleasure he found in her troubled him.

She dismissed them from the banqueting hall at what, in diplomatic circles, would be considered an indecently early hour. She pleaded the necessity to make preparations for the morrow's voyage and finalizing the details to legitimize her regency, but Jarrod suspected her of simply wanting to be rid of the formal pomp and ceremony with which the ambassadors filled their speech. When his turn came, he bowed low over her hand, bid her a formal good-night, and left with his delegation.

He didn't go to his room, though. He strolled out through the entry hall and exited the palace to stand in the tiny courtyard. This, he saw, had been carved out of the obsidian base of the extinct volcano that formed the palace. For a long while he stood gazing up at the multitude of stars, at the clusters that formed unknown constellations. The three moons hung low in the sky, their soft glows radiating color. The largest, Vergan they called it, really did pick up an amethyst tinge.

The time of the Amethyst Moon. The New Year. Winter. But coldness seemed to have no hold on this tropical paradise. Warm air ruffled his hair, tickling his neck. Almost, he could find peace here.

But the night wasn't over yet.

He made his way through the darkened entry hall and up the wide staircase. Lights still glimmered in the corridor, and behind several doors he heard the deep tones of voices raised in urgent discussion. A slight smile tugged at his lips. Dia's announcement hadn't pleased the other ambassadors. Yet she'd been right to plan this trip; seeing her confirmed regent would only enhance her bargaining position.

He palmed open his door and stepped into a room dark except for the rapid blinking of the green message light. He flicked on the screen and it sprang to life with static. A moment later it settled into an image of Dia, still crowned and robed, but in her sitting room.

"Ambassador tolArvik." The cool tone of her voice matched the distance of her expression. "There is a message I was supposed to deliver to you earlier. If you will call on me when it's convenient for you, I will rectify that oversight."

He knew she maintained her formality in case any-

one else saw the message, but it bothered him not
to see the flickering warmth in her eyes. It was like
looking at a stranger—which was exactly the impression she hoped to give. And perhaps strain added to
the reserve.

Her summons could only mean that the funerary
barge was ready to depart. He donned a cloak over
his uniform and moved quietly down the hall toward
her room. As he drew near, her door slid wide; she
must have been on the watch for him. He stepped
inside, then halted, stopping himself from closing the
space between them and gathering her into his arms.

She had removed her elaborate cape and ceremonial gown and now wore a simple sarong and cloak.
Her hair hung in two long braids over her shoulders,
their ends waving about her knees, making her look
absurdly young. Far too young to deal with the problems besetting her. Her maid, as if under that very
impression, hovered just beyond the door of the sitting room as if guarding the bed chamber from any
intruders.

The grim set of Dia's mouth softened as Jarrod
closed the door behind him. "Well? Did I do all right
tonight?" Her tone sounded casual—unconcerned,
in fact—but the rapidity of the question betrayed her
uncertainty.

"Very well." He joined her, taking the glass of
mulled wine she held out. "But keep your eye on
Madam Chevika."

"Chevika, Quy'dao. Chevika, Quy'dao," Dia murmured.

He nodded. "That woman has never been motherly
in her life."

A wrinkle formed in Dia's brow. "To see her
tonight, you'd think she'd never been anything else.

So she's trying to gain the upper hand by acting the loving parent, is she?" Her lips twitched into a half smile. "I'll bear that in mind. I wonder what the others'll try to pull."

"Well," and he matched her smile, "the Gavonian ambassador is probably going to try to be your friend and confidante."

She shook her head. "Too blatant. He hasn't a chance of succeeding."

"I should hope not. Now," he added, studying her face, "what prompted the jaunt to Waianoa? That line about the regency came off as a good excuse, but I'm not buying it. If that's all you needed, you could have sent for your ministers and done it here. And under the circumstances, that would have been the safer course. So, what's the real reason?"

She let out a deep sigh. "I want to make a tour of the outlining atolls, perhaps visit one or two of the floating cities, just to let people know I've got everything under control."

"Good try, but still a little glib. You've had news of unrest, haven't you?" he demanded.

She looked away, avoiding his gaze, which was answer enough for him. He swore softly. "You've had enough problems," he declared with unusual force. "You don't need more." For a moment he stared unseeing out her window into the darkness beyond. "How are the mercenaries doing?" he asked abruptly. "Arranged transport for them yet?"

"I—" She twined her fingers. "I think it's best to keep them here a bit longer. They seem comfortable enough in the gym."

"You mean you don't want to turn them loose so they can come back? What makes you think they'll try to finish the job here?"

She shook her head. "We better go. The barge will be waiting for us." She picked up a basket of large, sweetly scented perri blossoms and headed for the door.

She wasn't talking. Resigned, he followed her.

Together they took the service lift down to the main floor, where two guards awaited them. Jarrod studied their visored faces, but could see too little of their features to determine whether or not they were the same two who'd stood at Dia's side in the Audience Chamber.

"Leave your helmets," Dia said. "They'll only be in your way tonight."

"Thank you, Lady," one of them said, his voice heavy with relief. He unfastened the strap and dragged the metal visor from his head.

Sorin, Jarrod realized. Eelam emerged a moment later. He set his head gear on a table, adjusted his cloak, then assumed something that might have been an attention stance.

"At least you're keeping a loyal guard with you," Jarrod said under his breath as they exited the palace.

"In their case, I think loyalty more than makes up for lack of training. Besides," she added, and a ghost of a smile sounded in her voice, "they're enjoying themselves."

So was he, Jarrod realized with a touch of surprise, in spite of the solemnity of their errand. He took Dia's arm and guided her down the steps carved into the volcanic rock. A steep descent. More than once he caught at the railing to steady them both.

Plasti-form floats made up the landing, and they swayed gently beneath his feet. The smell of the sea surrounded him, and the sweet scent of water lilies mingled with the tangy odor of kelp. Dia moved ahead, stepping onto the floating walkway that led them to the palace dock.

Here the water lilies gained full sway, filling his senses. Dia, still a step ahead, reached the end of the dock and stopped, staring for a long moment into the canoe that rocked gently with the tide. From the basket she took a single large blossom and tossed it into the little boat, then threw several more after the first. The last she held for a moment before casting it after the others. Abruptly she turned away and climbed into the waiting motorboat.

Jarrod looked over the canoe's side. By the light of the stars, he could just make out the outlines of two bodies beneath a covering of fur and feathers. The flowers lay at their feet. Whispering the words of the Gavonian prayer for the dead, he sketched the accompanying salute, then followed Dia aboard.

She stood in the bow of the ship, staring resolutely out into open water. Jarrod took up a position just behind her; if she wanted comfort, he would be there. The sound of lines being untied from their cleats reached him over the gentle lap of the waves against the hull as the captain cast off.

Dia's shoulders trembled and he placed his hands on them, feeling their slenderness—their fragility for carrying such heavy burdens—through the light fabric of her cloak. Amethyst light washed over her, setting a glow to her cheek, brightening the blackness of her hair. He touched it with one callused finger, and felt the silkiness slip across his skin.

"The amethyst moon," Dia said. She gazed upward to where the three moons now rode in their triangular pattern higher in the sky. "It's usually a warm ivory, you know. See how it picks up its color from the sapphire and ruby tones of its two sisters."

"A sign of good omens," he reminded her.

"Not for them." With her head she indicated the canoe that trailed in their wake as they headed out into the sea.

"On Gavin, death isn't seen as an end, but a transformation, a rejoining with the elements."

"Recycling," she said, and a fleeting half-smile just touched her lips.

Her very full and tempting lips. Lips he wanted to explore in detail, to unlock and delve— He broke off the thought and eased himself away from her, so her warm body no longer brushed against him with every bump as they cut across the breeze-stirred wavelets. He'd always had too vivid an imagination for his own good.

They continued their steady progress for approximately one standard hour. Dia remained where she stood, unmoving, as if unaware of his presence. Lost in memories, he supposed. He did nothing to disturb her.

At last the captain stopped the engine. Dia shifted, straightened her shoulders, and made her way over the rocking deck to the stern. The captain disappeared below into the small cabin, only to re-emerge the next moment carrying a bucket filled with glowing coals.

Sorin handed Dia a torch that was two meters tall. She drew a steadying breath, then plunged it into the bucket. A blaze sprang to life, casting a dancing light across the deck as she raised it high above her head. For a long moment she stared at it. "Return to the elements," she whispered, then cast it into the center of the canoe.

The captain, who had unfastened the tow line, tossed it into the flame. Using the boat hook, he shoved the canoe away, setting it drifting in a gentle spiral through the dark waters. The flames blazed, shooting high in the sky.

A rumble sounded beneath Jarrod's feet and he jumped before he realized the captain had restarted their engine. The motor boat swung in a wide arc, turning back toward Kerrian-Isla. Mission accomplished.

Dia stood in the stern, head high, gazing back toward the flaming canoe. A line glistened down the cheek he could see, reflecting the orange fire, tears to which she paid no heed as she watched her cousin's funeral pyre. Jarrod folded his arms, torn by the longing to comfort her, to take her into his arms and wipe away those tears. But grief was sacred; it must be allowed to run its course. She would turn to him if she needed him.

Not until they slipped into the berth at the palace dock did she leave the post which she had taken. She faced the captain, her features a blank mask. "Thank you, Rork," she said softly.

"Lady." He pressed her hand, then helped her out of his boat.

Jarrod sprang to the dock, then caught Dia's arm as she stumbled on the floating pier. She cast him the briefest of smiles, then moved ahead, away from him. He allowed her this solitude, merely falling into step behind her. Sorin and Eelam assumed their positions of protective escort, not leaving them until they reached the service lift in the palace.

As the lift door closed behind Dia and Jarrod, sealing them off from their two companions, she turned to him. Sight of her brimming eyes proved too much for him; he gathered her close, his lips brushing her hair, his arms memorizing the feel of her pressed tightly against his body. He was a fool, he knew, but even a fool needed something to remember. Only when the door slid open did he release her, and then with reluctance.

"We—we go in different directions." She didn't look up at him. She turned and, with her back to him, whispered, "Good night," and hurried away.

Not a word of thanks, not a word of acknowledgement for his accompanying her earlier, nor for his comforting her just now.

A slow smile tugged at his lips. There'd been no need for thanks, their bond had been too close. They knew without needing to speak.

And that closeness, he realized with a sinking feeling, might well spell trouble for them in their interactions with the other ambassadors in the negotiations to come.

Chapter Thirteen

Morning found Jarrod once more on the dock, this time in the company of the other ambassadors. Dia had been there already when he'd arrived, a slight figure moving from one of her guests to another with a grace that captured the eye. She wore a simple sarong and light cloak, her only adornments a choker of amethyst pearls, her bracelet, and entwined in her hair a silver circlet crown set with amethyst Dahmla coral. She looked pale to Jarrod; he doubted she'd slept much.

He'd hoped for a message from her when he awoke, an invitation to share breakfast, a chance for them to talk. Great Artis, a chance for him to gaze at her! He could hardly do that here, with everyone looking on, seeing for themselves how the Gavonian ambassador worshiped this fragile beauty who pretended to be a tough negotiator.

The motor boat was no longer moored at the dock. Instead, the lines which fastened to the cleats rose to a thirty-meter long luxury yacht, a sleek vessel promising both speed and comfort. Looking it over, Jarrod could understand why Lomax, a restless hedonist, enjoyed his frequent visits to Kerrian.

The captain, a slightly built honey-skinned man, every inch a Kerrinian, strode along the dock from the palace and spoke with Dia. She smiled, thanked him, then turned to the waiting diplomats. "We're ready to depart. Please, come on board, and thank you for taking this journey with me. Our captain assures me we should be in Waianoa by late tomorrow morning." With a smile that owed more to years of training as a gracious hostess than any inner happiness, she ushered her guests toward the gangway.

Today, he must act as if he were just one of these other diplomats, as if Dia meant nothing more to him than a head of state with whom he must deal. Last night, with its emotions and needs, he must put from his mind. Not for a moment could he let himself think of Dia held close in his arms, of her silken, scented hair tickling his nose, of her hands clinging to his shoulders. . . .

He strode up the ramp somewhere in the middle of the group, passing Dia at the top. It cost him a severe pang not to let his arm brush hers.

Cabin assignments took a little time, but no one had any complaints except Jarrod, who kept his to himself. He could hardly object on the grounds his room was located at the opposite end of the boat from Dia's. Probably an act of wisdom—or self-preservation—on her part, if she'd made the arrangements. He could think of too many possibilities if only one thin wall separated them.

Even before the porters deposited the last of the luggage in the appropriate cabins, the captain cast off and the yacht motored along the artificial harbor lane. When it approached the buoys marking the mouth, a subtle change occurred in the engine thrum. The volume decreased to the merest whisper, the breeze increased, and the great vessel rose up on its skis and all but flew across the rising swells.

Dia walked up behind several of the ambassadors, who stood in the bow, arguing in hushed voices. "Yes." She directed a cool smile at the group. "You are experiencing coral power. We will achieve a speed of a little over two hundred kilometers an hour. Not fast, I know, but it will allow you to see some of Kerrian."

And allow Dia to achieve whatever purpose she had in mind. Jarrod couldn't help but wonder what it was.

"The fuel, it is—interesting." The Bertolian ambassador, Lord Feldar, kept his voice neutral. The others murmured agreement and wandered off.

Jarrod followed in their wake. Whatever had made him think Dia needed help in dealing with these people, even if they were seasoned diplomats? She'd been trained in tourism, which seemed to be as exacting a science as his.

It didn't surprise him in the least when she proved to be the perfect hostess throughout the day. Not for a moment did the others have cause to suspect her inner worries; he knew, of course, and perhaps read more into a sudden glitter in her eyes or the way her fingers strayed to her bracelet. Her weapon. What news, he wondered, had she learned yesterday? And why hadn't she shared it with him? Did she feel some need to maintain appearances of control of her planet, even before him?

They made six short stops throughout the day, two at atolls and four at floating cities. These Jarrod found

fascinating, made up as they were of the most unbe-
lievable collection of barges, tugs, and suspended
platforms. Dia spoke briefly with the men and women
who awaited them at the docks, obviously by pre-
arrangement. Jarrod could only wonder what they
said, for whatever it was caused Dia some measure of
satisfaction, yet no joy.

Only the Cerean and Rualdan ambassadors displayed any signs of impatience. It showed in shortened tempers when the Cerean Lord Xar, pacing
the deck, stumbled against Lord Pieral. The Rualdan
sprang away, glaring, but his sharp words died on his
lips as Dia intervened.

"You don't have any wine." The warmth of her
smile would have melted an ice cube. She waved to
one of the yacht's staffers, who shimmered up to her,
his tray outstretched. She took two glasses from him
and pressed them onto her angry guests. "Come, give
me your opinion on this vintage. Have you visited the
vid room? You haven't? Then I think I can offer you
a treat." She ushered them down the companionway.

Jarrod watched in amusement. He'd heard from
Lomax the range of exotic—and erotic—vids available on even the simplest of the luxury yachts. Neither
Cerean nor Rualdan cultures tended toward the prud-
ish; he wagered it would be some time before either
man emerged again.

Jarrod found himself content with sampling wine,
food, and watching the incredible variety of marine
life. More than one of the junior members of the
diplomatic staffs expressed a desire to return here
for their vacations. Jarrod, to his surprise, found himself as pleased as if this were his planet showing off
its treasures and meeting approval.

For evening entertainment, Dia had arranged for

native musicians and dancers. The diplomats lounged about the low-set tables, their precious dignity for once not uppermost in their minds as they relaxed. Jarrod, alone of the company, remained on his guard. The moment he eased his control on himself, he would gravitate toward Dia. The struggle to keep his gaze from her proved hard enough. When they at last retired to their cabins for the night, he lay awake, thoughts of Dia burning themselves into his mind and body.

He arose early, heavy-eyed and tired, yet too restless to remain in the luxuriously spacious bed. It called for company, and that—at least the company he wanted—he couldn't have. Not with his two junior staff members sharing the giant cabin. The more he recognized that he couldn't have Dia, the more he longed for her, to touch the softness of her skin, to feel the racing of her heart and to know the sweetness of her love.

He leaned on the rail, gazing at the near-arctic waters they had entered during the night, wishing their icy touch would cool the fires that burned within him. With furious intensity he watched a pod of cetaceans, the individuals larger than any he'd seen near Kerrian-Isla. They moved slower, as well, with an elegance that commanded admiration.

A flock of some small variety of gull swooped and dived about the boat, fishing among the tiny kelpies and orik schools stirred by the vessel's passage. Their hull slashed through huge patches of snow-flowers, flashes of wintry green, blue and pink which spread out from the floating chunks of ice. Off to the left, a family of sea lions slid gracefully through the waters in pursuit of breakfast; on the right, otters and water bears played a form of tag amid the floating gardens.

A padded footstep sounded behind him, and he turned to see Dia, her legs protected by sleek boots of some supple black leather, picking her way across the spray-slicked deck. A cloak of deep amethyst wrapped about her, its brooch fastening the warm material at her neck. The furred feathers of the snow goose trimmed hem and hood so that her face peeked out at him through a ruff. He wanted to kiss her, let the plume tips tickle his nose. He forced the desire from his mind.

"Enjoying our winter?" She leaned on the rail next to him, staring out across the white-peaked waves.

"Nothing in Kerrian-Isla prepared me for it." He positioned himself a prudent distance from her. "I suppose winter water sports feature heavily in your travel ads."

She smiled. "Second section on the vids. There's a garden down there you wouldn't believe." She gestured toward a massive chunk of floating ice. "There're warm currents about a hundred meters below the surface. They sculpt the bottoms of the bergs, and there's a type of barnacle that grows in incredible colors that fastens in the ice. Submarine tours run two hundred fifty standard credits."

"Pretty steep."

"Worth every credit of it. The guides earn it, too. Maintenance on the subs is astronomical. Those barnacles are partial to plasti-form."

He grinned. "There seems to be something on every planet that loves the stuff. One of these days the scientists will develop a *really* inedible substance."

"They have." She wrinkled her nose. "Stewed gyrok root. It's on the breakfast menu if you want proof. It's supposed to be a Quy'doan delicacy, but not one of them has touched it."

"I'll take your word for it. Come on, I could use a large dose of hot stimi right about now." He took her arm, drawing her away from the incredible view, back toward the cabin where he could see the other diplomats moving about, plates or mugs in their hands.

She slowed as they neared the doorway. "We'll reach Waianoa in a little over an hour." Her voice wavered.

"Are you expecting trouble?" She hadn't mentioned the possibility to him, but then there might be any number of things she kept to herself. That probability bothered him, though he knew it to be only reasonable.

"No." She hesitated over the word, as if it didn't hold quite the meaning she'd intended. She straightened her shoulders and strode ahead as if eager to put some distance between them.

His only responsibility was to guide her through the negotiations, he reminded himself. Of course, he could stretch that a little to cover the political upheaval caused by the coral. His tharl, he knew, regarded Dia as a much-loved niece. Dysart would have no objection to Jarrod's helping her in any way he could. In fact, he was surprised he hadn't received any messages to that effect.

And now that he thought about it, it seemed odder than ever.

He closed the door to the lounge against the biting wind. Dia strode lightly across the room toward Lord Feldar, the Bertolian ambassador. The man looked up, smiled at sight of her, and allowed her to draw him toward the comfortable chairs that faced the plasti-clear wall.

Jarrod wended his way among the people still standing and reached Dia's side. "A question, Lady?"

She looked up, a slight frown that might have been vexation wrinkling her brow. "What is it, Ambassador?"

He held her gaze. "Have you spoken with the tharl since the recent troubles?"

Lord Feldar directed a withering glance at him. "Does he trust his ambassador so little that he must intervene on his own?"

The lines in Dia's forehead deepened. "I haven't. That's odd. I'd have expected—something. Maybe he doesn't know."

"Know? Know what?" The Bertolian's sharp gaze darted back and forth between them.

Dia turned to him, an artificial smile on her lips. "Tharl Dysart has been a frequent visitor to Kerrian. But it's possible, because of the nature of the negotiations, he felt any personal contact for condolence on our brief troubles might be inappropriate." She glanced over her shoulder. "Maybe he's contacted the palace at Waianoa. That would be the diplomatically correct approach, to send messages to the ministers."

A gleam lit Lord Feldar's eyes. "As I am sure the Supreme Councilman of Bertol has done, Lady." He rose and, with a slight bow, left them to join his two junior staffers.

Dia leaned forward, her voice urgent. "Do you think—" She broke off as the Quy'doan ambassador—Madam Chevika—swept up to stand half a meter away, staring out the window at the ice caps they sped past.

Jarrod directed a formal bow to Dia and went in search of much-needed stimi. He would take Dia's unspoken suggestion and use the comm room at Wai-anoa to contact Dysart. This time, he'd try for a vid-to-vid conversation with him, rather than relying on the chanciness of recorded messages. One could never be sure of proper delivery. And right now, he very much wanted to reassure himself that all was well on his homeworld.

Dia huddled in her fur-feather lined cape as the icy wind sought to penetrate its warmth. A crowd stood on the pier, to which the yacht drew closer every moment. She could make out shapes, muffled by their parkas and cloaks into unidentifiable, andro-genous clones. She shivered as her imagination turned them into enemies who would throw off their disguises to reveal alien military uniforms and imploders.

She fought against the sick feeling of dread. She should never have done anything so foolish as to sail blithely into the capital without a loyal army at her back. She had only Sorin and Eelam, though their courage and spirit made them worth a dozen men each. In her eyes, at least. To a trained soldier, they probably resembled nothing more than two scared household staffers armed with unfamiliar weapons.

Jarrod would have protested if this were dangerous. She tried to comfort herself with that thought. She wouldn't mind a glimpse of him, either. That wouldn't do, though. The ruler of Kerrian could not appear so weak as to need constant reassurance from an alien ambassador. That would hardly inspire her ministers with faith in her.

The great yacht slowed, eased into position, then nosed into the berth at the end of the pier. Several of the hooded and cloaked figures hurried toward them: an honor guard or arresting force, Dia couldn't be sure which. She straightened, throwing her shoulders back in defiance, and strode to the gangplank the crew raced to ease into position.

On the wharf, the leader of the huddle of figures drew back his hood, revealing a mane of tangled black hair liberally shot through with gray. His hawk-like nose burned red with the cold as his narrow mouth broke into a crusty smile. Rastor sett Danies, Chief Minister. Uncle Rastor. Friends, not foes.

Rastor gave a short bow of acknowledgment, while those standing behind him followed with deeper salutes. A touch of sadness lurked in the elderly man's expression, but he started forward in his usual brisk manner, hand extended to take hers. "Well, child. So you decided to come home. Your father—" He broke off, every muscle of his face tightening.

"My father is still missing." She tried to match the crispness of his tone. The prospect of seeing Rastor betray emotion proved too disturbing to contemplate.

"Very well, Lady." He awarded her another short bow. "The ministers of Kerrian accept your request to enter the capital and acknowledge your right to take part in the choosing of a regent."

"So formal," she murmured, for his ears alone. As if he hadn't scolded her when she was a child for sneaking off to sail when she should have been at her lessons, or smuggled her chala cookies after her father's subsequent punishments.

The Cerean ambassador—Lord Xar—pushed forward. "She will not be regent, then? Lady, you deliberately gave us to understand—"

Rastor jerked his head up to fix the man with his piercing glare.

"Don't you have a similar ceremony?" Jarrod asked, his tone amused. "Or do claimants to your highest offices simply barge in and announce they're taking over?"

The Cerean's lip curled. "A mere female—"

"Can accomplish far more than some idiot male," Madam Chevika broke in. She bestowed a condescending smile on Rastor, where he stood rigid on the gangplank before Dia. "Please, continue with your ceremony. We are honored to be witnesses to it."

Rastor opened his mouth, a gleam burning in his eye.

"I believe my guests may be tired from their journey," Dia said quickly, before the old man could deliver the blistering retort he could barely contain.

Rastor shot her a baleful glare, bowed, and turned on his heel to lead the way to the wharf. Dia fell into step behind him, and following her came Eelam and Sorin. The others she allowed to follow as they would.

The wharf didn't sway; it remained frozen in a cake of ice that stretched as far as Dia could see. Home, sweet frozen home. She'd probably choose to stay here in the winters if the demands of the tourists didn't require her presence in Kerrian-Isla. She loved the icy chill, the way her breath puffed out in a misty cloud, the simple delight of wrapping up in a fur-feather cloak and sipping hot stimi or mulled wine in front of a blazing brazier.

Five men and six women waited in a welcoming semicircle: the remaining ministers. They had turned out in full numbers for this greeting. Even if the visiting ambassadors didn't recognize this sign of honor and support, she did, and she greeted each in turn with fervent warmth.

"Have you read up on the ceremony?" she whispered to a woman a scant ten years older than herself, Gisa innis Movan, the minister for internal affairs.

Gisa gave her a conspiratorial wink. "We've all been memorizing our parts. We'll show those aliens we're united, never you fear."

Dia squeezed her hand and moved to the next, a gloomy-faced old man who'd served as minister for fishing for as long as Dia could remember. He merely bowed before her, his countenance gray. His heart trouble, Dia guessed, and turned away. As soon as she could, she'd have a talk with his aide, make sure his doctor had seen him since the revolution had occurred.

Gisa shifted position to stand beside Dia. "Old Rastor will lead the procession to the palace, with the ministers following. Then you come with your guard. The ambassadors will be surrounded by the rest." She nodded to where a crowd remained on the main wharf, pressing against the rail to see the newcomers. "We've got a few plain-clothes guards planted to make sure nothing gets out of hand. Ready?"

Dia nodded, and at a signal from Rastor the ministers fell in behind him. The ambassadors consulted with their aides, and somehow took up their correct position as everyone moved forward toward the wharf. The crowd that waited there separated, flowing apart to allow passage for three walking abreast. As Dia entered the gateway they made, those at the back of the crowd circled around and fell into step flanking those who came at the rear.

A sensation of protection and love surrounded Dia, startling in its intensity. This wasn't just a ceremonial escort put on as a tourist-pleasing display; her people honestly sought to guard her from these aliens. They watched out for her, like Sorin and Eelam. Emotion welled in her throat, choking her.

A flicker of pale yellow fluttered in front of her and landed at her feet. Then more, pink and blue as well. Snow flowers. The people threw them to form a carpet on which she would walk. Blue for mourning the dead—or in this case missing—ruler. Yellow for honoring the new ruler-elect. Pink for the heart, for sworn loyalty.

And orange. A blossom of this rarest of snow flowers fell at her feet and she stooped to pick it up. Orange symbolized a champion, a selfless doer of great deeds. She clutched it, her gaze searching the crowd which stood in silence, watching, expressing their sentiments with the flowers they threw. She could see baskets brimming with pale blossoms, enough to escort her the whole way to the palace. And amid the profusion of pinks and yellows and blues, she saw a number of orange.

Had they really such faith in her? Her heart clenched with fear, the dread that she might not live up to all they needed, all they wanted from her.

A man raised his arm in salute, then another, and a woman, then a child and several more men. One after another as she passed, her people awarded her their highest honor. With head held high but fingers fumbling, she fastened the stem of the orange blossom in the clasp of her cloak, so it rode at her throat.

She couldn't let them down. . . .

The procession slowed, and she put her foot on the low, arched bridge that led to the volcanic mound on which Symon the Mercenary had constructed his first palace. It rose above her a bare three stories, a solid utilitarian structure formed from obsidian blocks. No fairy-tale palace like the one at Kerrian-Isla, which served as the tourist capital. Here in Waia-noa the real business of government took place.

And here the ministers sheltered, shunning the noise and bustle of the tourist industry in favor of the peace required to get their jobs done. Had it been any time other than the depths of winter, the coral treaty negotiations would have taken place here. Now, she needed these more sober surroundings to lend credibility to both her position and that of her planet.

Where was Jarrod? She paused at the top of the steps to the palace and turned around to face her people, her gaze sweeping over their faces, then covertly searching the ambassadorial delegations for his figure. She didn't need him for this, she had her own advisors who knew better than he how to conduct this official business. Still, his presence comforted her. She spotted him and, reassured, turned to the entrance.

Inside, the palace showed none of the touristy excesses which had been allowed full sway in Kerrian-Isla. The floor tiles lay in a simple checkerboard pattern of deep purple and white, and the walls held giant display cases showing off some of the incredible shell specimens. Heavy drapes hung at the ice-frosted plasti-clear walls, insulating against the frozen wind without.

Dia followed her escort along a short corridor, then stopped outside the door of the council chamber while the ministers went in and took their places around the great table. A guard ushered the diplomats around her, gesturing for them to take seats along the wall. Dia stood alone, with only Sorin and Eelam. At a word from the guard, they fell back a pace.

She stood stiffly erect, breathing deeply to calm herself. The ministers spoke amongst themselves so quietly that only the low hum of their voices reached her. Rastor delayed on purpose, she wagered, to give the diplomats a good show. Tourist-pleasing ran deep in the blood of every true Kerrinian.

At last, all twelve heads nodded and Rastor rose. "Dialora rys Pauaia," he intoned. "Step forward."

Oh, damn, what was she supposed to say? She couldn't remember. She'd have to wing it. She took two steps into the room. "I present myself before the council as summoned," she announced, and hoped it didn't sound idiotic.

A muscle twitched at the corner of Rastor's mouth. "King Dysart rys Pauaia is unable to fulfill his duties at the present time. The council has voted to appoint you as regent until such time as the king is able to resume his position or his death is confirmed. Do you accept?"

"I do." And what would he say if she screamed no, and ran from the room? She forced that possibility from her mind, and her fingers strayed to touch the pale orange blossom at her throat. Whoever threw it must have guessed the courage this took.

A man stepped forward from where he'd stood half-hidden by the thick drapery at the back of the chamber. Colonel vis Otral, head of the guard. He carried the crown and ceremonial robe she had brought with her. She'd forgotten about them; she could only be grateful others attended to details.

Rastor himself arrayed her in crown and robe, then

offered his arm. She placed her hand on it and allowed him to lead her from the chamber, across the hall and into the corridor leading to the plasti-clear pavilion. At the door she hesitated, but Rastor drew her inexorably forward.

Show time. And never had she had such a case of stage fright. Out of the corner of her eye she caught a glimpse of Jarrod, and suddenly it didn't seem so bad.

See-through plasti-panes formed the octagonal structure. The walls rose ten meters, then slanted inward to form a peaked roof. A fountain splashed in the center, surrounded by a reflection pool in which floated an exotic array of water lilies. Braziers burned brightly, scattered about the room.

And people. She stared about, amazed that so many could crowd together. There were more here than she'd ever seen before in one place on Kerrian. They must have come from all over the outer atolls and floating cities. Curiosity seekers? Or as a show of unity? She hoped the ambassadors were as impressed as she.

Rastor took his place on the raised dais before the fountain. Beside him stood the elderly Tallan sett Dahmla, minister of science, holding the scepter of office wrapped in heavy cloth. Dia stood before them, one step below. A hush fell over the room. Somewhere above, the vid cameras would already have begun recording the event. This was, after all, history being made. Never before had Kerrian needed a regent.

"Dialora rys Pauaia," Rastor intoned.

Dia bit back a hysterical desire to giggle. Poor Rastor, he always grouched about formality. He must hate all this. She tilted her head back and kept her expression appropriately solemn. "I am here."

"Repeat after me. 'I. . . .'"

Dia closed her eyes. "I, Dialora rys Pauaia, daughter of Dysart, king of Kerrian, swear to protect Kerrian, its people and its interests until such time as the rightful king returns, or his death is declared and his heir is presented before the council."

Tallan sett Dahmla stepped forward, unwrapping the scepter as he came. Not very touristy, Dia reflected as she accepted it. Only a meter long, of plain metal, its only decoration a small branch of Dahmla coral at its top. When things calmed down, she might have a metal-smith install a tiny chamber of jellactic acid. These days, you could never have enough personal weapons, it seemed.

Dia turned to face the salutes of those of her people who had been able to gain admittance to the ceremonial pavilion. Short, sweet and over. She was regent. Now she must mingle with the crowd and take the opportunity to find out what had been going on in the outer atolls, the ones not on her route here from Kerrian-Isla. Someone, she hoped, might have word of the missing Columbine Liaison, Karla innis Mecca.

The ambassadors crowded toward her at the foot of the dais. She had no choice; she had to accept their renewed congratulations and acknowledgments. They seemed to thrive on this sort of thing.

Jarrod's hand closed over hers as he bowed before her. Her fingers twisted in his, clinging, seeking the comfort that contact with him always seemed to bring. He awarded her no more than a fleeting smile, then stepped back. Still, it helped. But she wanted more, much more. Unable to move away, seeking an excuse to linger just a moment longer by his side, she broke into speech, asking the first inane question that sprang to her mind. "Did you enjoy our ceremony?"

"Very moving." The softest of caresses sounded in

his voice. "Surprisingly lacking in touristy trappings," he added *sotto voce*.

"Normally the tourists wouldn't be invited." She moved away, her spirits lifted by that brief exchange. Now her people pressed forward, offering words of condolence and hope. The ambassadors, she noted, had retired toward the back of the pavilion, watching.

Good, that got them out of her way. Unfortunately, it also kept Jarrod at a distance, but perhaps that was for the best. She didn't want him learning too much of the problems that still plagued her planet.

One middle-aged woman stepped in front of Dia, her face set in tight lines. Dia hesitated, trying to place her vaguely familiar features. She should know her. . . .

"Lady." Her guttural voice rumbled forth. "A word?"

"Certainly." She took the woman's arm and drew her aside, murmuring excuses to those they passed. It took several minutes, but at last they stood behind the fountain, partly screened by a large brazier. "What is it?"

She looked a trifle uncomfortable. "Didn't mean to disrupt things like this."

"You wouldn't have spoken if it weren't important. What's wrong?"

A young man joined them, followed by a girl, a mere child, who drew a young woman with her. A shawl covered most of this last person's face, a sign of mourning. Dia looked from one grim expression to another, and her heart sank.

The young woman unwrapped her scarf, allowing it to fall about her shoulders. Beautiful, fine-chiseled features, thick black hair falling in waves over the folds of the shawl, an aura of grief that Dia found all-too familiar. A small dari-keet nestled against the girl's neck, its body purple, its throat violet-pink, its wings and tail rainbows of every shade from blue through red. It nuzzled the girl's jaw, then set about inspecting a partially webbed foot.

"You—" Dia began, then broke off as recognition struck her. "Karla!"

Karla innis Mecca nodded. "The Columbines knew of the trouble before I did. We took each other into hiding."

"Thank the Great Net for that." Dia took Karla's chilled hand. "I'd heard you were missing—" She broke off, seeking the source of the other's grief.

"They killed her family," said the older woman who stood at Karla's side. "Jenna, her sister, was still alive when Karla got back to their boat. She didn't live for more than an hour."

Karla, the empath who could communicate so completely with the jells. Dia met the girl's gaze, reading the horror and pain in her eyes.

The little bird on the girl's shoulder fluffed its feathers and peered up at Karla in a worried manner. Karla touched it with a finger, and it rubbed its head against her and snuggled closer to her neck. "My link isn't as strong with people as it is with the jells," Karla assured her. "Or the birds. Otherwise I'd have known. I could have gone back—"

"You couldn't have betrayed the jells, not for anything," the young man declared, his voice harsh. "And your family felt the same way. Jenna said even your brother wouldn't have told them where you'd gone, even if he'd known."

Karla nodded, then drew in a shuddering breath. "Jenna said they dressed as natives, came on a hydroplane disguised as a fishing boat. They could be anywhere, and—and there's no one left to identify them."

"We'll do it somehow. We've captured the ones who tried to take Kerrian-Isla. We'll get the others, as well."

"If I can help—" Karla left the offer unfinished. She turned and, with her three companions surrounding her, walked away, toward the exit to the pavilion.

"What was that about?" Jarrod's voice sounded softly near her ear.

Dia watched the retreating figures. "More murders."

"Who was that?" He indicated Karla with a nod of his head.

"The salvation of our jells, but at too great a personal cost to herself. I'm not the only one who's had to set a flaming canoe adrift." She looked up at Jarrod, her heart aching. "How many more will there have to be before this is all done?"

Chapter Fourteen

Dia stood for a long moment, steadying herself. She couldn't dissolve into helpless anger and frustration. She had to keep control, to act. She had to call an urgent meeting of her ministers.

She looked around the assembled company and spotted Rastor standing with Madam Chevika, listening to her comments with apparently rapt attention. She hurried through the milling crowd, murmuring apologies as she went. "Rastor? You'll excuse us, Ambassador." She drew the elderly man aside. "Assemble as many of the council as you can in the next five minutes and meet me in the comm room."

"The comm—" He blinked strained eyes at her.

"We have to start a search. At once. Five minutes." She left him to the task and made her way into the corridor and along the short maze of halls. Outside the comm room she halted and closed her eyes. No weaknesses. Not now. She had to act swiftly and decisively, assure these alien diplomats she could care for her own. She drew a deep breath and strode into the room.

One of the techs looked up. "No messages, Lady."

"I'm sending one. Get me the guard captains."

The tech cast her an uneasy glance, then keyed the command into his console. Seconds passed, then first one, then two other screens sprang to life, each portraying the image of a helmeted officer. The tech stepped back, offering his chair to Dia.

"No, thanks. I'll stand." She turned to the screen. "A moment, gentlemen. My ministers will be here shortly."

The door slid open, and three men and two women hurried in, following Rastor. They surrounded the console, their gazes shifting from Dia to the screens. "Lady—" one of the men began.

Dia held up her hand and addressed everyone, including the captains. "Two nights ago, two mercenaries, dressed as fishermen, murdered four of our people. All I know is they have a hydro-plane. They could be anywhere. I want shuttles launched at once to search for them."

One of the captains cleared his throat. "It won't be easy to find them."

"I know. Chances are pretty slim we'll succeed. But we're going to try. I'm not going to let what happened to the innis Mecca people be ignored."

Another of the captains nodded. "We'll launch in ten minutes. Standard search pattern. We won't quit 'til we find something."

"Thank you." Dia keyed the link off. "Now, all we have to do is wait." She looked up at the ministers' frowning faces, and a slight smile touched her lips. "Should I have asked your permission first?"

Rastor shook his head. "If they're mercenaries, it's an act of war. Your father would have done the same."

"I've got another job for you all, I'm afraid. I want to stay here for a while, make sure there aren't any problems in getting the search underway. Will you convey my apologies to the ambassadors and keep them company for me? Entertain them?"

Minister Gisa innis Movan rolled her eyes. "I'll take anyone but that Quy'doan female."

"Right." Dia actually smiled. "Rastor, she's all yours. Show them around, arrange for dancers or a concert or something. Show them vids. Just keep them busy, but let them know we act swiftly to right wrongs on Kerrian."

She ushered her ministers out, then turned back to the tech. "Put the searchers on the main screen, will you?" She dragged up a chair and sat sideways on it, her arms over the back. One after another, lights began blinking in a clump over a spot that would be Waianoa. A minute later, more lights blinked from other bases around the planet. Slowly they began to move. The search had begun.

Dia drummed her fingers on the chair. What else could she do? She couldn't let her people down, she couldn't let Karla down. They had to know she supported them, would stand for no such invasion. She couldn't—wouldn't—allow cold-blooded killers to roam her planet, seeking coral and the beautiful, intelligent Columbine jells!

The inactivity of waiting, she decided, would drive her insane.

Jarrod palmed open the door of the comm room, then stopped. Dia paced the chamber, hands clasped behind her, her heavy formal robes swaying with every restless step. She hadn't even stopped to shed those uncomfortable garments. Something tugged at his heart, something warm yet painful. He thrust it aside.

She tried so hard to manage, to carry a burden too great for any one person. Damn it, he wanted to help, to protect her, to shield her from so much strain. Even now, she kept her shoulders straight, her head high, as if nothing could quell her spirit. He hoped the other ambassadors had noticed the aura of camaraderie between her and her people, one that went beyond the formal relationship of subject to monarch. He'd sensed warm friendship, which was far more Dia's style. That, though, the other ambassadors might see as a weakness.

She turned in the course of her pacing, faced him, and stopped. Pleasure flickered across her features, only to fade. "What are you doing here?" Strain sounded in her voice.

"Need to send a message."

She nodded and continued on her way.

One of the comm techs spun around in his chair. "Can I help you, sir?"

"Gavin-Secundus," Jarrod told him. "Merylar Citadel. Urgent for the tharl."

"Right." The tech keyed in a series of numbers and the screen blurred, then sprang to life with an image of Gavin-Secundus as seen from orbit. "For the tharl, direct vid, urgent," the tech announced.

The screen blurred again, dissolving into the image of a Gavonian tech. "Sorry, the tharl isn't available for consultation. I'll have any message delivered to either Tharl Dysart or Lomax tolDysart."

Jarrod gritted his teeth. Deliberate avoidance or coincidental? The urge grew in him to return home, to find out in person what he couldn't assure himself of by vid. He didn't want to entrust his message to persons unknown. He glared at the screen. "All right, tell Tharl Dysart tolErrol there's a damned Gavonian mess on Kerrian, and I want some answers. Fast."

The Kerrinian shot him an impressed look. The Gavonian tech merely nodded. "Recorded for delivery as soon as possible."

"I want an answer faster than that," Jarrod muttered, but to himself rather than either of the poor techs. He signaled for end of communication, thanked the Kerrinian, and crossed to join Dia in her restless walk.

"You're getting the run-around, aren't you?" Her steady gaze rested on him.

"If I don't get answers soon—" He broke off, struggling to control his temper.

She nodded. "There's nothing worse than not knowing."

The single chime of an incoming message sounded, and Dia spun to face the mid-sized screen. "Put it on here," she directed.

The tech keyed it up, and a moment later Darmin's eager young face appeared. "Is our Lady available? I think I've got something for her."

"Darmin." Dia positioned herself behind the tech, where the monitor would pick her up. "What is it?"

"We picked up a message about half an hour ago. On the mercenaries' comm link."

"Good work," Dia breathed.

"Thank you, Lady. We've traced the signal to Zannon Atoll. The message was coded, and so far the mercenary commander has declined to translate. We've got the computers working on it, though."

"I'll get more than that on it. Thanks. We'll let

you know." Dia nodded to the tech, who broke the
connection and keyed up the guard. Dia relayed the
information, then turned to watch the giant screen
where the blinking lights revealed the progress of the
search. Less than a minute later, four lights veered
off their courses, converging on a single point.
"Determine which one will get there first, then switch
to their visual," Dia called to the tech.

Again, the screen shifted, passing through black
static to a swirling amethyst blur. The ocean at high
speed, Jarrod realized. At least Dia's wait would soon
be over.

The door hissed open behind them, but he didn't
turn until a faint squeaking caught his attention. A
staffer rolled a cart laden with covered trays to a halt
beside them. The young woman stepped back, eyeing
them uncertainly.

"I didn't know you were in here, Ambassador. The
meal has already been laid out in the dining hall,
with Minister sett Danies presiding. If you'd rather
stay here—" She broke off, her gaze drifting to Dia.

"They're already eating?" Dia demanded in dismay. "Oh—nets! I'd better go." Still, she made no
move to do so. "Ja—Ambassador?"

"Lady." He bowed to her. "If you don't mind, I'm
waiting for an answer to a rather urgent message. If
anything important happens," he nodded toward the
wall screen, "I'm sure they'll alert you immediately.
The other ambassadors are more important to you
right now. Here there's nothing you can do but wait."

"Like you're doing?"

He inclined his head. "No one will miss me."

She nodded. "If anything happens—"

"At once," he promised.

She turned from him, leaving him with the oddest

notion that his remaining comforted her in some way. He must be imagining it—yet he had to admit, he would feel better if *she* were able to monitor something in his absence. It would be almost like being there himself. He glanced back to find her standing in the door, staring at him with a perplexed, pleading expression on her face. Solemnly, he raised his arm in the Kerrinian salute to her, and a half-smile tugged at her lips as she turned to leave.

He carried her lunch tray to a chair and, while sampling the contents, continued watching the wall-sized vid screen. He could see little of the waterscape; everything flashed past in a blur of speed. Still, it held his fascinated gaze.

An hour passed, during which time he munched broodingly on a roll and a strong-flavored cheese, the best he'd ever tasted. He asked a tech where it came from, then was sorry he did. Sea bear cheese? Well, it could be something worse. For that matter, many of the foods he accepted as normal on Gavin might be considered outlandish or distasteful here.

The movement on the screen slowed so that he could make out a dark speck in the distance. An island, he realized as it raced closer. "Have you signaled . . . your Lady?"

"Just now, sir." The tech leaned forward, his gaze intent on the screen.

The image of the island grew larger, slowed, then vanished as the shuttle passed directly over it. Then all movement ceased; the shuttle had come to a hovering halt.

"Aren't they going to land?" Jarrod demanded after a long, tense moment.

"They'll be looking for their quarry, sir."

The view tilted, righted itself, then lowered, pro-

ducing a blur of amethyst-tinged sky, clouds, the
green and beige of palm trees, and the purplish hues
of the coral sand of the atoll. The images rocked
gently; the shuttle had landed in the water, Jarrod
realized. He opened his mouth to demand answers
to innumerable questions, but realized the tech could
only see what he, too, saw, and whoever sent that
coded message wasn't in sight.

"Why don't they switch on audio?" Jarrod
demanded.

"They—" The tech broke off as the view swung
about, then raced forward through the amethyst sea.

A boat rose up from the water, a hydro-plane gaining speed until it almost flew, shooting ahead, becoming smaller and smaller as it vanished in the distance.
Then it grew larger, and the ocean spray all but oblit-
erated the images on the screen. The shuttle raced
in pursuit; then the hydro-plane shuddered and
dragged to a halt, settling back into the swells.

"Got it." The tech leaned forward, his fists
clenched, his triumph shining in his face. He glanced
over his shoulder toward Jarrod. "Tractor beam, sir.
They won't be able to pull free. The Lady—"

"Right. I'll find out what's keeping her." Jarrod
turned on his heel, ignoring the tech's stammered
protest, and strode from the comm room. He paused
in the corridor, frowning, then turned right. The
pavilion stood across the main hall, if he remembered
correctly, but he could think of no reason why they'd
return there. Now, where—?

A door hissed open and Dia, followed by Madam
Chevika, Lord Feldar, and one of the assistants to the
Cerean team, hurried toward him. Every line of her
slender body radiated tension. "I couldn't get away

from them," she whispered. "What's happening?"
Strain tinged her voice, making it curt.

The Bertolian studied Jarrod with a piercing gaze.
"You did not join us for lunch."

"I've been waiting for a reply to a message." Jarrod
allowed Dia to lead the way; the hostility of the other
diplomats made itself all too clear. He didn't want to
compromise Dia's position.

When they entered the comm room, Jarrod made
a point of going to another tech and holding a low-
voiced if pointless conversation, allowing Dia and the
others to receive the report. He remained in the
background, watching, while the screen image spun,
then blurred with mounting speed. Dia stood stiffly
erect, her hands clutching the back of the tech's
chair, her knuckles white.

Minutes passed, then a tenor voice announced
over the comm unit: "Waianoa, this is Rysis. We've
taken two prisoners and have their ship in tow.
Will return to dock E-T-A in one point five seven
standard hours."

Dia leaned forward and tapped the switch. "Rysis,
this is Regent rys Pauaia. Can I have visual on them?"

Static filled the screen, then cleared to reveal two
men garbed in sarongs and parkas decorated with
shells. "Gavonians, wouldn't you say, Lady?" came
the voice once more.

"Yes." Dia's voice sounded flat. "I would say. Any
papers on them?"

"None, Lady. But don't worry." The voice sounded
cheerful. "They'll be *dying* to tell you everything by
the time we get home."

The slightest tremor crossed the features of one of
the two men; the other straightened his shoulders.

"If you're implying torture," he said, "that is in violation of the Interplanetary—"

"That's a war act code," broke in the unseen Kerrinian, the amusement in his voice growing. "You've just been telling me how you're not part of any military team. That means you're common criminals. And probably on the planet illegally, at that. That makes you fair game. Doesn't it, Lady?"

Dia's shoulders rose, then lowered with her slow, deep breath. "I have reason to believe they're partial to torture for interrogation. All I want to know is whether they're the ones who killed the innis Mecca clan. If they are—" She broke off.

The silence stretched for several seconds.

"Don't worry, Lady." This time, the Kerrinian's voice sounded tight, all traces of enjoyment gone.

Dia turned from the screen, her face an unreadable mask.

Madam Chevika folded her hands into the sleeves of her blue and silver robe. "You will have them tortured to death?" Her tone held approval.

Dia glanced up as if shaken from deep reverie. "To death? No. Not even tortured. It's not our way."

"Principles?" The Quy'doan's mouth curled into a condescending smile. "They do very well to keep tourists happy, my dear . . . regent, but I fear you are entering a different level of interplanetary relations. A reputation for decisive action will be your best defense."

"That, and a careful choice of ally." Lord Feldar cast a significant glance toward Jarrod. "Gavonians tend to stick together, even in their greatest follies."

"As the Cereans have had reason to discover," put in that junior diplomat. "Consider well where you put your trust."

"I do." Dia gave him her sweetest smile. "I've

noticed Cereans, Bertolians and Quy'doans among the mercenaries. But that doesn't mean I think all of your planets were behind that attempted revolt. Then, of course, I haven't discounted that possibility, either. Shall we return to the others? Ambassador tolArvik? You will be more comfortable waiting with us, I'm sure. My people will notify you as soon as your answer comes in." With that, she swept from the room, not bothering to look behind her to see if the others followed.

Jarrod fell into step beside Madam Chevika, who shot him an assessing glance. "Disturbing, is it not?" she said. "That these two murderers were *both* Gavonian?"

"Not disturbing." Jarrod allowed the Quy'doan to precede him through the doorway. "I'd find it disturbing if one had been Gavonian and the other, say for example, Cerean. That would be an unnatural pairing, even in a mercenary outfit."

Madam Chevika inclined her head in acknowledgment.

Jarrod lagged back. It *did* disturb him. Far too many Gavonians worked for this mercenary army. Did that mean it was Gavonian-based? He'd expect it to be better run if that were the case. He couldn't deny that his planet—or some faction on his planet—lay somewhere near the root of Kerrian's troubles. Just *how* near troubled him.

Dia, he realized a little over an hour later, avoided him. Not directly, true, but with a subtlety that proved as effective as it did inoffensive. She was simply charming—to everyone. To his annoyance, Jarrod realized he didn't like sharing her attentions, seeing her smile as warmly at others as she did at him. Or maybe that was as coolly.

He listened with an outwardly polite interest to the concert hastily assembled for their entertainment, but his thoughts remained on Dia, on whether or not she had reason to distrust him. His honor—the honor of his planet—lay at stake, and he wanted it cleared. He sat in the dark, glaring at the musicians, barely aware of the intricate melodies played by each of the instruments as they chased one another in a musical game of tag.

The chime of her comm link only reached him because he'd been waiting for it. He turned at once to where she sat several seats away, but she didn't look at him. She merely rose, spoke a quiet word to one of her ministers, excused herself to them all and slipped out of the chamber.

Jarrod clenched the arms of his chair, wanting to follow, wanting to know what went on—damn it, wanting to set things right between them. But he couldn't, not without compromising her integrity as far as the other ambassadors were concerned. He settled against the cushioned back, gritted his teeth, and determinedly enjoyed the remainder of the program.

He didn't see Dia again until dinner time, when she swept into the dining hall's antechamber. Her deep amethyst sarong swirled about her ankles, drawing his eye to her slender figure. A delicate coronet, mounted with a piece of Dahmla coral, sat on her brow, its ends intertwined in the thin braids that hung over her shoulders. The rest of her thick mass of hair tumbled loose below her knees.

"I'm sorry I had to leave you earlier." Her cool smile included them all in her apology. "The shuttle returned with its prisoners. I wanted to hear what they had to say."

"And that was?" Lord Pieral, the Rualdan ambassador, prompted her when she fell silent.

Her smile tightened. "It's nothing that need concern any of you. The situation is settled, that is enough. Tomorrow we can start back to Kerrian-Isla where the climate—I'm sure—will be more to your taste. And we'll waste no more time. I intend all treaties to be fair and equal. The right to trade, and the amount of coral we will sell, will be based on the size of your populations and on your intended use."

"Our intended use?" Lord Xar, the Cerean ambassador, lowered the glass from which he'd been about to sip. "You would dare to dictate to us how we can use what we have purchased?"

"Yes," she said simply. She crossed to where one of her elderly ministers poured wine for the ambassadors and accepted a cup from him.

"That seems a bit excessive," Lord Pieral pointed out.

Dia straightened her shoulders which had begun to sag as if with weariness. "I know what devastation coral-power can produce. I also know what greed can do. There is very little of the coral. I'm not about to let it be used to destroy when there are so many worlds it can help. Part of what I negotiate for is protection of the coral and jells, and proof of how it is to be used. And now," she added as a deep, resonating gong sounded through the chamber, "dinner is ready. Shall we go in?" She led the way through the open door into the long hall beyond.

Jarrod gritted his teeth. What, if anything, had she learned? He took his seat across the low table from her, and surreptitiously studied her face, her eyes, seeking clues. Did she agree with the other diplomats, that Gavin might be a treacherous ally? He couldn't blame her; he shared those fears. Which made him want to protect her all the more.

She reached for the decanter of Rualdan wine that stood before her, and he forcibly prevented himself from taking it and serving her. She ate sparingly, he noted, and he seethed with the frustration of not being able to talk to her. Something weighed on her mind, and he wanted to know what.

She kept up polite conversation with them all, then rose as the last of the diplomats set down his fork. "If you will excuse me? I believe we should all retire early tonight. A written proposal from each of you will be helpful for me. I'm sure none of you will mind. We will—" Her comm link chimed, and she broke off to touch it. "Yes?"

"Lady, a message for the Gavonian ambassador. Is he at table with you?"

"He is." She raised her eyebrows at Jarrod. "Live or vid?"

"Live, Lady."

Jarrod rose, dropping his napkin on the low table. "If you will excuse me?" He bowed to Dia, then included the other ambassadors. "Perhaps I'll have the answers to the questions we're all asking when I come back." He tried to catch Dia's gaze.

She merely nodded. "I will wish you all a good night, then. We leave at seven—which this far north is long before dawn, I fear. Breakfast will be brought to your rooms." She exited the dining hall through a back door, leaving her ministers to usher out the diplomats.

Repressing a desire to chase after her, to shake her, to force her to look at him, Jarrod stalked from the room. The sooner he spoke to Dysart, the better it would be.

It wasn't Dysart's image that stared impatiently from the smaller vid screen in the comm room, but that of a tech. Jarrod moved behind the console and touched the link to initiate. "Tell Dysart I'm here."

The Gavonian tech studied him with an air of mild interest. "The Tharl isn't available, sir. He has asked me to inform you that he has received your messages and is personally looking into the matter. He will send you word as soon as there is anything to know." The tech sketched a salute. The screen flickered, then filled with static as the connection broke.

"Sir?" The Kerrinian tech stood at his side. "Is there anything more?"

"No. Yes. Is there a gymnasium in the palace?" Somewhere—anywhere—he could work off his building frustration.

He followed the tech's directions and shortly found himself in a long, high-ceilinged chamber. A number of exercise machines stood near one wall; the others bore a variety of lines, hoops, nets, and bars, allowing for a wide range of games. Jarrod stripped off his uniform coat and shirt, located a small ball and a netted racquet, and proceeded to slam the former against the wall with the latter in a manner designed both to exhaust and to relieve temper. When at long last his leg muscles no longer raced him across the court with sufficient speed, he retired to a steaming bath filled with jet sprays that seemed to find and ease every one of his stiffening aches.

The chronometer on the wall indicated it was only a few minutes before twenty-hundred hours, midnight by the Kerrinian reckoning. He toweled himself off, dragged on pants and shirt, draped his coat over his arm, and set off in search of the apartments set aside for his delegation's use. He felt better, he had to admit, but one yearning ache remained which the exercise had done nothing to alleviate. He wanted to see Dia.

Tired as he'd made himself, he suspected thoughts of her would keep him long from sleep. Just as well, he supposed; he still had a written proposal to prepare for her.

A sleepy staffer directed him toward the guest quarters. He started along the corridor, but the brilliance of the night beyond the curtained plasti-walls slowed his steps. He paused in one of the alcoves that let out onto a terraced patio. A rectangular reflecting pond, now frozen over, stood in the middle.

For a long minute, he stared into the night sky where the three moons rode high, still in close proximity. Already, though, the amethyst glow dimmed from Vergan as they separated once more. The new year had begun.

Movement caught his eye, and a cloaked figure emerged from the shadowed walls and stood at one end of the iced water, staring down with a concentration that could almost melt the freeze. Long hair shimmered in the light as it fell over the figure's shoulder. Very long hair. Dia.

He touched the panel and the plasti-door slid open; a blast of icy air swirled about him, and he dragged on his coat. He could use a cloak like the one that wrapped about Dia. He strolled up behind her. She never moved except for the rise and fall of her shoulders as she breathed.

He stopped a couple of meters from her, studying

her straight figure, and an emotion so intense as to be painful swept through him. So much endurance, so much bravery, so much honor. Love for her, for her strength, for the way she had hidden her fears and conducted herself before the alien ambassadors, filled him. He took a step forward.

"If you look carefully enough," Dia said without glancing over her shoulder, "you can read omens in the sky."

"Can you?" Jarrod joined her, standing just far enough away so he didn't actually touch her. As it was, the temptation proved almost overwhelming.

"Umm hmmm." She let out a sigh. "See there? That reflection of light in the shadows of Rhysta— the largest moon? That's a ship, battle cruiser size. One of the ambassador's transports, undoubtedly, but I'd be willing to wager it's fully armed."

"Not a pleasant omen."

"No," she agreed, and fell silent. A slight tremor shook her shoulders.

"You're cold. What brought you out here? Omen watching?"

She shook her head. "Waiting for you. There hasn't been a chance to talk to you when the others weren't around."

He glanced about the walled patio, but saw only a single lighted room to their left, up one floor. "Have they all gone to sleep?"

"They're probably up writing their proposals." Amusement touched her voice, then faded. "Visitor's rooms face over the ocean. Only the family apartments and government offices look down on the pond." She turned to face him, apparently not minding that only centimeters separated them. Her breath formed a pale cloud, hovering between them, mingling with his. It dissipated, only to be replaced with the next. "What did Uncle Dysart have to say?"

"He sent a message that he's looking into things." His hand started to rise, and only with an effort did he keep from brushing her loose hair back from her forehead. "What did you learn from those two Gavonians?"

She grimaced. "They're mercenaries, but we knew that. One insists their admiral is Rualdan, the other swears she's Bertolian. They were sent to capture Columbine jells, and insist they didn't mean to kill the innis Meccas, but those poor people wouldn't say where Karla had taken the jells into hiding." She drew a shaky breath. "It was the other way around, Karla says. The jells knew about trouble before she did. They were so upset they took *her* away. Her family never knew where." She turned away, hugging herself. "I wish we'd never discovered—" She broke off.

"Just think about how much good the coral power can do."

She nodded, but when she spoke a quaver sounded in her voice. "Provided we can keep it from doing harm. I don't see how we can monitor the use."

"You sounded pretty certain earlier."

"I'm getting good at bluffing."

He laid his hands on her shoulders and turned her gently to face him. "Are you sure you should be telling me that?"

She didn't meet his gaze. "You're supposed to be my advisor, aren't you?"

"Do you still trust me?" His heart seemed to be pounding with unusual force.

"Yes." She studied her hands. "Whatever your planet might be involved in, you're not part of it."

At last she looked up, her troubled gaze meeting his. "How am I to deal with them tomorrow?"

He took her chilled fingers in his. "Just remember one thing: the key lies in understanding your adversary, both his strengths and his weaknesses."

Her lips twitched into a wry smile. "Oh, sure. Simple. Now, all I have to do is figure out what they are."

"They'll let you know. In subtle ways. You just have to be alert." If she were, she'd be aware of his weakness. Her. But she was his strength, as well. What she made him feel he could do. . . . He released her hands abruptly and strode to the edge of the pond, staring down at the ice. If he touched her, held her the way he wanted. . . .

"Jarrod—"

The sound of her voice tore at him, undermined his intentions. He turned, allowing his gaze to rest on her face as it peeked out at him from the ruff of downy feathers that bordered her hood. He had to resist, he couldn't give in to the raging desire to drag her into his arms, carry her up the steps to her room and tumble with her amidst the silken pillows and feather-fur throws that made up Kerrinian beds. Every part of him burned to negotiate an agreement with her, one in which coral would play no part—yet, the explosions generated would dwarf those of the tiny branches in their jellactic acid.

"You'd better get some sleep." The words came out harsher than he'd intended. "Come on, I'll see you to your room. Then I've got a proposal to write." He caught her arm and headed toward the steps, pulling her along with him. He reached the top and palmed the door open. "You get in there and get warm. I've got work to do."

He took her hand and raised it to his lips for a brief kiss. That extended into a very long one. He retained his hold, his fingers caressing hers, danger alarms clamoring in his mind that his body refused to acknowledge. "I—go to bed. I can't think when you're near me. Or rather, I can. *Too* much." A short, derisive laugh escaped him. "Great Artis, what you make me think of."

"You're giving me a pretty vivid imagination, too." Her words sounded hoarse, as if they dragged themselves out against her will.

For a moment, he didn't breathe. He gazed down at her as her hands turned in his to return his clasp. It had been a mistake, he realized, to touch her. His control wavered, crumbling. She'd been through too much, lost too much, naturally she'd turn to the one person who offered her help. He couldn't take such advantage of her vulnerability. Yet, the smoldering light in her eyes spoke of passion more than dependence, of inner strength rather than clinging weakness. He freed one hand only to trace the line of her cheek.

"I'm not a child looking for comfort," she whispered as if reading his thoughts. "I don't need—or want—some strong man to sweep in here and solve my problems for me. I can take care of myself, and with my ministers' help I can take care of my planet. Without you."

His mouth tugged into a smile. "Where does that leave me?" He smoothed back her hair, dislodging her hood as he did so. Unable to resist, he brushed his lips across her forehead. The delicate scent of water lilies filled his senses.

"With no political or business ties between us." Her response sounded a trifle breathless.

"What about personal ones?" His mouth worked its way over her eyes, down her cheek, along her throat to the enticing hollow at the base.

"We're both free agents. Ties of any kind can prove tricky, though." She moved her head, finding his mouth with hers.

"You're telling me," he muttered. His hand slid beneath her cloak as he dragged her against himself.

"It's cold out here." Her cheek brushed his as she nuzzled her face in his hair.

"You'd better go in." He pushed her through the doorway, but she kept hold of his hand, drawing him after her into her room.

"I'll still be cold—without you."

The longing in her voice proved too much for what little control he retained. He swept her tightly into one arm, the other groping at her throat for the tie to her cape. It slid with a feathery rustle to the tiled floor, and her soft sigh sounded in his ears.

Behind them, the fagots of dried seaweed crackled in the brazier. Its fire burned bright, though it dimmed in comparison to the one that consumed him. Dia filled his senses, her softness, the tantalizing scent of water lilies that clung to her skin, the silkiness of her sarong as it slipped away from her body. He buried his face against her skin, inhaling deeply, carried beyond conscious thought as he lowered her to the bed, his hands already exploring her yielding curves.

Some hours later, she stirred against his chest where he held her close. "This won't influence me any at the negotiating table," she murmured sleepily.

He chuckled softly, kissed her waving hair, and drifted into the deepest sleep he had experienced in years.

Chapter Fifteen

Dia stood in the pre-dawn darkness at the stern of the ship, watching the ambassadors and their assistants board the yacht. Lights dangled from the lines, swaying and snapping with the chill wind. The icy sea tang stung her nose, and she wrapped her heavy cloak closer about herself. She could make out little of the diplomatic parties as they scurried for the protection of the lounge.

She knew the moment Jarrod came on board, though she didn't know how. He looked the same as the others, a parka-shrouded figure moving swiftly through the wavering light. Yet, with little effort, she picked him out of the growing crowd. His height, his proud carriage, his overwhelming presence, all combined to make his figure unmistakable. That, and the rush of sensual awareness that raced through her.

He did no more than award her a slight bow in passing—a bow that nevertheless wrapped about her with the tenderness of a loving embrace. They'd agreed, in the early hours of the morning, that they would have to stay apart this long day. Disguising what they felt, the reactions they created in one another, would be almost impossible under any circumstances. With the penetrating stares of the other diplomats upon them, they would be certain to betray themselves.

Resolutely, Dia turned her back on him and moved forward to speak to the captain. She would collect the written proposals from the ambassadors, then retire to the privacy of her cabin to read and compare their documents. That should keep her busy—and most importantly, alone. Then, if thoughts of Jarrod intruded, as she knew they most assuredly would, no one could see her distraction.

"Five minutes, Lady," the Captain called to her. He signaled two sailors, who disengaged the gangplank and gathered in the lines which now hung limp beside their cleats on the rocking dock. "Is everyone safe in the lounge?"

"I'll herd in the last," she shouted back. Leaning into the wind, she crossed the polished deck toward the door where two of the cloaked and hooded passengers stood in conversation. "We're about to take off," she announced as she neared. "Let's get inside where we won't freeze."

The closest man looked up, one of the junior Rualdan diplomats. "It's no wonder you winter in the southern clime, Lady Regent. Why have you centered your capital here, in these frozen seas?"

"Easier to carry on the real business of government without the constant interruptions of the tourists." She offered him a smile which she hoped he would take to mean she didn't include him in that statement. "Kerrian-Isla is the center for tourist business."

"Wise to separate them," the junior diplomat murmured. He bowed to her and entered the lounge.

Dia turned to the remaining man, Lord Pieral, the Rualdan ambassador. "You'll be more comfortable inside."

"Comfortable, yes, but private, no." He fixed her with a steady gaze from his oddly gold eyes. "I would very much like a word in confidence with you, Lady."

Dia hesitated. She couldn't take him to one of the cabins. The lounge offered little chance for uninterrupted or unheard speech. That left the observation deck. "It'll be cold," she warned, as she led the way toward the bow of the yacht, then clambered up the ladder that rose along the side of the bridge. Here no roof protected them from the elements, but at least a high plasti-clear wall surrounded them, providing a break in the wind.

A brazier stood in the center of the shielded area. Dia struck a light, the dried bundles of Urus plants smoldered, then flames sprang to life. As the Rualdan swung up behind her, the salty-spicy scent of the seaweed surrounded her.

The yacht vibrated with the starting of its engine. They pulled away from the dock, picked up speed, and salt spray splattered the plasti-wall, freezing into intricate patterns of frost. Dia held her hands to the blaze before her. "What did you wish to say?" she asked.

"One feels like a bird, perched so high above the deck," the ambassador observed. He, too, held out his hands to the brazier. For a long minute, he said nothing more, merely warming himself. "What I wished to say," he continued at last, "is not for the ears of the others. Perhaps I speak out of turn. If I do, I hope you will forgive me. But it seems to me that in spite of your brave appearance, you are in a somewhat vulnerable position."

Dia choked back her dismay at his perception, and awarded his comment no more than raised eyebrows. "I assure you, the tourist trade has trained us better than you might imagine for dealing with the galaxy."

Lord Pieral made a dismissive gesture with his hand. "I don't doubt it. I am also aware, though, of the long-standing ties of friendship between your planet and Gavin-Secundus. I believe you, personally, have always regarded their tharl in light of a close relative?"

"I know him very well," Dia admitted. "That also implies I have few delusions about him."

A smile broke across the Rualdan's face. "Then you know he is a warrior chieftain and places a high value on honor. But," and his eyes narrowed, "honor is relative. The betrayal of friendship for the advancement of one's planet might well seem an honorable action."

Dia inclined her head. "I've considered that possibility. I am also aware that coral lies in a very different category from recreational facilities. No one goes to war for the right to water ski or take underwater tours. But the principles of negotiating for them remain the same for both. Fairness, honesty, mutual benefit?"

"May I be blunt?" Lord Pieral met and held her gaze. "Your first action seems to have been to convert weapons to coral power. Under the circumstances, that is the wisest move you could have made. Every system in the galaxy would give a great deal for an excuse to annex your planet."

Dia merely nodded and hoped her expression wouldn't betray her, let him know that they had no such weapons.

"You would be wise," he went on, "to form a treaty for protection with a powerful system."

"If you're suggesting I hand over my planet to someone else, just so they won't take it by force—"

"No! No, I assure you, that is not what I meant. I had something else in mind. You see, in a sense, you will probably be doing just that, anyway, in the near future."

Dia's hands clenched. "You mean with the treaties? I am not so gullible—"

"No, not gullible. What you are is marriageable."

She stared at him, too stunned to respond.

"You, it appears, have not considered the matter yet. Your ministers, however, have. One in particular, Rastor sett Danies by name, was very interested in the unmarried heads of state and their families on my planet. I'm sure he asked the other ambassadors, as well."

"A marriage treaty." Dia stared into the flames. "Of course, they're considering it. A tie with a strong planet from a strong system."

"One that can protect your planet and its precious coral from avaricious parasites." He cleared his throat. "It is well known that the most binding of all treaties lies in the marriage bed. I'm surprised," he added after the slightest pause, "the Gavonians haven't already approached you on behalf of their tharl's son."

"Lomax?" Dia's flesh prickled. They hadn't made any such suggestion because Lomax knew full well she considered him a particularly slippery and voracious specimen of razor-eel and had done so, since they were both small children. A man less like his open, good-hearted father she could hardly imagine. Now, if it were Jarrod—

She broke off that thought. Jarrod, though an ambassador, would not be considered suitable by her ministers. She must have realized that, even last night. Was that why she'd drawn him to her bed, to share what they could before it was too late? That opportunity, she realized with a dull ache, might never come again.

"I'm sure your ministers will take the greatest care in their selection of a husband for you." The Rualdan gave her a reassuring smile. "You are quite a marriage prize, if you will forgive me for putting it in such blunt terms. Any would-be head of state would assure himself of a dynastic reign on his planet if he were lucky enough to secure such a close tie to the coral as you represent."

She turned away to stare across the sea that flashed past as the yacht skimmed the surface of the purple waves. She'd always expected to make her own choice in marriage. Rules for royal alliances on Kerrian weren't stringent—a simple majority vote of the Council of Ministers approved the ruler's choice of consort. Never, in the planet's history, had that been denied. But now, because of the coral and the threat it brought, she must look off-world for a husband—to buy protection for her home with her body and life.

An arranged marriage. Her beloved Kerrian, annexed by another planet through her marriage bed. She was nothing but a pawn.

And Lord Pieral was right. Marriage to the Kerrinian coral would indeed be a dynasty-maker for whoever secured it—and her. Would she be besieged by upstarts and power-grubbers who saw her as an easy way to realize their ambitions?

And Jarrod. . . . She looked down to the bow, where

somehow she knew he'd be. She could see his parka-clad figure staring ahead at the floating chunks of ice that the ship pushed aside as it surged south through the freezing sea. Jarrod could be tharl, after Dysart, if he succeeded in capturing the coral matrimonial prize. Was that his plan? Did he consider last night to be an audition for the job of her consort?

No. Warmth surged through her at the thought of those perfect hours spent in her bed. There'd been no lies in the love they'd shared. His honor would never permit him to act in so dishonorable a way. Whatever else happened, whatever else she must do or sacrifice for her planet, that memory would sustain her. No one could take from her what she and Jarrod had known together.

She turned back to the brazier, to find she now stood alone on the observation deck. Apparently, Lord Pieral had accomplished his purpose and left her to think about what he'd said. If he'd hoped to unsettle her for the upcoming negotiations, he'd succeeded far too well.

Depressed, she made her way to the lounge. She noted Jarrod had also returned. She tried not to look at him, but her gaze seemed drawn as a lodestone to the north. His very presence created a tumultuous reaction in her, fueled by far too vivid memories of the night spent in giving and seeking joyous love.

Lord Xar came up to her at once, bowed deeply, and presented a vid disc to her. "Our proposal, Lady."

"Thank you. As soon as I've seen them all—"

The Cerean bowed once more, clicked his heels together, and strode off. One down, four to go.

The others were not to be outdone by Xar. Lord Feldar hurried toward her, disc in hand, followed closely by a junior diplomat from Quy'dao. Jarrod, his face a disinterested mask, came after Lord Pieral. She took each disc with smiling thanks, though she refused to look at Jarrod.

She studied her handful, then glanced up to find all gazes resting on her. "You will excuse me for a little while, I'm sure. Please make full use of the entertainments we have to offer. I'll return as quickly as I can."

She spent the next two hours closeted in her cabin, poring over the vid screen, making charts of the various offerings and planned uses. Transport, of both goods and people, seemed the primary concern. It amused her that not one of the five proposals included mention of any military ships to be converted to coral power. But the number of commercial vessels seemed inordinately high. .

How was she to assure that coral served only peaceful purposes? She leaned back in her chair, rubbing her aching forehead with her palms. Only the Quy'-doans mentioned converting selected cities to coral-fuel. Cities with military bases, she'd wager, though the proposal called them medical and research-oriented.

As for what they offered in return, a variety of proposals lay before her, ranging from the Cerean suggestion of an inter-planetary militia to remain in protective orbit around Kerrian to the Bertolian offer to train Kerrian personnel in peace-keeping technology. Peace-keeping technology. She liked that term. It masked a wealth of militaristic overtones.

Yet, her people were sadly backward when it came to contemporary technology. If it didn't please tourists, they'd seen little need to learn it. That would change, now. It would have to. She hesitated over her comparison file on the screen, then highlighted training. In exchange for the coral, she would see her people sent to top universities on these planets. She liked the idea of protection, too—but *not* a militia in orbit. She'd ask for warning beacon satellites, and a more sophisticated communications system that would allow screening to detect weapons at a safe distance.

She took more notes, made her way to the bridge, had the comm tech call Waianoa, and sent it all to her ministers. Let them come up with more ideas. She had the ambassadors to entertain. And she couldn't bear another minute without at least seeing Jarrod.

The afternoon proved torture for her, to be so near him yet unable to acknowledge in any way the yearning that ate away at her. As they sat around a table, holding the six-sided cards used in playing lyroq, she could sense his tension. He drummed his fingers on the table, made rash bets, then folded early. Slamming the cards down, he paced outside to stand in the freezing air. She wished she could do the same, anything to cool the heat of desire that burned within her.

Not until they retired for the night did she get a chance for a private word with him. She excused herself early, pleading the exhaustion of the last couple of days. Madam Chevika accompanied her into the corridor leading to the cabins, and had barely entered the one assigned to her when Jarrod emerged from the lounge.

Dia paused before her door, deliberately delaying, hoping he would approach. Yet, what could they do? Others might appear at any moment. She fiddled with the palm plate and the panel slid wide.

"Excuse me." Jarrod pressed against her side as he moved past in the narrow corridor.

Dia leaned against him, her body thrilling with the contact. "I thought I'd go mad today," she whispered.

"Meet me before dawn, on the observation deck," he whispered back, and was gone before she could do so much as answer.

That contact only made the night harder to bear. She lay in her bed—easily wide enough for two intertwined bodies—longing for him. Yet he couldn't come; she might have a stateroom to herself, but the male ambassadors shared with their male staff members. Jarrod could hardly slip away during the night without the others noticing. Long before morning, though, she would have willingly risked discovery for just a few minutes in his arms, touching him, reassuring herself that what they had shared the night before had been as real and wonderful as she remembered.

She awoke with his name filling her heart, as if she had sung it in her dreams. Her cabin remained dark, for despite the great distance they had traveled south, it was still too early for the sun. Jarrod, she knew, was awake also. Awake and waiting for her.

She rose quickly, dressed, and slipped out of her cabin. Already the sky softened from deep purple to the amethyst glow of approaching dawn. The chill spray from the ocean dampened her cheeks, and she wrapped a light cloak about her shoulders as she made her way to the observation deck.

He stood on the far side, back against the rail, gazing toward the first rosy streaks that proclaimed the dawning of the new day. Clouds, tinged pink and amethyst, hovered at the skyline. His gaze came to rest on her, and Dia hesitated at the top of the ladder, suddenly nervous. He held out his hand to her, and she took it, the warmth of his firm clasp reassuring.

He drew her toward him, against his side, and smoothed back the wind-ruffled hair from her eyes. "We have plans to make, you and I."

"Not yet." With her free hand, she caught the fingers that twined playfully in a strand that had come loose from its pins. "It's too soon."

Gently he freed himself and tilted her chin upward to study her face. "I knew the first moment I saw you, crawling out of the water and lying on the dock that night."

"Yes, a bedraggled heap strewn with seaweed. You make me wonder about your taste." She rested her cheek against his palm, and her smile faded. "My choices may no longer be my own."

"But if they were?"

She tried to look away, but his tone commanded an answer. Yet how could she give one? What good could it do to avow her love when the needs of her planet, not the desires of her heart, dictated her path?

The corners of his mouth tugged into a sad smile. "I never realized how eloquent silence really could be. Oh, my beloved. Would that I had found you six months ago."

She gazed into the depths of his shadowed gray eyes, unable to speak, unable to look away, lost in the enveloping awareness of him. If life were different . . . what she would renounce . . . how much could they still share? Questions only half expressed, not fully understood, jumbled through her mind.

A chair scraped on the deck below, and Dia started, pulling away, until she realized it was only a crewman. How long had they stood there, simply staring at one another? She could only wish they had a little longer before they had to return to the others and pretend to the barest acquaintance.

"Go first." Jarrod drew back, his expression somber.

With a last, lingering look at him, Dia turned and made her way down the ladder. The diplomats would be awake, some probably already venturing forth from their cabins in search of breakfast. Another day. At least, she wouldn't have to entertain them for long. A couple more hours only, then they would dock at Kerrian-Isla, and she could plead duties and her being away as an excuse to escape for awhile. And in the palace, there would be more opportunities for privacy, for stolen words with Jarrod.

As she drank steaming stimi with the junior Rualdan attache, the ship's steward strode into the lounge, spotted her, and hurried forward. "Lady. A message from Kerrian-Isla. From the palace."

She smiled at the Rualdan, whose name she had yet to hear distinctly. "Probably a welcome back. If you'll excuse me?" Once out of the lounge and heading toward the bridge with its comm screen, she asked the steward, "What's happened? Has something gone wrong?"

Before he could answer, she pushed through the door and headed to where the comm tech sat before his vid. He looked up, then rose and gestured for Dia to take his chair. She slid in front of the screen, and the tech reached over her shoulder and keyed it to life.

For a moment, only the saronged shoulder of a man appeared in the image, then he straightened and Darmin looked straight at her. "Lady, may I offer you our congratulations on the regency?"

"Have I offered you my thanks for your help in securing it?" she countered. "What's up?"

"Message from Gavin-Secundus."

"For me? Or for Ja—Ambassador tolArvik?"

"You. From Lomax tolDysart."

Dia's eyebrows shot up. "What does he want? To see if he can weasel some profit for himself out of our negotiations? Thank the Net, he doesn't go in for politics."

Darmin grinned. "It's coded and sealed for you alone, Lady. Urgent priority, but not to be transmitted for security reasons."

"Security reasons? Lomax always did have a flare for drama. Just bear in mind, this is a man who thinks buying a cup of stimi should include high pressure bargaining techniques."

Darmin chuckled. "I'll remember. It's here and waiting for you, as soon as you get in. So are your answers from Waianoa. They came in late last night."

"Bless them," she said with heartfelt sincerity. "See you in a couple of hours." She keyed it off herself, then went to join the others.

Jarrod, she noted as she entered the lounge once more, stayed some distance from her. Only when she toured the breakfast buffet, browsing for rolls stuffed with kala fish, did he come near to her, and then in company with the senior Bertolian assistant. Dia studied the selections on the table, hoping her self-conscious awareness of Jarrod wouldn't be apparent to everyone.

He paused for a moment beside her. "Good morning, Lady. I've enjoyed our voyage very much, but I must say I'll be glad to return to the solid ground of your palace again." He moved on, continuing his conversation with the Bertolian.

She allowed herself a brief glare at his back, then

turned to the fresh fruits. She wished she could appear so casual.

The next hour passed rapidly, what with repacking then standing on the deck, once more in the tropical warm breeze, watching the fishing and excursion vessels scattering across the endless sea. A shadowy shape appeared on the horizon, gray against the pale amethyst-blue of the morning sky. As they drew closer, it resolved into the palace spires, tall and pointed, carved from the volcano's obsidian peak. Dia leaned against the rail, watching it race closer.

As soon as they disembarked, Dia excused herself to the ambassadors with a promise to rejoin them for lunch with Kerrian's treaty proposal. With only a quick stop-off at her room to exchange her spray-dampened cloak and sarong for fresh garments, she hurried to the comm room.

Three techs sat at various stations, lounging back in their chairs and drinking from steaming mugs. Merris, with the stimi cart before her, sat on one of the counter tops laughing at something one of the young men said. She sprang to her feet as Dia stepped inside, and the techs jumped to attention.

"Back to your break," she called. "Unless there's something urgent? Darmin, are these from Waianoa?" She picked up a few sheets of hard copy and glanced through them. Her ministers, she noted with relief, had annotated everything she'd sent, then offered a revised proposal. If Jarrod approved. . . .

"Ready for Lomax tolDysart's message?" Darmin keyed it up from the file where he'd saved it for her. "There, it's in the booth, your access code."

"Probably all that secrecy is just to make me look at it." Dia wended her way through the work stations

to the back of the room, where a single vid screen
stood enclosed in plasti-clear. She palmed open the
door, entered her personal code on the unit, then
leaned back against the wall to observe.

The screen flickered, then the official seal of Gavin-
Secundus appeared, overwritten by the image of Merylar Citadel and the stamp of the tharl. Dia's brow
furrowed at this bit of posturing. Lomax always had
liked playing with his father's trappings of power,
though she'd expected him to outgrow it. But then,
Lomax took his games seriously.

More flickering, then Lomax's face, with his thin
brown hair sleeked back from his forehead, filled the
screen. His eyes seemed to glitter; he'd probably just
concluded another successful—if questionable—
business venture.

The image of the sharp features wavered a moment
as the computers unscrambled the encoding, then
returned to focus. On the screen, Lomax leaned forward, intent. "Please forgive all the security nonsense,
Dia, but I don't want anyone else seeing this. I'm
counting on our lifetime of friendship in this matter."

Friendship? A derisive laugh escaped her. Lifetime
of veiled insults and avoidance, more like.

"This is a tricky matter for us, as you must have
realized by now. It concerns our ambassador, Jarrod
tolArvik." Lomax drummed restless fingers on the
desk before him. "We're charging the man with treason. Now wait—" He held up a hand. "I know what
you're thinking, that my father sent him there to help
you negotiate, but he didn't know at the time. The
charges are two-fold. One is for planning and bringing about the revolution on your planet. The other
is for attempting to establish a personal relationship
with an alien head of state—that's you, Dia—as a

ploy to gain power on Gavin-Secundus.'' He looked down for a moment, then up again, straight at her. ''You're probably on to him already, and damn it, Dia, we're all sorry someone from our planet's caused so much trouble. I'm formally requesting that you take him into custody for us until our authorities can place him officially under arrest. I've already dispatched a guard.'' The image froze, then blurred; the Gavonian seal returned, signifying the end of the message.

Dia stared at the screen, stunned. With a hand that trembled, she touched the control panel and replayed the recording. She hadn't been mistaken. Lomax really *had* accused Jarrod of treason. How could he get it so wrong? Usually, Lomax weeded out his bad ideas at their earliest stages.

But occasionally—rarely—a blunder slipped through and ran rampant, hurtling toward disaster.

She hugged herself, her mind racing. Guards already sent to arrest Jarrod. Too late to stop this idiocy; she'd have to circumvent it. But how? She had no idea when the guards set out. They could be here at any time.

She had to warn Jarrod, help him get away until she could reach Dysart and convince him how wrong Lomax was this time. Jarrod couldn't be taken.

Treason, on Gavin-Secundus, carried the death penalty.

Chapter Sixteen

Dia hurried into the circular solarium to see Jarrod already there before her. He stood beside the central fountain, his back to her as he studied a huge ficus. The crystal-clear water splashed against the side of its obsidian bowl, setting glistening sparkles across the arm of his coat.

He must have heard the soft scrape of her sandals on the tiles, for he turned, his entire countenance brightening at sight of her. "Dia," he said softly, and strode forward, hands extended.

She started to respond, to rush into his arms, only to come to an abrupt halt. She couldn't let herself be distracted. This was too important.

It wasn't going to be easy, either. Somehow, she had to convince him of the seriousness of the situation. And somehow, she had to convince him to behave in a manner that would seem to him dishonorable.

He, too, halted, his narrowed gaze studying her.

"What is it? You didn't send for me to wile away a spare half hour, did you?"

"No." That one word was hard enough to get out.

"More troubles," he muttered. "Dia, my beloved, what can I do to help?"

She shook her head, fighting the horrible urge to burst into tears. She wanted the comfort of his arms about her. "Jarrod—" She broke off.

His thoughtful gaze rested on her. "Best to just blurt it out, whatever it is. Get it over with."

She nodded. "I had a message waiting for me from Lomax. Listen, Jarrod. You've been accused of treason, and I'm supposed to hold you prisoner for your Citadel guard to collect sometime this morning."

"Treason?" He sounded incredulous. He drew in a deep breath, then asked, "Were the charges specified?"

"Instigating our revolution, and—" She stumbled over finishing.

"And?" he demanded.

"And courting me as a means of gaining power on your own planet." There, she'd said it. "They'll be arriving any time, now. You can stay here, of course, but it would be safer if you went away, maybe to one of the atolls."

"Safer?" he demanded. "What are you talking about?"

"I don't want them to take you." She was making a mess of this, saying it badly, but she forged on. "Not until we convince Uncle Dysart there isn't any truth in it!"

"My wonderful Dia." He cupped her face between his hands and gazed down at her. After a very long minute, his lips twitched into a wry smile. "Actually,

I suppose there is the veriest grain of truth in that last charge.''

"The—" She broke off, searching his face, willing him to deny what he had just admitted.

"No, my dearest." He smoothed a loose strand of hair back from her forehead. "The only part of it I'm guilty of is courting you. And loving you. Your revolution—no. And there's only one type of power that interests me when I'm with you, and that has nothing to do with politics. The charges are false, I promise you."

She wrapped her arms about his waist and pressed her cheek into the rough fabric that covered his shoulder. "We'll explain it to Uncle Dysart. Loving each other isn't a crime."

He rubbed his chin along the top of her head. "Love—" He broke off.

She drew back to look up into his face, and saw the tenderness of his expression fade to a frown. "What's wrong?"

"Love. In our case, it just may be a crime." He didn't look at her, but his hands caressed her shoulders. "Not legally, but morally." He released her abruptly and strode a few meters away, coming to a stop before the fountain. "Conflict of interest," he said at last. "That's my true crime."

"What do you mean?"

He shook his head, then looked toward her, his ironic smile tugging at his mouth. "My loyalty is divided, and therefore my integrity is compromised."

"But—" she began, only to break off when he held up his hand.

"It is. I've sworn to serve my planet, and that's an oath I cannot and will not renounce. It's part of me, serving Gavin's interests. And my dearest love, I want to help you, as well. When we go to the negotiating tables, which will win out? Will I sacrifice the advantages for my own planet to assure you the best treaty? Or will I try to influence you, subtly and perhaps even unintentionally, to favor Gavin?"

She opened her mouth, then closed it again. After a moment, she said, "I wouldn't want you to do either."

"No." His hands clenched. "At this point, I can no longer trust myself to act as I should. A man of true honor," he added, "would leave."

"I—I don't want you to go. It isn't *safe* for you to go."

He shook his head. "Running or hiding isn't the way. I can see only one viable course—to return to Gavin to clear my name of the charges." He made no mention of the one he'd made against himself.

Dia drew in a shaky breath. "What if you fail?"

His shoulders straightened. "I won't. I'm not guilty, and Dysart must realize that."

"This whole thing is ridiculous! Why would they trump up these charges in the first place? You should stay here until it's settled."

"Dia, love—" He broke off, his brown furrowing. "Great Artis, you're right. The charges *are* obviously trumped up. They wouldn't hold for a minute in our courts. So there's a reason for all this, and for it being Lomax who contacted you. He never involves himself in matters of state. So—" He stared into space, frowning. "So maybe," he continued slowly, "it's the only way they could find to warn me that Dysart's in trouble. I have to go to his aid."

She caught his hand and held it to her cheek. "I *want* to help Uncle Dysart, but is it safe for you?"

That slow, slightly twisted smile tugged once more at his mouth. "If I don't go, I'd only stand condemned of dishonor and disloyalty, both in their eyes and in my own. And in yours.''

She nodded, understanding yet hating the code of ethics that would take him from her—that might draw him into danger as deadly as any she'd faced here. She blinked back the moisture that stung her eyes. "When—?"

"Now." He drew her against him, enveloping her in his strong embrace, his lips brushing her hair. "I don't want them to feel like they're capturing me. I'll meet my escort at the spaceport, alone."

She drew his head down to hers for a long, heart-wrenching kiss, then clung to him, memorizing the feel of his thick hair tickling her face, the way her forehead tucked comfortably under his chin, the way his arms pressed her body tightly against his. He kissed her eyes, then her lips once more, then released her. Through blurred eyes, she watched him leave.

She sank onto the bench surrounding the fountain, clasped her hands tightly together, and began to breathe in the controlled pattern that would bring ease. At last, a form of peace settled over her, an acceptance of the inevitable, of the rightness of Jarrod's choice. She rose, knowing she had to return to the ambassadors, had to continue with the negotiations, had to pretend nothing had occurred. Knowing that Jarrod could not now influence her one way or the other.

Or did she even need him physically in the room with her for that? His presence lingered, filling her, tantalizing her, no matter how far from her he went. Conflict of interest, Jarrod called it, and blamed himself bitterly. If she were honest, she must confess to that same crime.

And why had she not recognized it before? She might tell herself she would not have favored Gavin over the other systems, but how could she have helped it? By thinking only of the love that filled every part of her, she had betrayed her people, her own honor—and all that Jarrod stood for.

Trees and mountains. Everywhere. Jarrod halted as he emerged from the shuttle and inhaled deeply of the familiar air. The spicy, pungent aromas surrounded him, filled his lungs. Pines, redwood, spruce, vacawood, cedar.

And the colors. Hills rolled beneath carpets of green. Mountains towered above them, purple and gray and peaked with white. From their slopes, myriad trees stretched toward the deep cerulean sky, each a blaze of yellows, golds, reds and every conceivable shade of green.

Home.

So very different from the endless amethyst seas and the salty ocean air that permeated everything on Kerrian.

A hand clapped on his shoulder, shoving him forward toward the top step. "Get along, there." The sergeant's grating voice held impatience now that the journey neared completion.

Jarrod caught his balance, a feat made difficult by the light but efficient shackles that bound his wrists behind his back. He descended the first stair, his step caught short by the inadequate length of the chain connecting the ankle bracelets. He was a prisoner, disgraced and unjustly accused of treason—but he was home.

Once on the paving, the guard caught his arm and

hustled him across to the waiting ground skimmer. Jarrod shuffled along as best he could, struggling to stay on his feet, mentally devising retribution for this overgrown muscle brain. Two more guards—neither displaying higher intellectual capabilities but both sporting brand new corporal stripes on their collars—brought up the rear.

The front passenger door swung upward, and a lieutenant unfolded his long, lanky body. A young man, newly commissioned, still suffering from youth. His freckled cheek showed the reddened rash of skin still unaccustomed to depilatories. A shock of unruly brown hair fell across his eyes. With a self-conscious gesture, he tugged at his uniform, straightening the set of his coat. "Give you any trouble?" he called.

The sergeant gave a derisive laugh. "He was just waiting for us at the spaceport! Would you believe it? The damned fool actually went there on his own to meet us! Unarmed, too. Not so much as a protest when we arrested him." Here he sounded disappointed.

He had been, too, Jarrod remembered. He'd taken the sergeant's measure within moments of laying eyes on the man. The guard's whole manner had begged his suspect to flee, to put up a fight, to provide any excuse whatsoever to rough him up a little. That kind of guy thought with his muscles and had the intellectual potential of a carrot.

The lieutenant looked Jarrod over, and nervousness spasmed over his long, narrow face. "Ambassador?" The kid swallowed. "I hope your journey was as comfortable as possible."

"Under the circumstances." Jarrod kept his voice genial, his face expressionless.

"Yes. Just so." The kid cleared his throat. "I'm

under orders to escort you to Merylar Citadel to face the tharl himself." He sounded awed at the prospect.

Jarrod allowed himself a slight smile. "I should hope so. That'll be the quickest way to clear up this business."

The lieutenant stepped back, gesturing toward the skimmer. The sergeant, unimpressed by his superior's deference to their prisoner, shoved Jarrod forward. One of the corporals ran to open the back door, and Jarrod found himself thrust inside the bright interior; the smoked plasti-roof of the skimmer let in full light.

The others climbed in, and the skimmer shivered as the engine roared into life. Odd, Jarrod had never noticed how much noise these cumbersome old engines made. Conversion to coral power would lighten the vehicles, increase their maneuverability, power and range. All this, without harming the atmosphere or creating hazardous by-products.

At the moment, the coral and acid lay under the control of the most honorable and caring person he'd ever met. But for how long? Could she remain in charge of the situation, outbluff those practiced diplomatic teams, maintain the upper hand in the negotiations? Dia, inexperienced, still uncertain about the fate of her father and bereft of competent counsel—

For the first time since facing the guards at the Kerrinian space port, he chafed at his shackles. He couldn't delay here; he'd have to speak with Dysart, give him whatever aid he could, make sure the tharldom was safe, then return to Kerrian. The mere thought of seeing Dia again sent a surge of elation, of desire, through every part of him.

With a tremor punctuated by a rising whine, the skimmer shot forward, lifting a meter from the ground where it remained. At first only the emptiness of their sector of the landing field shot past, then they threaded their way past other shuttles, other disembarking passengers, then offices, warehouses, factories. The residential area with its massive apartment complexes stood in the distance.

So many people, crammed into such close proximity. For a moment, the vast unpopulated seas of Kerrian rose in his mind. Purple seas, with masses of colorful lilies and hyacinths, and towering tufts of grasses and reeds growing from the shallows around the coral atolls. Lonely. A man could think there, come to know himself, find his soul. But he'd miss the towering pines and vacawoods.

The buildings thinned, and now they passed through sparse fields, which gave way rapidly to the rocky, brush-covered foothills. A scattering of trees sprang up on either side of the road, thickening to forests, heavily covered by undergrowth and boulders. Somewhere ahead, hidden by the towering tops of the redwoods and spruce, stood Merylar Citadel, the capital, the fortress. The prison.

His hands had gone numb, Jarrod realized. He shifted in his seat, trying to bring back the circulation. It was damned uncomfortable sitting this way, but he wasn't about to mention that fact to the sergeant. It would probably please the man immensely.

The terrain changed little except for the steepening of the angle at which they climbed. Jarrod clenched his hands against the sting of returning blood, forcing back his impatience to arrive. There would be delays enough in reaching Dysart once they entered the courtyard of the Citadel.

At last, they rounded the final curve and faced the high stone wall. Silver flecks gleamed in huge white

blocks hewn by stonemasonry tools in the ages long
before the advent of lasers. Old and powerful. Impene-
trable. Returning here after a visit to more recently
developed planets always gave Jarrod a sense of solidity,
of history, of permanence.

The iron-barred portcullis shrieked its protest as
unseen mechanisms dragged it upward. The skimmer
slowed, eased through the wide, arched tunnel of the
massive wall, then nosed to a halt on the cobbled stones
of the enclosed courtyard. Behind them, the bars
clanged back into position.

The skimmer door hissed up. Jarrod's escort scrambled out, then turned to drag him from the seat.
Jarrod stumbled on the uneven paving, caught his
balance, then strode as determinedly as his eclipsed
step could take him toward the steps leading to
the Citadel's door. The guards hurried to surround
him, trying to regain control of the situation, but
they seemed shaken by Jarrod's external display of
confidence and composure.

Good. That suited him just fine. He mounted the
shallow stone steps, and the sentry hurried to swing
the steel-enforced wooden door wide. Jarrod strode
through the arched entryway, and the cool darkness
of the marbled hall surrounded him.

"Where is Tharl Dysart?" Jarrod demanded of the
sentry.

The man opened his mouth, but subsided under
the sergeant's glare. "Forgetting yourself, aren't
you?" The sergeant jerked Jarrod's arm. "Prisoners
go where they're taken."

The nervous lieutenant cleared his throat. "Ambassador—"

"Temporarily relieved of duty," Jarrod assured
him. "I understood I came here to talk things over

with the tharl," he went on in a reasonable tone. "We might as well get all this straightened out at once. Where is he?"

The sentry looked relieved and nodded to the lieutenant. "The tharl is expecting you. He's in the Chamber of Justice."

The lieutenant's eyebrows rose. "I'll be glad to have this out of my hands," he admitted. "Am—Mor tolArvik?" He altered the title to a term of simple politeness.

"I know the way." Again, without waiting for his escort, Jarrod moved ahead. It gave him perverse satisfaction to hear them scramble after him.

Normally he could have outdistanced the guards easily with his long, swinging stride. The shackles hindered him, and the soldiers surrounded him once more before he'd gone five shortened steps. The lieutenant directed a reproachful glance at him, which Jarrod returned with a brisk nod, denoting neither apology nor defiance.

Their booted footsteps echoed through the stone hallway. The tapestries helped muffle the sound, but large threadbare patches now marred the colorful depictions of pivotal battle scenes, and moths and cheepas had chewed innumerable holes, leaving the yarns to unravel. Dark, heavily banded chests stood at intervals against the walls, still in position from a time when they stored supplies against the threat of siege.

The Chamber of Justice lay on the ground floor in the east wing, where the rising sun could shine through its tall, arching windows. Glistening shields redirected the rays so they would fall fully on the raised dais against the far wall where the accused

stood in the polished wooden cell, awaiting the pro-
nouncement of the verdict. That Dysart met them
here now, in mid-afternoon rather than the significant hour of dawn, reassured Jarrod.

The lieutenant threw the door wide, and Jarrod
preceded his escort into the long, shadowed room.
He peered through the dimness, seeking the shape
on the throne at the opposite side. Then lights flashed
on, two beams, one directed at the throne, the other
at the prisoner's dock.

A soft click announced the turning on of the sound
system, and a deep voice thundered over the speakers:
"Place the accused in the dock."

Jarrod advanced on his own, pulling his guard with
him. What the devil did Dysart think he was about,
using this ancient pomp? If it were his idea of a joke—

Jarrod's eyes narrowed. The glittering, golden
Robes of Justice hung oddly on Dysart. Limp around
the shoulders. The hood protruded forward, hiding
the face. The crown, an ancient war helm studded
with amber stones, held the hood down.

One of the corporals opened the polished cenna-
wood gate to the dock, and the sergeant shoved Jarrod
inside. The gate swung closed behind him, followed
a moment later by the sound of the bolt shooting
home. Only two possible ways out lay open to him
now: the door in the back wall on his right led to
the Gardens of Vindication, with their flowers and
fountains and singing birds; behind the door on his
left a black-hooded jailer would wait to lead the way
along a darkened corridor to the dungeons—and far
too frequently in the old days, to immediate execution.

Jarrod straightened and turned to face Dysart. "I'm

flattered." He had to raise his voice to be heard clearly in that vast chamber. "You're giving me the whole show."

The golden-robed figure leaned back on the throne. "I doubt you'll appreciate it for long."

Jarrod's brow snapped down. "Lomax? Great Artis, what the fire devils are you doing in that get-up? Where's your father? I came here to see the tharl."

"You *are* seeing the tharl." The haughtiness of the voice wavered, then returned. "My father is dead, and I have taken the tharldom in his place, by right of inheritance."

"Dead?" Jarrod demanded, incredulous. "How? When? He was fine less than a week ago. What happened?"

"He was murdered."

Murdered. Jarrod had come too late. Treachery! For a long moment he stared at Lomax, assimilating the news, knowing he had failed his tharl. Dysart, murdered.

His brow furrowed. That meant Dysart hadn't trumped up these treason charges to summon him home. And this charade of Lomax's—

"What's been going on?" Jarrod demanded. He leaned forward, and for the first time he tugged at his shackles, trying to free himself. "What do you mean, he was murdered?"

"A deeply laid plot," Lomax told him, "managed by a coward who wouldn't face either my father or me in ritual combat for the throne."

Jarrod ceased struggling. "But you *have* become tharl. You caught him, then?"

Lomax nodded, and the great war crown shifted on his head. He rammed it down into place. "We caught him before he could complete his mischief."

He turned to the low table that rested beside his throne and picked up the silken black cloth that lay there. He shook it out, then pulled it on over the crown so the folds completely covered his head and shoulders. Only slits showed the faintest gleam of his eyes, reflecting the powerful lights aimed at him.

With slow ceremony, Lomax rose to his feet. "Jarrod tolArvik, you have been found guilty of the highest treason—the murder of your sworn warrior chieftain and overlord, Tharl Dysart tolErrol, and stand condemned to death."

Chapter Seventeen

For a long, stunned minute, Jarrod stared at Lomax, unable to command his voice. At last, he said, "Me? *Me?* Kill Dysart? You're mad. You know how loyal I am to him. Think for a minute. I've been on Kerrian this past week. I even received a message from him after I arrived there."

"Obviously not from him. He was found stabbed in his rooms only minutes after you left the Citadel for the spaceport."

Jarrod stared straight ahead, his thoughts racing. "Someone *could* have manufactured that vid, I suppose—" He glared at Lomax. "Why wasn't I told? You should have reached me. Damn it, I've been trying to get through to you since that whole Kerrinian mess started. Why wouldn't you talk to me?"

"I wasn't taking any chances with anyone." Lomax adjusted the eye holes of the hood. "Not with treason of that nature afoot. And as it turned out in your case, I was right."

Jarrod's jaw tightened. "You know me better than that, Lomax. I've never wanted the tharldom. Take off that damned silly hood, and let's get to the bottom of this."

Lomax ignored the last. "Never wanted the tharldom? You swear to that, do you? Do you?" he repeated, intense.

"Of course I swear to it. Does that satisfy you? Dysart was a good man."

"So, you never wanted it." An angry purr sounded in Lomax's voice. "You think I have that short a memory? What about the games we played when we were kids?"

"The games— By the fires, Lomax, you just said it. We were children!" His eyes narrowed. "And as I remember, what I said was that you'd make such a rotten tharl, it was to be hoped *someone* would defeat you in combat before you got control of Gavin."

"You'd defeat me yourself, you said." Lomax's restless fingers toyed with the jeweled dagger hanging at his belt. "Well, you won't get the chance. You murdered my father, and you won't get away with it."

"*Why* would I murder him?" Jarrod demanded. "If I did it for the tharldom, I'd have made it a formal duel with the proper witnesses. And I wouldn't immediately leave the planet and—"

"But you had to, for the main part of your plan. Gaining the tharldom was only the means to your real end." Satisfaction sounded in Lomax's voice, as if he sprung his trap. "It's no secret you've been trying to court the Kerrinian princess. And it's equally obvious her ministers would never give her to a mere *ambassador*. Marriage to her means control of the richest prize in the galaxy. They'll want nothing less than the ruler of a planet for her. So you had to become tharl.''

Jarrod's bound hands clenched into useless fists. "I didn't kill Dysart."

"Don't try to deny it. I have proof. Not only of your murder of my father, but also of your little revolution on Kerrian."

"My—" Jarrod broke off, incredulous.

"You think we couldn't find out how you hired the mercenaries? Your dealings with the Cereans—"

"I spent two years in a Cerean slave mine," he said through gritted teeth. "I don't deal with Cereans."

"You'd do anything with a prize like coral at stake. Stage a revolution, set yourself up as Kerrian's hero, usurp my father's throne—"

Jarrod stared at him, silent, questions tumbling over each other in his mind. The plot sounded logical, but why choose him as its villain? Because of his role on Kerrian? What "proof" did they have? What made Lomax, or Dysart's guard, suspect him?

Lomax leaned back on his throne. "You've caused Gavin-Secundus considerable embarrassment. I've already extended my apologies to the princess, but that isn't enough. No, I'll make her proper reparation. I'll marry her myself."

"You'll—" Jarrod bit back the words that sprang to his tongue. "She'll never agree."

"My dear Jarrod, of course she will. She'll be so very grateful to me for saving her father's life."

"Saving—"

"I was on Kerrian when your revolution broke out, didn't you know? With King Harryl, in fact, when he was wounded, right at the start of the fighting. I managed to take him with me when I escaped."

"Why didn't you tell her? She's been sick with

worry, half-convinced he was dead, refusing to believe it—"

"I didn't want to ruin my little surprise."

"Your—" Jarrod took a step back, shaking his head. "By all the fire demons in Mount Beleron, I've been blind. *You* did it. All of it. You even killed your own father."

Lomax gave a short laugh. "Accusations won't do you any good. I've got all the proof I need. Your treason is over. You've lost. Tomorrow morning the charges against you will be publicly proclaimed, and your execution will follow at once. I'm sorry it's come to this." A touch of genuine regret sounded in his words.

"You'll live to be sorrier," Jarrod breathed.

"Possibly. But one does what one must for the good of one's planet, no matter how great the sacrifice. My father's brother knew this."

"He died while a prisoner of war in the slave mines on Ceres Alpha, trying to lead us in an escape," Jarrod reminded him. "He didn't murder his own father."

Lomax's hands clenched. "You don't see the similarity? Each is a form of slavery, a form of sacrifice, suffered for the greater good."

"Flaming Artis, you don't really believe that drivel, do you? You offer up your patricide on the high altar of Gavin? The planet would be offended."

"Not patricide. Regicide. And not for politics, but for business. But we digress. The crime is yours, not mine. You forget yourself. Guard!" He raised his hand in summons. "See the prisoner settled for his last night, in some cell where his ravings won't disturb anyone. He continues in his treason, and will try to spread his poison about me everywhere."

Jarrod shook his head. "I'm not letting you get

away with this," he breathed. "Dia—" Rage welled in him at the thought of her having to submit to Lomax to save her father's life. He struggled against the shackles, trying to tear his hands free, but only managing to shred his flesh. He couldn't reach Lomax, couldn't strangle the man as the lying traitor deserved.

"Take him away," Lomax repeated. He rose, dragged off the black silk hood, and left the chamber.

If the Rualdan ambassador patted her hand one more time, Dia reflected, she would throw something at him. All of them, even the junior members of their staffs, hung about her, unashamedly flattering her, since Jarrod's departure. And Madam Chevika. Dia refrained from looking at her. The Quy'doan woman positively smothered her with motherly advice. Every one of them wanted to assume Jarrod's officially unofficial place as her advisor.

Tarquin tolRendal, Jarrod's second-in-command, now ambassador-elect in his superior's absence, rose from the table and paced to the window. "This is a planet of serenity," he announced to the company at large. "I'm surprised you haven't had a number of spiritual sects begging permission to build temple boats here for retreats."

"We have." Remaining polite grew harder every minute.

He turned back to her. "How unpleasant all these negotiations must be to anyone from this planet. You should be allowed to devote your time to meditation and contemplation."

"Those who are given to such activities do," she snapped. "The rest of us get on with the very profitable business of an extremely well-run tourist industry. Don't fret on our account, *Acting* Ambassador. We're much sharper than our sarongs and shell necklaces lead people to suspect. Now, we're still discussing the fifth clause, about setting up a board to monitor the use of coral power."

"Impossible!" Lord Feldar declared, and many heads nodded in agreement.

"Only if we rely on honor." Dia held the Bertolian's gaze a moment. "That seems to be a commodity sadly lacking in our quadrant. From your reactions, it seems I can't count on any of you to keep your word that you won't build weapons with our coral."

"It would be necessary, for the defense of Rualda!" Lord Pieral came to his feet in his intensity. "Those— those others—" He broke off, satisfying himself with a wave of his hand that encompassed the entire table, and the staffers who sat behind. "*They* will build weapons in secret, hoping to gain an advantage over those of us who desire to comply with your wishes. Are we to let ourselves be destroyed, to be made slaves—" his gaze settled on Xar, who ignored him, "—at your whim?"

"So you would purchase coral in good faith, then sadly be forced to break your promise to assure your own safety." Dia allowed her voice to go flat, as if defeated.

The Bertolian cleared his throat. "It *might* prove our only option, Lady. We wouldn't want to, of course—"

"No, of course you wouldn't, Lord Feldar," she agreed.

He smiled at her. "Of course not. But if you could have prevented the recent bloodshed here, saved your father from whatever fate has overtaken him, simply by creating one deterrent weapon, wouldn't you have done it? No matter what you might have naively believed when you agreed not to do so?"

"In other words," Dia said slowly, "if I insist on that clause in the treaty, you all warn me you may have to break it because you can't trust each other?"

"There are those who cannot be trusted," Madam Chevika told her.

"It would not be done easily or lightly, but one must assure the protection of one's planet," Pieral agreed.

"I see. Then since you can't trust each other, it seems I can't trust any of you." She stood. "It seems we have nothing to discuss. Goodbye. I hope you all have safe trips home."

Complete silence met that gambit. Then Madam Chevika laughed. "Your tactics are too blatant, my dear regent. We are used to more subtlety."

"I'm used to straight-forward honesty. I have control of something you want. You want it for something I find morally wrong. Therefore I can't let you have it. Simple, isn't it?"

"But there are so many other uses for the coral power!" Pieral objected. "You cannot deny Rualda— all our systems—the advantages it could bring!"

"I'm not denying them," Dia pointed out. "You are. Decide amongst yourselves a way to monitor its use—and to keep all of you from agreeing together to try to fool me. I'll let you think about it for a few minutes."

She rose and strode to the plasti-clear wall to stare across the ocean. Twenty-six standard hours. One full day and six long hours into the next since she'd last seen Jarrod. He'd be on Gavin-Secundus by now, probably even at Merylar Citadel. Possibly, he'd even

seen Uncle Dysart and found out the reason behind
Lomax's accusations.

How long would it be before he contacted her, told
her everything was all right, that he was coming back?
She closed her eyes, conjuring up his image in her
memory. He stood so straight, so proud. In her mind,
his eyes gleamed as they had the last time he kissed
her. This evening, she decided, if she hadn't heard
from him, she would try to contact Dysart herself.

Voices rose behind her, and she glanced back to
where the ambassadors and their staffs argued. A
smile tugged at her lips. She wouldn't trust a single
one of them out of her sight. Trust. She trusted Jarrod.
He, alone of these diplomats, had proved himself
honorable.

And that, she realized, vindicated her love for him.
They were both aware of the split loyalties created by
the bond between them. They wouldn't have yielded
to it to grant one another unmerited concessions.
On the contrary, they would have fought against it
at the negotiating table, driven harder bargains in
their treaties to assure fairness. But any agreement
Jarrod made, she could trust him to keep.

For the rest of these vultures, she needed an elaborate system of checks and balances. In the end, even
the Cereans would be forced to agree to it. But, by
denying the quadrant coral as a fuel for weapons, she
would have to make other concessions to keep them
happy, to keep them from going to war against her.
She'd make it where they least expected it but most
wanted it—in their credit accounts.

She had no intention of price gouging, anyway; the
poorer systems needed coral even more than did the
wealthy ones. Coral and jellactic acid were rare com-
modities. The amount each system could purchase

would be based on population, not on how much they could pay.

The discussions continued throughout dinner, by which time Dia only wanted to escape the noise and argument. At least they'd reached the stage of discussing the statistical demographic makeup of the inspection teams. She excused herself as early as she could without openly giving offense, and left them to work out the details of the proposal they would give her in the morning.

Three techs sat around the comm room, only one, a young woman, actually at her vid screen transferring progress reports to and from Waianoa. The other two, a man and woman, played cards and drank stimi. They looked up as Dia entered. The man jumped to his feet, his expression one of agonized guilt, but the woman merely saluted.

"All quiet, I take it?" Dia waved to the tech at the screen, poured herself a mug from the steaming pot, and joined the other two. "Can you raise Merylar Citadel for me? I need the tharl. Himself. In person."

"I can try." The girl, whose nametag proclaimed her to be Rhetta, spun in her chair to face a console. "He's apparently been in seclusion of some sort. Wouldn't even take messages from his ambassador."

"He'll talk to me." Dia folded her arms. "There's more than one kind of coral power." For the first time in her planet's history, they held the trump card. She intended to use it, if need be.

Rhetta grinned as she keyed up Gavin-Secundus. She made a quick check on the read out, and uttered an exclamation of disgust. "It's the middle of the night at the Citadel, Lady. Do you still want me to try?"

Dia swore softly. Not the best time to beg—or

threaten—for favors. "Four standard hours 'til normal business time," she muttered. "All right, wake me at oh-three-hundred. We'll do it then."

Rhetta tapped in the wake-up call, then spun around in her chair. "All set. See you then."

Four hours. But she'd make Dysart talk to her, make sure he understood Jarrod's innocence. And maybe she'd be able to talk to Jarrod, as well, tell him they'd betrayed no one, not even each other. He could stay away until the negotiations were finished, then . . .

But she couldn't let herself dream, not yet. She had to face her ministers, find out where they stood on the issue of marriage treaties. If they felt it necessary she marry a head of state—well, who said Kerrian needed a royal family? She could resign, and the ministers could commandeer some other poor soul to delight the tourists.

Oh-three-hundred hours came way too early. Her comm chimed insistently until she dragged her eyes open wide enough to see where to shut it off. For a moment she lay in her bed, gathering the thoughts that had scattered at the rude jarring from her dream, then memory clicked on. Time for a quick conference with Dysart.

She pulled on a sarong and regretted not having stimi sent up instead of the comm-call. With her hair combed and braided, she at least looked passable. At this hour, that would have to do. She made her way along the dimly illuminated corridors to the comm room.

Rhetta looked up from the monitor as Dia strode in. "I've already got the Citadel for you. Want it up there?" She nodded toward the wall-sized screen.

"Where you've got it'll do fine." Dia slid into a

chair beside the girl. The image of the Citadel filled
the screen. "Have you told them it's for Dysart—and
urgent?"

"Will now." Rhetta's fingers flew over the keys, the
screen blinked, then a Gavonian tech stared at them.
Rhetta relayed Dia's message.

The tech inclined his head. "Tell the Lady of Kerrian the tharl will be with her in a moment."

So she hadn't needed her trump after all, her threat
to withhold coral. She sat back, relieved and happy.
He was still her Uncle Dysart, everything would be
all right. He'd tell her he never believed Lomax's
nonsense about Jarrod.

The screen blinked again, and this time Lomax's
face stared at her. He regarded her solemnly for a
long moment while she stared back, too surprised to
speak.

"Where—where's Dysart?" she demanded at last.
"I want to talk to your father."

Lomax shook his head. "Sorry, Dia. You said you
had an urgent message for the tharl."

"So where is he?"

He leaned back in his chair. "*I* am tharl."

She clenched her jaw. "Listen, Lomax, I don't have
time for your power games. In case you're not aware of
it, it's the middle of the night here. This is important.
Where's your father?"

"No game. My father's dead. Murdered."

"*Murdered?* Lomax, I—I'm sorry." Uncle Dysart,
murdered. . . . And her own father. . . . Numbness
seized her brain, and she shook her head to free her
thinking. "How?" she demanded. "When?"

"The worst kind of treachery, stabbed by a man
he trusted. One who tried to get his claws into you,
too, Dia."

She drew in a shaky breath. "What do you mean?" Though after his message of the other day, the horrible possibilities clamored in her mind.

"His supposedly loyal ambassador. Jarrod tolArvik. We found proof that he was behind your revolution and my father's murder."

"Jarrod—"

"I'm sorry you can't have him for trial and punishment. My claims on him were greater. You'll be glad to know he's already been executed for his crimes. At first dawn, this morning." He glanced at his wrist chronometer. "Two hours ago."

Two hours. Jarrod. Dead. . . .

"We're safe from his schemes now, Dia, but I think there's a way we can assure it stays that way."

She shook her head. He had to be lying. Jarrod couldn't be dead. He hadn't committed any crimes, he hadn't murdered Dysart, none of this made any sense. . . .

"Dia?" Lomax, frowning, studied her. "There's one of that traitor's schemes that didn't work. Your father."

She sat up, gripping the edge of the desk. "My— Where's Dad?"

"Here." He motioned with his hand and the view shifted, drawing back to include three other figures who had been just out of sight before.

"Dad," Dia whispered. Hope surged through her, shattering the last remnants of her composure. "Dad?"

He appeared half asleep, leaning heavily against the shoulder of one of the two guards who stood on either side of him. Older, she thought dazedly. Ill. His eyes remained unfocused, as if he weren't aware of the monitor.

"He was wounded before I could get him to safety," Lomax informed her. He swiveled in his chair and studied her father. "He's in pretty bad shape, I'm afraid. In fact, I'm not sure how much longer we'll be able to keep him alive."

A chill settled over her heart. "What do you mean?"

He spun back to face the monitor, his mouth pursed in a tight line. "I think it's safe to say he's got only one real chance to pull through. One," he repeated for emphasis.

"What's that?"

"For you to marry me."

"Marry?" She broke off and shook her head. "By the Great Net, what are you talking about? How would that help him?"

Lomax's jaw set. "I've done a great deal of thinking about it, Dia. Let's just say he'd like to see the union of his daughter and the son of his best friend."

"He wouldn't like anything of the sort!" Her eyes narrowed. "Just what are you playing at?"

"I think you know what I mean." His fingers tapped restlessly on the desk. "If we sign a marriage agreement, your father will recover to live a long, healthy life. If not— Well, there's only just so much doctors can do."

"You mean if not, you'll kill him!" Dia slashed her hand across the control panel, cutting the connection, then surged from her chair. Her shoulders shook as she stood with her back to the monitor, hugging herself, wanting to scream. Jarrod dead, her father not ill but drugged, a prisoner, his life hostage to her agreement to wed Lomax.

Her trump card. Her wonderful win-all trump card. Useless. Lomax held the only hand that could beat it.

Chapter Eighteen

Dia could guess now what had happened to Uncle Dysart, why there seemed to be a Gavonian connection to the revolution. Even why Jarrod had to die. But Lomax wouldn't get away with it.

She had to stop him. But how? She paced to the wall then back again, hands clenched, still hugging herself. She had to plan, she had to think, to get her brain out of this numbed state and functioning again.

"Lady?" One of the techs—Lector, according to his nametag—stood in front of her, a mug of hot stimi in his hand. "Drink this, Lady. Good for shock."

"Thanks." Her voice barely made a sound. She grabbed the beverage, aware of heat. In the back of her mind she knew she must be burning her hands, her mouth, her tongue, but it didn't matter. Nothing mattered. Jarrod, Dad— She drained the cup and he refilled it, pressing it once more into her hands.

Half way through this one, the blur that formed her world began to clear. A plan, she reminded herself. She needed some way of defeating him, of rescuing her father without giving Lomax what he wanted. If she married him—no, that prospect was unthinkable. Even if she did, she had no guarantee he'd free her father. More like, he'd keep him under his domination, a drugged puppet, leaving Lomax in control of the coral.

Why couldn't she think of something? She might have so little time. . . .

The comm unit chimed with an incoming message. Dia clutched her stimi and nodded to Rhetta. The tech keyed up the screen; Dia stayed well out of sight.

Lomax, his expression intense, regarded them. "We lost our connection. No matter, you may tell your lady it's been re-established. Ah, there you are, Dia," he added as she stepped into view. "What, no warm greeting for your bridegroom?"

She clenched her teeth, twisting her mouth into a caricature of a smile. "It's all so sudden."

He gave a short laugh. "It's about to become even more so, I'm afraid."

Her hands clenched on the back of Rhetta's chair. "What do you mean?"

"I'm worried about your father. To be blunt, I don't think he has a minute to waste. There's a very good chance he might not survive if you don't come to see him quickly."

"How quickly?"

"Be here within twenty-three standard hours. That should give you time to pack a few necessities and order a ship to meet you at the spaceport. Twenty-three hours, no more. You may be very sure I'll count every minute of them until you're here—and the marriage document's signed."

"Twenty—I can't. I have a palace full of ambassadors and their staffs. We're in the middle of treaty negotiations!"

He raised his eyebrows. "How very sad. I was sure you'd want to do everything in your power to give your father the will to live. Really, Dia, I never thought you could be so selfish. Twenty-three hours," he repeated, and broke the connection.

Dia sank onto a chair and rubbed her aching eyes. "Twenty-three hours," she said. "By the Net, how—" She broke off, worrying her lower lip between her teeth.

"He's trying to force you into this before you can get one of the other systems to help you." Lector boosted himself up to sit on the table top behind him. He cocked an eyebrow at her. "Any of them likely to be of any use?"

"Without weeks of negotiating and a lifetime of payoffs?" Dia shook her head. "One of them would have. Ambassador tolArvik. But Lomax had him killed." There, she'd said it. So why didn't she cry or rant or just *react*? Why did she have to feel so numb, so empty, as if it couldn't be true? Lomax would never have attempted this outrage if Jarrod had been alive to challenge him.

"Twenty-three hours." Rhetta drew in a deep breath and let it out on a sigh. "That leaves you just over an hour to get out of here."

"If we had a space fleet—" Lector began.

"We don't," Rhetta snapped back. "And if she took our armed merchant transports with her, that would leave us wide open for an attack from our diplomatic friends."

"So we let her marry that—that—wampa bait?" Lector demanded.

Dia rubbed her arms, chilled, and her fingers brushed across her rys-bracelet. The rys-bracelet.

Lomax was one of the few who knew its secret. For once, she couldn't count on it; for her it would be nothing more than an adornment, a piece of jewelry.

A piece of jewelry.

She straightened. A piece of jewelry. One her honor guard could wear. They'd have time enough for target practice on the twenty-two hour journey to Gavin-Secundus. She only had to have something made, something innocent-seeming, something an unarmed, ceremonial guard would be expected to wear.

A brooch, to hold his cloak.

"Jewelers," she declared. "Rhetta, I need jewelers and an armsman. Quickly! Lector, I want an honor guard. Eelam and Sorin, and four others. In the workshop here, in ten minutes." She strode out the door, her mind racing. She needed Agathas, someone to buy her time with the ambassadors. She grabbed the door frame and swung about to face back into the room. "Get me Rastor sett Danies in Waianoa. Fly him here by shuttle, make sure he's in the palace by morning. He'll have to tell everyone I've got some virus."

"Caught from one of those mercenaries," Lector called after her. He leaned over his vid screen once more, linking up for more messages.

Dia ran down the corridor. Agathas could deal with the household, plan the proper meals, keep up the fiction that Dia lay in her rooms indisposed. All should progress well here, at least.

A door opened just ahead, and her maid Loris stumbled out, dragging on a dressing gown. She blinked tired eyes. "Lady? Rhetta signaled you needed me."

Bless Rhetta. In a few words, Dia explained the situation. "Within the hour," she finished. "We're— Oh, damn! Transportation to the spaceport! I forgot to ask for it. Can you make sure we have some skimmers ready?"

Loris nodded. "Will I be going too, Lady?"

"I—" Dia broke off, then shook her head. "I'd love the company, but you'll be needed here, to keep up the fiction I'm sick."

Loris folded her arms. "Which means you think this mission is dangerous and you don't want me along."

A reluctant smile touched Dia's lips. "Well, that too. Get going. I've got a lot of planning to do still."

She could count on Loris. That only left seeing to the brooches. She made her way along corridors lit only by the dim glow along the floor, at last letting herself into the throne room.

Third turtle, she reminded herself. Her fingers searched the muraled wall panels, at last uncovering the hidden locking mechanism. She keyed in her code and a section slid open. No lights illuminated the contents; she reached inside, letting her fingers find what she needed. A moment later she drew out a velvet bag filled with odd, sharp shapes.

She sealed the emergency safe and once more made her way through the maze of corridors. As she neared the workroom, she saw the door stood open. A man, running from the opposite direction, ducked inside. Dia hurried to join him.

Two men already stood at one of the long tables. The newcomer, still panting just inside the doorway, looked up at her and grinned. "Got a job for us, Lady?" Sorin demanded.

"Could be a suicide mission." She looked over the other two. "Carel, thank the Net you're here. Did Lector tell you what I want?"

"That he did, Lady, but I can't give you six weapons. I only had four of these." The armsman held out his hand. On his palm rested four tiny laser pistols, each only three centimeters long.

"Four," she repeated. "Well, that will have to do. At least that's four more than our friends will be expecting."

Sorin perched on the edge of the table, his eager gaze on her. "Do I get to know why I'm offering up my life? Not that I'm not pleased to serve you any way I can, of course, Lady, but—"

"Rescue mission for my father. Lomax took him captive."

Sorin gave a soundless whistle. "I knew he went in for cut-throat business deals, but kidnapping? What's he demanding, the deed of sale for our planet?"

"He's settling with marrying me. I—" She broke off as Eelam entered, followed a moment later by another man carrying a tool box.

Sorin straightened. "I'd like to hear more when you get the chance," he said, and drew back, out of the way.

She caught him. "Right now, I'd like you to find Agathas. Four ceremonial cloaks, from the storerooms. The more feathers, the better. And get anything else that looks ridiculously touristy, will you? We want to put on a show, distract them from the fact that part of the costumes are weapons."

Sorin nodded, grinning. "Come on, Eelam." He caught the new arrival. "How long do we have?" he called back over his shoulder.

"Forty minutes. You'll have to pack, too. And warn whoever else will be acting as my honor guard. Remember, our getting back alive will depend on our wits." She turned to the jewelers. "Four brooches," she said. "They have to work like this." She stripped off her rys-bracelet and showed them the mechanism.

Dia sat on the lounge chair in the shuttle's cabin, staring straight ahead. The bracelet hummed on her left arm, sending an uneasy shiver through her. She'd used it before, it would be easier this time; she'd had practice. Only this time, her father's life lay at stake.

She touched the ornament and every sense came alive with the vibration that only her inner ear could hear. Power. Raw, vibrant power. But it was only as good as its channeling, as its user. She couldn't depend on it, but only on herself.

A sharp rap sounded on her cabin door, and she drew a shaky breath. Time, already. They hadn't practiced nearly enough, so much of their plan remained at the whim of chance. She rose and faced the door. "Enter," she called, pleased that her voice didn't shake.

The door slid noiselessly apart in the middle and Sorin, garbed formally in his purple guard's sarong, bowed low before stepping over the threshold.

Her lips twitched. "Practicing your part?"

He grinned, full of youth and eagerness. "I don't think I want to go back to being an assistant cook when this is all over."

She shook her head. "Being a ceremonial guard is a lot flashier and a lot more fun, but being a cook is infinitely safer."

"Maybe I need a reprieve from 'safe.' And it looks like we've all got one, now. The captain just initiated landing procedure, Lady."

"Show time." She managed a smile. "Just think of them as particularly disagreeable tourists, and let's go give them the business." He raised his arm in a salute, and she moved past him into the corridor.

The command room stood at the far end. As Dia neared it the door whispered open. She stepped inside, only to stop short at sight of the image on the giant vid screen. A large ball, mostly blue but with vast patches of brown, swirled overall by a delicate mist of white. She recognized the last as clouds. The blue would be oceans. And the brown . . .

"Land?" she breathed. She strode forward, staring. She'd seen pictures in her learning programs, examined models, but she'd never *seen*, not like this. She'd never been off world before. On Kerrian, every season was tourist season, the royal family always on display, and spare money simply didn't exist to take vacations away from the quadrant's primary vacation destination.

"There's got to be water breaking up all that land," Sorin declared. He stood just behind her, staring over her shoulder. "No one could exist on anything that *dry*."

"You'll find out for yourselves in a few minutes," the captain called to them.

Eelam came up on her other side. "According to the stat reports, it's rich in minerals and has an animal population like we've never dreamed of."

"Umm. Like traitors." Sorin turned away as if unwilling to find anything to interest him in this planet.

Dia touched his arm. "We're going to free my father, Sorin."

"You bet, Lady," Eelam stuck in. "We're not leaving this place without him."

Dia glanced at him, surprised by the intensity in his voice.

He shrugged, as if trying to pass it off lightly. "Well, what's wrong with a bit of loyalty to our king? All the guards wanted in on this one."

"On a probable suicide mission?" she demanded.

Eelam looked down, embarrassed. "He's our king. You're the princess. It's an honor to be chosen."

"Great Nets," Dia breathed, and turned away. She'd never suspected such loyalty. And now she felt doubly responsible for their safety. Well, she'd just have to bring them all back alive, she supposed.

She strapped herself into one of the lounge chairs for landing, and stared blindly at the screen as they sped down to Merylar spaceport. Unbidden, against her will, Jarrod's image rose before her eyes, tall, dark, laughing. Jarrod—dead, because of Lomax's treachery. No, she wouldn't let Lomax win all; he had cost her too dearly already.

"Lady?" Sorin snapped loose his harness and swung out of his chair. "As you said: Show time."

"Cloaks." She looked around and saw one of her guards passing out the ankle-length garments with their intricately embroidered pattern of feathers. To her he offered the last, the heaviest, the one actually constructed from toroq egret feathers. She draped it about her shoulders, then fastened it with a brooch identical to those of her four honor guard—except hers lacked the laser pistol. She'd have to rely on her rys-bracelet, keep it hidden and hope its deadly use slipped Lomax's memory.

She checked her four companions, adjusted a couple of the cloaks, then nodded. She stepped forward; the captain saluted her, then palmed open the hatchway. It hissed outward and down, becoming a short flight of stairs.

Dry, pungently scented air filled her lungs. No salt, no spray on her face, just this itchy, *dusty* sensation. She coughed, then coughed again, and drew in another lungful of this unfamiliar air.

She started forward, down the steps. Once on the paved landing pad, she paused and regarded her reception committee. No Lomax in sight. That relieved her. Only six men faced her, the new Tharl's honor guard by their dress. They stood stiffly at attention, their imploders crossing their bodies and clasped in both hands. Armed. But her four men wore coral brooches, primed with jellactic acid. That made the odds almost even. No, better for her, for the Gavonians wouldn't be expecting the jewelry to be lethal.

The captain of the Gavonian guards stepped forward and bowed deeply to her. "Welcome, Princess. The tharl awaits you."

He might be awaiting her, but she could only hope he wasn't expecting what he was getting. The bracelet vibrated again, as if reacting to her inner hatred, and Dia closed her fingers over one of the metal wires. The less attention it drew, the better.

The captain's gaze settled on the coral medallion that rested on her forehead, suspended from a band of pearls. Greed flickered across his features, and several moments passed before he looked away, down to her brooch. His darting glance took in the ones fastening the guards' cloaks. Good. Let him think the jewelry nothing more than an ostentatious display of wealth. Other fragments of coral already sizzled away in the implosion chambers, out of sight, arming the weapons.

He led the way to where three skimmers rested just beyond the pad. Dia followed slowly, looking about. Even her eyes felt dry, she realized, blinking to bring them needed moisture.

But what sights there were to see! Sharp, high peaks that must be part of mountain ranges. They looked impossibly long, taking up so much room, stretching endlessly like a horizon, only much higher in the sky. And trees. All shapes, all sizes, covered in leaves of a multitude of colors and patterns. Even the sky looked different, a brilliant blue without even a trace of amethyst. A cloud drifted overhead, and she stared at it, wondering where the moisture could have come from to form it.

"Princess?" The captain recalled her attention. He stood beside the middle skimmer, its door raised and waiting for her.

She accepted his hand and allowed him to help her into the middle row of seats. The upholstery was soft and yielding, but she couldn't stand or move about. More like a canoe than an outboard, she decided, and fought off the unpleasant feeling of being encapsulated. Sorin entered next, winked at her, and settled back to study his surroundings. One of her other guards—Jorn, a seasoned trooper in dealing with tourists—took a seat behind them. The other places filled with Gavonians.

She glanced back through the windows, but couldn't see the rest of her escort. Where were Eelam and her other experienced guard, Rixhard? In the skimmer in front of them, or the one behind?

The door hissed downward, closing them inside,

and the engine vibrated as it sprang to life. The skimmer eased forward, lifting from the ground, then shot across the paved area of the landing strip. They followed a wide road, hovering about a meter above it.

Rocks, Dia decided, spotting the large, rounded gray lumps where they protruded between trees and underbrush. They didn't look anything like the volcanic stone of Kerrian. But this was Gavin-Secundus, and a very different collection of minerals, ores, and who knew what all else lurked in the planet's core. Geology was not her specialty. She was better at analyzing tourists.

Never had she dreamed so many trees could be packed so close together, that she couldn't even see through them. And tiny specks of color that must be wildflowers, for they reminded her of the patches of water lilies floating on the surface of her familiar seas.

Jarrod. Everything here reminded her of Jarrod. He'd talked of trees, of rocks, of bushes, and now she saw them for herself, perhaps the very ones of which he'd spoken. This was his planet, and here she could sense him, almost feel his presence again. Here, she could be a part of him. Here, she could almost forget he was dead.

Anguish rose through her, a lessening of the numbness that had choked off her heart and enabled her to function. Jarrod . . . For a long moment she gave way to the ache of longing, the unbearable emptiness that opened like an unfillable void within her. Jarrod. . . .

Not now! Part of her mind, some residual scrap of logic, took hold. She couldn't sink into that unending pit of loneliness and emptiness, not yet. She had first to avenge him, avenge her cousin and all the others

who had died or suffered on her planet because of
Lomax. She had to rescue her father. Only then could
she allow herself the luxury of grief.

Something moved among the trees at ground level,
off to her left. A light flashed, followed by another,
then an eerie whining noise crescendoed over the
thrum of the engine, deafening her. Imploders.

She tensed, clutching the back of the seat before
her. Sorin grabbed her arm, dragged her down to
the skimmer's floor, and threw himself on top of her.

"I can't breathe!" she managed to gasp as his
weight crushed her.

"I suppose you'll be able to with an imploder blast
through the chest?" But Sorin shifted his position a
little, easing off her so his arms covered her instead.

Dia peered over his shoulder in time to see one of
the Gavonians in the back seat crumple, his hands
crossing over his neck where the imploder blast
seared his flesh. The other skimmers seemed out of
control, darting this way and that on evasion courses.
She couldn't see any heads, had no idea how many
had been hit.

A high, anguished cry broke from their driver. For
a moment he sat perfectly erect, then slumped over
the control panel. Their skimmer lurched, spun sideways with reckless abandon, and Dia stared in horror
at the massive tree that raced toward them. It filled the
front window, then the collision threw her forward,
slamming her into the other seat. For a long moment
nothing existed except the scream of tortured metal
and the splintering of glass, then even these faded
into the blackness that engulfed her.

Chapter Nineteen

Shouts, the hissing whine of imploder fire, a dull ache that filled every part of her head and neck— Dia opened her eyes to find herself surrounded by darkness. Soft, velvety darkness punctuated by sharp prickles that pressed against her cheek. Cloth, she realized, as her senses returned. Cloth decorated with feathers. She drew back from where her face had been pressed against Sorin's cloak.

"Lady?" Her guard held her on the floor of the skimmer, his body shielding her.

"What?" She moved her head gingerly, and the throbbing pain settled in her left temple. "We were attacked?"

He nodded. "I haven't spotted the others, yet, but all the cars are down."

"Welcome to Gavin-Secundus." Dia gave a short laugh. "Think this is the normal greeting, or do you suppose someone other than me intends to prevent my marriage to Lomax?"

Abruptly, the outside noise stopped. No flashing lights, no crackling hiss of imploders. Nothing. For several long moments no sound reached her at all, not even the shrieking complaints of birds. Not even the moans of the injured. She shifted, but Sorin held her down.

"I want to see what's—"

"Lie still," he hissed.

The underbrush rustled, and Dia tensed. "Anyone in here able to use a weapon?"

Sorin eased from her and looked into the seat behind them. His jaw tightened. "Jorn?"

A shaky breath sounded. "Yeah." A pause. "This guy's dead. I'll—there, got his imploder. What about the ones up front?"

Dia dragged herself to a sitting position and fumbled for the pulse point on the driver's neck. Nothing. Her hand came away covered in blood. She glanced at Sorin, who checked the other guard. He grimaced and shook his head.

"Eerie," Dia said. "Three Gavonians dead, three Kerrinians alive."

"Yeah." Sorin craned his neck to look at the skimmer in front of them. Two Gavonian guards lay sprawled across their vehicle, lifeless. Others slumped inside. Only one figure moved. "Eelam," Sorin breathed. "He looks okay."

"So's Rixhard." Jorn sounded relieved. "He's in the car behind us. That makes all Kerrinians alive. But none of the Gavonians are moving."

"Then—" Dia broke off.

She hadn't heard any movement, yet ten figures had emerged from the protective trees and surrounded the downed skimmers. The men moved slowly forward, closing the circle. Each held an imploder at the ready.

Dia raised her arm, the thrumming of her bracelet her source of courage. Ten against two—unless her other three guards could get their hands on weapons. The brooches would be no good at this range.

One of the attackers raised his hand, and the band of guerrilla fighters stopped. Their leader moved forward a pace, then grabbed his helmet and dragged it off. He cast it on the ground and continued toward them, heading for the center car where Dia sat, steadying her aim.

He was tall, with thick, waving brown hair tumbling about his shoulders, secured from his eyes by a band about his forehead. His features— She shook her head. "Jarrod?" she whispered, not quite daring to hope. Then, "Jarrod!" His name tore from her, half a sob, half a cry of triumph.

She struggled with the door, unable to open it. Then Jarrod reached her, leaned through the front window, touched the skimmer's control panel. The door hissed up, opening, freeing her. She stumbled out, falling into his arms, and he clasped her tight, lifting her off her feet.

She found his mouth, kissed him, clung to him, and kissed him again. He lowered her slowly until her toes touched the ground, but never eased the tightness of his hold. She buried her face against his chest and realized she had started to cry.

"Dia," he murmured. His mouth nuzzled along the side of her face, near her ear. "It's all right, love. I didn't mean to frighten you, but under the circumstances, there wasn't any other way."

"Frighten?" She pushed back to stare up into his face. *"Frighten?!* You idiot, he told me you were dead! I've been sick, thinking I'd lost you, and now you think some imbecilic stunt like this could—could—'' She broke off, shaking so hard she couldn't control her voice.

"Oh, love." He dragged her against himself with a rueful laugh. "Great Artis, I'm sorry, Dia."

She sniffed, and held him tighter than ever. "You owe me an explanation."

"That I do. These men—" He nodded his head toward the guerrillas, who busied themselves dragging the bodies of the Gavonian soldiers from the skimmers. "They're friends, loyal to old Dysart. We served together, under Dysart's brother, in the Cerean war."

"Dysart?" Dia studied his face, and her heart sank. "He's really dead, then?"

Jarrod's jaw set. "Lomax killed him."

"His own father?"

"I doubt he planned it. Dysart must have found out about Lomax hiring the mercenary army, or maybe he discovered your father had been brought here as a prisoner. I don't know. But with his father dead, and the tharldom thrust on him, he must have discovered how unpopular he is—and how necessary it was to change that, and fast."

"Marriage to the coral," Dia stuck in.

Jarrod nodded. "I was likely to interfere with that, so he told me his father's murder took place earlier than it really did, and blamed me for it. His only mistake was that the captain of the Citadel guard was an old friend of mine."

"So he let you escape." Dia relaxed against him.

"Actually, he came with me. But now, love, I need to get back into the Citadel. And you're going to have to help me."

She shook her head. "*I* need to get in to rescue my father, and I suppose *you're* going to have to help *me.*"

He grinned. "All right, we help each other. Step one, get us all inside."

She smiled, too. Relief at having him back, with her, alive, flowed through her, but it was more than that. In Jarrod and his friends, she had found powerful, dependable allies in this dangerous undertaking. For the first time, real hope began to replace her grim determination. "Step one," she told him, "you're going to be recognized at the door."

"Already thought of that. One of those ceremonial helmets you Kerrinians wear should do the trick. Mind if I change places with one of your guards?"

A quick comparison of size determined that Rixhard came closest to Jarrod's large build. Already, Jarrod's companions changed into the clothing appropriated from the dead Gavonian guardsmen. Rixhard and Jarrod joined them, and in a surprisingly short time six Gavonian honor guards, three drivers, and four seeming Kerrinians took their places in the hastily cleaned skimmers. The one remaining guerrilla set about the task of hiding the bodies.

"Do I look Kerrinian?" Jarrod asked as he settled in the seat beside Dia. His hand closed over hers, and his fingers traced tantalizing circles in her palm.

She studied him, an occupation that gave her considerable satisfaction. "Large," she pronounced at last, "but I doubt anyone will pay any real attention to you. The nose piece hides your face well enough. Feeling bereft without a weapon?"

His mouth twitched into a wry smile. "Nothing like a good imploder in your hands to build the confidence."

"How about a brooch fastening your cloak? Take a good look at the clasp, then make sure the hasp stays at the top. Touch the bottom—no, don't! It's already armed. Just see where the mechanism is. It fires straight ahead. Limited, but the best we could rig up in the one hour he gave us."

A soundless whistle escaped him. "What's the range?"

"My bracelet's good at four meters, but you won't have the accuracy of aim that I do. Close up only, I'm afraid."

He brought her hand to his lips for a quick kiss. "Clever. And infinitely better than nothing."

The engine roared to life, the skimmer shuddered, then they swept forward and into the air. Dia's nerves raced, but somehow, with Jarrod beside her, touching her, anything seemed possible. For now, just being with him seemed enough. She clung to his hand and wished this journey would last forever.

All too soon he leaned forward to speak to the man in the borrowed captain's uniform. "Make sure you escort us inside the Citadel."

The man looked back, grinning. "That much I can manage. Then what?"

"Depends on what we find. I'll stick with the princess and her guard. You take the others and cut off Lomax's line of support."

As Jarrod leaned back, Dia fixed him with a stern glare. "No plan, I take it?"

He shook his head. "Plans tend to lock you into one line of thinking and make you miss opportunities. Sorry, I suppose you worked out a complete one."

"Of course." She inserted a haughty note into her voice. "Get in, kill Lomax, get my father, and get out. In any order that works."

"Your attention to the minutest detail awes me."

"Thought it would. We—" They rounded the last curve, and she broke off at sight of the huge silver-flecked block wall. "I've seen vids of it, but I never realized how—how daunting it is."

"Meant to repel a siege. Thanks to your arrival, we'll get a free pass inside the walls." He squeezed her hand. "Best start playing our roles." He released her with a last, caressing touch and sat straight in his seat.

"Show time," she agreed.

They slowed before the barred gate, and with a grating creak, that very impressive curtain rose. They entered the long tunnel, then emerged into the light of the courtyard. The first skimmer pulled up just beyond the massive front doors, and the car in which Dia rode stopped even with the entrance. The third pulled in and settled to the ground just behind them.

The locks clicked, and the skimmer doors swung outward and up. Jarrod unbent his long legs and climbed to the paving stones, then turned to take Dia's hand. She allowed herself to clasp it for a fleeting moment, then moved away from him to examine the formidable facade.

A citadel, indeed, she reflected. A damned great fortress. She could only hope it wasn't designed to detain prisoners within as well as keep intruders out. She'd be getting in with no trouble; leaving again might well prove another matter.

"No windows wide enough for escape on any of the outer walls," Jarrod murmured as he took up a position just behind her.

"Was it obvious I was looking for something like that?" she shot back.

"How well does Lomax know you?" he countered,

his voice barely audible. "Enough so he'll know you aren't just submitting tamely?"

"I don't know. We've spent more time exchanging insults than anything else. We—" She broke off as the doors opened.

"I'll be right behind you," Jarrod murmured.

Dia strode forward toward the steps, her four companions keeping close. The six Gavonians—Jarrod's mini-army—kept pace with three on either side. The men who had served as drivers remained with their vehicles. Fast getaway? she wondered.

She mounted the shallow steps and strode into the marbled entry hall. "What now?" she whispered to Jarrod.

"The honor guard probably had instructions." Jarrod cast a sideways glance at his friend now dressed as their captain. "I'll bet he's playing up the ceremony. The throne room?"

The man gave an almost imperceptible nod and led the way across the austere hall. A double door stood before them, and as they neared, two uniformed figures rose from benches hidden behind pillars and swung the great oak doors wide. Her party started forward, but the two men blocked their way.

An official garbed in a deep green robe and high mitered hat appeared in the doorway. "Welcome, Princess Dialora. Tharl Lomax awaits you." He made dismissive gestures toward the others, then held out his arm to Dia.

After a moment's hesitation, she placed her fingers on his elbow and allowed him to lead her forward. The others, to her dismay, didn't follow. Jarrod— The sound of the doors closing, separating them, echoed through the great chamber.

Dia tilted up her chin. She had her bracelet. She

would make Lomax release her father. She *would* succeed. But she needed to get him alone.

He sat on a massive wooden throne at the far end of the chamber, a tall, wiry figure impatient with the imposed majesty. He wore dark green robes, decorated with narrow bands of gold braid. Restless, his gaze darting to follow her movement, he looked more than ever like one of the deadly razor eels.

She quickened her pace, and her attendant broke into a jog to keep up with her. She marched forward, leaving no doubt as to who led whom, then halted in front of the dais. Hands on her hips, she glared at Lomax. "I want to see my father."

Lomax's steady regard held mild reproof. "My dear Dia, is that any way to greet your bridegroom?"

"It seems fitting enough to greet *you.*" She spat out the pronoun. "Now quit being such a pompous idiot. You know why I'm here. Where is he?"

Vexation flickered across his angular countenance. "Try to observe the nicities, Dia. That might help make this unpleasant situation a little more bearable."

"Very well." She gave him an exaggeratedly sweet smile. "Where, by all your filthy fire demons, is my father?"

His lips twitched. "I don't think you're really trying, Dia."

"No, *you're* the one who's trying. My patience! If you think I'm going one step farther with this ridiculous charade without knowing whether he's safe and you haven't killed *him*, as well as your own father," she broke off for breath, then forged on, "you're out of what little mind you have left."

"He's perfectly all right," Lomax snapped. "He's

resting. Doctor's orders. You can see him when he wakes up."

"Fine. Call me." She turned and started back toward the door.

He rose. "Where do you think you're going?"

"Somewhere. Anywhere." She looked back over her shoulder. "You don't think I'm going to stay here talking to you, do you?"

"Dia!" His voice took on a harsh note. "If you expect to see your father again, you'd better accept the fact that I'm calling the shots here. You don't leave my presence until I tell you to."

She turned slowly to face him. "If you kill him, you'll have no control over me."

Lomax's mouth tightened into a thin line. "Oh, I'll keep him alive, never you fear. But how comfortable he is will be up to you. Now, shall we start over? I believe you were about to bow to me, as befitting a bride's greeting of her new lord."

Dia's hands clenched at her sides. "You wouldn't dare—"

"Things have gone too far, Dia. I don't want to be stuck with you any more than you want me, but I *must* have the marriage tie to the coral. Do you understand? If I'm to hold Gavin, I've got to have you."

"Gavin would be a damned sight better off without you," she shot back.

"So I thought, too, until I suddenly found myself tharl. But a planet is really nothing more than a business, on a larger scale. You, of all people, should know that. What it needs is stability, in this case the continuing of the dynasty. Damn it, Dia, you know my planet's history. If someone challenges me, we'll be thrown back into decades of violence while anyone with any power at all tries for the throne. There's only been peace since my grandfather claimed the tharldom. It's got to be me, now. Me and my heir who'll be tied to the coral."

She stared at him, her fury growing. "You and your heir? And just who did you think would produce it for you when you ordered Linore and me killed?"

He waved that aside. "The situation was different, then. It should never have come to this. It was control of the coral I wanted then, not the tharldom. My father—" He broke off, his jaw tightening.

"You hadn't had to kill him yet?" she hazarded.

He ignored her interjection. "A tie with Bailan should have been enough. He'd have made any concession I wanted to keep me from producing your father alive. But you ruined that when you took over again."

"I'm glad I ruined something," she shot at him.

"Actually, since I've got the tharldom now, this works out for the best."

"More dynastic?" she suggested, her sarcasm heavy.

"More practical. A dynasty *and* the coral. That will give my people confidence, keep the business operation of the planet running smoothly." His gaze narrowed on her. "Never doubt me, Dia. If I have to use your father as a weapon to gain what I need, then I will." He drew a steadying breath. "I'd rather not use threats, though. Think about it. Peace and prosperity on my planet in exchange for security for yours. Gavin's strong. We can hold off take-over threats from other systems. No one will dare attack Kerrian once you're my bride."

She stood silent, strained. He had no illusions about

his popularity with the Gavonian people, about the precariousness of his position—and life. A challenge for tharldom meant a fight to the death. He wouldn't relax until he thought he'd gained her cooperation. She needed him to slacken his guard.

She allowed her shoulders to slump. "Are you sure we'd be safe?" she asked, allowing just a touch of wistfulness to creep into her voice. "Do you have any idea what we're up against right now? Four fully armed battle cruisers are circling Kerrian, just waiting for a chance to claim even a piece of us."

"They'll back off once we announce our marriage." He sounded more confident now. "Gavin has the reputation you need, especially since the Cerean war. Much as you don't want to admit it, Dia, it looks like we need each other. That's been the basis of a large percentage of marriages over the eons. At least we know each other to begin with. That should help."

"Maybe." She hoped she sounded half challenging, half resigned. She threw him an uncertain look, then studied her hands. "Can I go lie down somewhere until my father wakes up?"

"What you need to do is get dressed for the wedding, but you'll have time for a short rest first, I suppose. Come on, I'll show you." He descended the dais and offered his arm.

She ignored it, pointedly. What she wanted was to get Lomax alone, away from his minions, so she could kill him, find her father, and escape!

With an amused quirk to his lip, he led the way out of the throne room. Just outside in the main hall, six honor guards stood at attention. Not Jarrod's men, she realized the next moment. Had they gone to rescue her father, to undermine Lomax's support in the Citadel? She looked them over, noting the coldness of their expressions, and couldn't repress a shudder.

"Where're my own guards?" she demanded. "They should be in attendance on me."

"You don't need them. Come." He nodded to the guard, and the men fell into position around them.

Like being a prisoner, Dia reflected, then realized that was exactly what she was. Probably on her way to an escape-proof room, where she would be held until the wedding. That didn't leave her many opportunities.

They proceeded to the far side of the hall, then up the massive curved stair leading to the floor above. Banners and tapestries hung at irregular intervals, colorful against the silver-flecked white blocks that formed the wall. Only narrow slits allowed sunlight to filter inside, no wall-sized windows like they had at Kerrian-Isla. But Kerrian-Isla wasn't a fortress built in anticipation of a siege.

The guard escorted them through a gallery, then down a short corridor. They stopped before the second door, and one of the men in front drew it open, then stood back. Lomax gestured for Dia to enter. She strode inside; behind her sounded the soft click of the closing door.

Gavonian green, trimmed with gold. Dark, massive, overpowering. Dia swallowed and rejected the image of her own light, bright rooms. She should be glad she hadn't been shown to the dungeons.

On the whole, as prisons went, this really wasn't that bad. A huge canopied bed stood against one wall, opposite a cavernous fireplace. Heavy tooled wood chests and cabinets stood about the chamber, and elaborately worked rugs covered the floor. A cou-

ple of padded chairs stood on either side of a low
table, and a comm console sat on an ancient looking
desk.

No chance for escape, she noted. Numerous paned
slits lined the outer wall, but not one of them would
accommodate the passage of a body, even one as
slight as hers. If he bolted her in here, here she'd
stay.

"The door to my apartments lies behind that curtain at the head of the bed." Lomax's voice sounded
right behind her.

Dia spun about. "I—I didn't realize you'd come
in." He had, though, and they were alone.

Alone. If she wanted to kill him, she'd probably
never have a better chance. She allowed her gaze to
move over him, hoping she resembled a shy bride
while she took mental stock of his weapons. As far as
she could see, only a ritual dagger hung from his
belt.

"Afraid?" His eyebrows rose. "Please, spare me any
tragic airs. You don't have anything to worry about.
This is a business transaction. Aside from the fact I
need heirs born from you to inherit our planets, I
doubt we'll have much to do with each other. My
tastes run to the more exotic. Yes, I know you don't
approve of them." He looked amused. "I'll try not
to inflict them on you."

"Maybe it'll be better if we just skip the whole
thing." She raised her hand, and the power of the
coral thrummed through her.

Not just thrummed, her arm *shook*. And not with
the coral. Damn it, she couldn't go all weak and
helpless now! She had to kill him, for all he'd done
to her planet, for her father and Linore and all the
others. For what he still planned to do. She couldn't

let it matter that she'd known him all her life. He hadn't let sentiment interfere with *his* program.

He stared at her for a long moment, then burst out laughing. With one swift move, he reached out and caught her hand. "Really, Dia, your bracelet?" He shook his head. "What ever made you think you could actually kill me? Or anyone? It's just not in you."

She would lose to him. Desperate, she wrenched herself free, took frantic aim and touched the firing mechanism with her thumb.

Lomax staggered backward a step, gripping his upper arm. Shock, then outrage, flashed across his narrow face. Blood seeped sluggishly from what was no more than a flesh wound.

His mouth tightened and he lunged for her, grabbing her arm before she could aim again. Twisting her wrist backward, he tore free the heavy wire tracery of the bracelet. His fingers sought and found the implosion chamber, and with an exclamation of satisfaction he ripped it open. The jellactic acid poured out onto the carpet, where it sizzled.

He raised his furious gaze to her face. "Don't you ever try a trick like that again, my girl. Now, put on that robe. Looks like we'll just have to hurry the priest a bit."

She stared at the ruined bracelet he handed back to her. She'd wasted her chance. Numbly, she slipped the useless tracery of metal back on her arm.

"You think you only have to kill me, then summon your guards, don't you? Maybe I should have disillusioned you at once. Your guards, my dear Dia, are dead."

Her head jerked up. "Dead?" she breathed. Sorin and Eelam and Jorn . . . and Jarrod. . . .

Chapter Twenty

Lomax gave a short laugh. "You don't think I'd take any chances letting them roam around the Citadel, do you? Maybe trying a little rescue raid for your father? You forget I've dealt with treacherous business associates before. You're too valuable a prize to take risks with. Besides, you won't have any need of a guard here, not while you're under my tender loving care."

She turned away, sick. Sorin, Eelam and Jorn, dead. Dead because they followed her, trusted she could pull this off. Rixhard—he might have escaped, hidden among Jarrod's friends, but how long before his obviously Kerrinian features betrayed him?

And Jarrod. Jarrod. . . .

"Put this on." Lomax thrust a robe of Gavonian green at her. "Your wedding gown, my dear. Let's get this charade over with."

Numb, she made no protest as he dragged the fabric over her head. Her sarong remained underneath. How fitting, the thought flitted through her mind. Gavonian on the surface, but pure Kerrinian to the core. Yet she couldn't summon the rebellion she needed. To lose Jarrod a *second* time—it was more than she could bear.

Lomax fumbled with the ties at the back of the gown. She let him. She didn't care, nothing mattered now. Only Jarrod, and he was gone, torn from her. She could scarcely hope for him to miraculously resurrect himself a second time. Without him, only a dull ache remained that used to be her heart.

Lomax walked around her, studying her appearance. "You'll do," he said at last. "Under the circumstances, we're dispensing with pomp and sticking with the bare necessities. Short and to the point. Then you can see your father."

Her father. Slowly she straightened, her head coming up so that she stared blindly through Lomax. Her father. He, at least, was still alive. Jarrod—

She broke off thought of her love. Later she would grieve. Later. Not now. She had come here with a specific purpose in mind, believing Jarrod already dead. That hadn't changed. She had still to rescue her father, save Rixhard if she could, and make Lomax pay for the lives he had destroyed.

Her fingers strayed to her rys-bracelet. No hum, no reassuring vibration in her inner ear. Nothing. Only a dead tracery of wires. Beautiful, perhaps, but useless. Now she had only her wits.

And Lomax had only that ceremonial dagger. She cast a surreptitious glance at it. It hung annoyingly near to his hand. He could grasp it before she could— unless she got near enough. . . .

She slumped once more, covering her eyes with her hand. "I—" She broke off, swaying. If he thought she was about to faint, he might catch her. Then she could grab the dagger and stab him with it. She allowed one knee to buckle.

"Dia?" He sounded concerned, but he made no move to come to her.

"I—I feel dizzy." She turned slightly, crumpling, trying to fall against him.

He jumped back, away from her. She landed on her elbow, gasped with the pain, and slumped to her back. Determinedly, she kept her eyes closed.

Something prodded her in the ribs. "Dia?"

She rolled her head to one side and lay limp. It could still work if he bent over her. . . .

"Get up." The prodding came again.

His toe, she realized, furious. He kicked her. She remained where she lay, trying to figure out how to trip him. She still couldn't quite believe he had made no attempt to catch her when she appeared to faint. Had the man not a single mil of chivalry in him? Or was he even less trusting of her than she'd suspected?

The prod came again, and this time she grabbed his foot, jerking it upward with all her strength. He bent his knee, keeping his balance, then stomped down, pinning her wrist. A cry of mingled vexation and pain escaped her.

"You're getting tiresome. One more trick, of any sort at all, out of you, and your father receives a different drug. An addictive one, one that creates rather unpleasant hallucinations. Is that clear? Any trick at all."

Dia dragged herself to her feet, then tugged the robe into place. A long train tangled about her legs, and it took a minute to free herself. No more desperate risks, no more seizing at chances. The next time she acted, she had to be sure of her results.

When he grasped her arm, Dia made no protest.

This seemed to please him, but he didn't make the mistake of relaxing his guard. She could feel his tensed muscles. His eyes dared her to try something. Very well, for now, at least, she'd go along with his demands. She didn't necessarily *have* to kill him before they were married. Being a widow would suit her well enough.

He led her along the corridors back the way they had come. At the foot of the great curved stairs, they turned the opposite way, through an arched entry. Here the window slits ran from floor to lofty ceiling, spaced close together. The result looked deceptively fragile, with sunlight flooding in, casting an intricate pattern of shadows across the stone floor.

They stepped through another arch, and the hallway opened into an octagonal chamber, the walls made entirely of the tall, narrow windows. The ceiling cantilevered high above them, forming a dome. At the far side stood a raised dais on which rested a rectangular slab covered in a cloth of hunter green. Curtains hung in heavy folds behind it, tapestries depicting fires and smoldering volcanoes.

A temple, she realized. The seat of all sacred ceremonies. Like coronations and weddings. She was about to be joined to Lomax. The mere thought disgusted her.

A figure emerged from behind the tapestries, robed and cowled in Gavonian green. Embroidered flames shot upward from the hem, and down his back hung a mantle depicting a sacred fire. The priest.

He took up a position before them, in front of the altar, head lowered, his hands folded into his sleeves. Slowly he turned and knelt, facing the tapestries, and raised his hands. Whether in supplication or demand, Dia couldn't be certain.

Lomax took a step forward, dragging Dia with him. "Arise, priest!" he cried. His voice sounded heavy, as if he embarked on an age-old formulaic ritual. "I, Lomax, Tharl of Gavin-Secundus, bring Princess Dialora of Kerrian to this sacred place to be united with me in marriage." His voice echoed about the chamber.

Like a death knell. Dia cringed. Here, in the ceremonial and spiritual heart of his power, it seemed possible he might win all. He would bind her to him, force her to bear his heir, keep political control of his planet, turn her father into nothing but a puppet ruler, drugged and under his domination. . . .

Her father, she realized with blinding insight, would rather be dead, would rather endure any torture than have her submit.

Her gaze scanned the room, seeking any possible weapon, but found nothing. Her only hope lay in the dagger at Lomax's belt. She'd have to distract him, infuriate him. She pulled on her arm, trying to free herself from his grip. "No!" She shouted her denial, heard it reverberate about the walls. "I'll see you dead before I wed you."

The priest rose and turned to face them. With both hands he threw back his cowl. "The lady doesn't seem willing, Lomax," came Jarrod's deep voice.

Dia froze. Jarrod. . . . In disbelief, she stared at his beloved features, noted the blood-beaded slash along his cheek. Jarrod, alive, here. The man must have more lives than the proverbial weckel fish. . . .

She fought back her rising hysteria. Jarrod had survived. Together, they could defeat Lomax.

An arm closed about her neck, and she gagged as it tightened, choking her. The sharp point of Lomax's dagger dug into her collar bone. He held her body

before him, shielding himself. "You should be dead,"
he hissed at Jarrod, and his hot breath fanned Dia's
ear.

"Apparently it isn't my time yet." He descended
the first step from the dais. From beneath his robe,
he drew a cell imploder.

"Drop it! Stay where you are, or I'll kill her!"
Lomax dragged her a step backward. "Guards!" he
shouted, then repeated it as his voice tumbled about
the chamber.

Jarrod paused. "They're not going to come. You'd
be surprised—and chagrined, I'm afraid—to see how
eager they were to surrender to us. You're not popular."

Lomax's breath hissed. "Drop it. Or I'll kill her,"
he repeated.

"Then you'll have lost your shield," Jarrod pointed
out. "Let her go. It's over, Lomax. We've freed King
Harryl. He's safe in the hands of his own Kerrinian
guard." His voice sounded steady, reasonable. "This
is a matter between you and me, just us, alone." Very
slowly he stooped, bending down to set his weapon
on the stone step behind him.

Jarrod. . . . "Don't!" Dia screamed, but knew it was
too late.

From the belt of his priestly robe, Jarrod drew a
knife. He descended the last two steps until he stood
level with them. "Well? Do you accept my challenge?"

"Don't come closer!" Lomax's grip tightened on
Dia.

She forced back a cry as the point of the dagger
penetrated her skin. Warm blood trickled behind the
barrier of her collar bone, then down the front of
her gown.

Jarrod stopped, tensed, his furious gaze resting on Lomax. The pressure of the dagger eased.

A scream of frustration welled within Dia, but she held it in. Would Jarrod let the man escape because of her? He wouldn't risk her life, he'd let Lomax go free. But Lomax was not one to retire into quiet hiding. He'd wreak vengeance on those who denied him control of the coral. If he escaped, it would be to do more damage to Gavin, to Kerrian. And all because Jarrod loved her, wouldn't risk her.

She couldn't let it happen. She twisted her arm inside the heavy tracery of her bracelet until her fingers gripped an edge. With a tug it came away and dangled in her hand. It might no longer bear its deadly charge, but it still could be a weapon. Raising it, she brought it swinging down against Lomax's knee.

He yelled in surprised pain, and for a moment his grip on her loosened. She tore free, throwing herself into a roll, putting as much distance between them as she could. As she came up into a crouch, she saw Jarrod tackle Lomax with a flying leap.

The men fell to the stone floor, locked together, the hatred between them etched deeply on both faces. Dia pulled herself to her feet, watching with fascinated horror as they struggled. Jarrod knelt over Lomax, then Lomax lurched, throwing Jarrod off, rolling with him until their positions reversed. He slammed Jarrod's wrist against the stone, and Jarrod's knife flew in an arc, clattering to the floor several meters away.

Dia scrambled for the dais, and her hands closed on the unfamiliar imploder. She spun to face the men, but now Jarrod's back provided her only target.

She lowered the point, uncertain. She wasn't trained with this sort of weapon, she could easily miss, hit the wrong man. Better use it as a club. . . .

Lomax's vicious, gasping laugh sounded loud in the echoing room. His right hand drew back, and light glinted off the dagger as he swung it, slashing, down on Jarrod.

Dia lunged forward, but Jarrod had already caught Lomax's hand, forcing it back, away. Lomax teetered off balance, rolled to the side, then Jarrod was on top of him, blocking Dia's aim. Still Lomax retained his grip on his dagger, and slashed once more. Jarrod ducked under it; the heel of his hand caught Lomax's chin, forcing his head back as the dagger swung wildly, seeking its target.

An eerie cracking sound reached Dia. For a moment that seemed to stretch into eternity, Jarrod and Lomax remained frozen. Then Lomax fell back and lay still. Jarrod sat up, breathing hard, and dragged himself slowly to his unsteady feet.

"Jarrod?" Dia took a step forward, and her knees threatened to buckle.

"He's dead." Jarrod raised his gaze from his fallen adversary and turned to look at her. "He's dead."

"There hasn't been a duel for the tharldom in three generations," announced a man's voice from the archway.

Dia spun around to see a man garbed as a captain of the tharl's honor guard. Jarrod's friend. Several others stood behind him, watching.

Jarrod straightened, turning to face them. "Did you see what happened?"

The captain strolled forward to stare down at

Lomax's body. "We were about to intervene when you issued the challenge. After that, by the laws, we had to wait to see the outcome."

"And if I'd lost?" Jarrod demanded. A note of amusement crept into his voice.

A slow, grim smile spread across his friend's face. "Oh, we'd have arrested him for the murder of his father. That would have left us in a bit of a bind, though, with no one to replace him as tharl."

Jarrod's jaw tightened. "Wait a minute. I challenged him, but it wasn't for the tharldom. It was to settle old grievances. A duel, yes, but not—"

The captain shook his head. "Sorry, that's not how we saw it."

"It wasn't murder." Dia moved forward, reaching for Jarrod's arm, needing physical contact with him. "You can't accuse him of—"

"No, love. It's worse than that."

"But—" She looked from Jarrod to the captain, confused.

The captain cleared his throat, cast Jarrod a look brimful of humor, then turned to Dia. "He challenged the tharl to combat."

"A duel," she insisted. Surely he couldn't be arrested for that.

"A duel," the man agreed. "By the ancient laws of combat, the winner becomes tharl."

"Becomes—" Her gaze rotated to meet the mixture of anger and resignation in Jarrod's expression. "You're now tharl?"

"By all the fire demons—" He broke off. "If the duel was witnessed and attested to be fair, then I'm afraid I am."

"Witnessed and attested," confirmed the captain.

A cheerful note entered his voice. "May I be the first to swear allegiance to you?"

"Damn you," Jarrod responded. "I don't want to be tharl."

The captain grinned. "You should have thought of that before."

"If someone challenges me—" Jarrod began.

"A hero of the Cerean war, and protege of Dysart himself?" His friend shook his head. "Not a chance. You're stuck with it, pal." He clapped Jarrod on the shoulder. "We'll broadcast the whole story, everything Lomax has done. Your coronation is going to be the most popular event in decades. Come to terms with it, friend. There are a few advantages that'll go with the job, you know."

"Yes," Jarrod said slowly, and his gaze rested on Dia. "I can think of one. There's no way out of this?"

The captain glanced at the men who gathered about them. "There're a number of bureaucrats who'd be only to glad to take over. You want that?"

A deep sigh escaped Jarrod. "No."

"Then we'd better get busy." The captain gave his men orders for the summoning of various authorities and ministers, and the honor guard disbursed.

Jarrod took Dia's hand, clasping it, and led the way to the far side of the octagonal chamber, to one of the benches that lined the walls. Dia sank onto it, but Jarrod stood before her, gazing down at her face. "You heard what they said."

Dia nodded. "You're tharl—whether you want to be or not."

His lips twitched. "There's something I want you to understand. I don't need you. I don't even need a treaty for the coral. I *am* tharl. And it seems I'm going to have full, popular support.''

She inclined her head. "Fair enough.''

A very enticing gleam lit his eyes. He cupped her face with both hands, and his fingers caressed her throat with slow, tantalizing movements. "Glad that's settled.'' He dragged her to her feet and into his arms, and his mouth covered hers, demanding, teasing, passionate.

With an effort, she pulled away. "Just who says anything's settled? There are two sides to every negotiation, aren't there?'' She fixed him with as stern a gaze as she could manage. "You may not need me, but I don't need you, either. Is that clear?''

"Completely." He leaned forward and allowed his lips to just brush hers.

Her fingers tangled in the soft fabric of his priest's robe. "It's going into the treaties that every system that buys coral has to help protect Kerrian's autonomy—and help educate and train our personnel. So I don't need any Gavonian favors or strong-arming around the galaxy.''

"Damned right you don't, Lady.'' He drew her closer and rubbed his cheek in her hair. His mouth found the sensitive spot just behind her ear.

She caught her breath. "And—and I negotiated that on my own, without your help. So I don't owe you anything.'' His hands crept up her back, caressing, making it difficult to concentrate on what she said.

"Not a thing. We're both free agents.'' His fingers strayed into highly distracting territory.

"Free,'' she got out. She had to fight to keep back a soft moan of yearning.

"I'm honor bound not to influence you or your

father in the running of Kerrian—'' he broke off briefly to kiss her throat, ''—and you're honor bound not to try to bribe me with offers of extra coral. Right?''

"Right." Unable to stop herself, she pressed against him. Her hands folded into the thick waves of his hair, and she trailed a finger along the nape of his neck.

The embers in his eyes ignited, and his voice, when he spoke, sounded husky. "No political ties between us, whatsoever. Which leaves us free to deal on a strictly personal level, just you and me. What do you say? Shall we contract a marriage that's an equal partnership?"

"Agreed." She allowed the tip of her fingers to follow the line of his jaw, then down his neck. "That means equal time for each of our planets, you know."

"Agreed." He caught her fingers and pressed them against his chest. "That also means we'll have to have at least two children, one to inherit each planet, since we want our worlds to remain autonomous."

"Agreed." She leaned back in his strong arms and looked up into his face. Somehow, his hands still managed to roam in a manner that left her breathless. "Two ceremonies," she reminded him. "One on each planet. Our people will expect it."

"If you think—" his mouth returned to the hollow at the base of her throat, "—I'm going to wait to implement this contract—" his lips roamed across her cheek, "—while we satisfy everybody else's expectations—" he kissed her eyes, closing them, "—then—"

"Tharl Jarrod?" The voice of his old friend echoed through the temple.

Jarrod sighed against her hair and set her gently

away from him. She cocked an eyebrow, amusement bubbling through her. For a long moment they gazed at one another, then a rueful gleam replaced the exasperation of his expression.

"Right you are, love." Jarrod grinned as he took her hand and turned toward the people who had begun to gather. "It's show time."

HISTORICAL ROMANCE FROM PINNACLE BOOKS

LOVE'S RAGING TIDE (381, $4.50)
by Patricia Matthews

Melissa stood on the veranda and looked over the sweeping acres of Great Oaks that had been her family's home for two generations, and her eyes burned with anger and humiliation. Today her home would go beneath the auctioneer's hammer and be lost to her forever. Two men eagerly awaited the auction: Simon Crouse and Luke Devereaux. Both would try to have her, but they would have to contend with the anger and pride of girl turned woman . . .

CASTLE OF DREAMS (334, $4.50)
by Flora M. Speer

Meredith would never forget the moment she first saw the baron of Afoncaer, with his armor glistening and blue eyes shining honest and true. Though she knew she should hate this Norman intruder, she could only admire the lean strength of his body, the golden hue of his face. And the innocent Welsh maiden realized that she had lost her heart to one she could only call enemy.

LOVE'S DARING DREAM (372, $4.50)
by Patricia Matthews

Maggie's escape from the poverty of her family's bleak existence gives fire to her dream of happiness in the arms of a true, loving man. But the men she encounters on her tempestuous journey are men of wealth, greed, and lust. To survive in their world she must control her newly awakened desires, as her beautiful body threatens to betray her at every turn.

Available wherever paperbacks are sold, or order direct from the Publisher. Send cover price plus 50¢ per copy for mailing and handling to Penguin USA, P.O. Box 999, c/o Dept. 17109, Bergenfield, NJ 07621. Residents of New York and Tennessee must include sales tax. DO NOT SEND CASH.